BACK FOR REVENGE!

Delphinia walked across the yard, aware of the pistol still heavy under her shawl, holding the milk bucket easy, legs heavy with the urge to run, but not daring—not yet. And then a bullet slammed, loud and sudden, piercing the enamel bucket so that it tipped like a child's swing, turning in an arc, bottom up, and causing the milk to spurt through two holes like a sieve, splashing down her ankle and onto her shoe. Delphinia froze for a few seconds then, letting go of the bucket, attempted a dash toward the porch as heavy boots thudded behind her. She was stopped by the crash of a body against her own, as strong hands grabbed her waist and spun her around. In a wild stumble both she and her attacker tripped over the milk bucket and fell to the ground.

Raul Rivera's bad breath, smelling like onions and tobacco, scalded her nostrils. "I told you I would be back," he sneered.

She cringed, stiffened, turning her face away from him. Breathing hard, she was pinned under his heavy body.

"Your father killed my brother, *puta!*"

Sept - The all-girl filling stations last reunion

BOUNTY HUNTER'S
Daughter

BOUNTY HUNTER'S

Daughter

Phyllis de la Garza

The characters and events portrayed in this book are fictitious. Any similarity to real persons, living or dead, is coincidental and not intended by the author.

Printed in the United States of America.

Published by AmazonEncore
P.O. Box 400818
Las Vegas, NV 89140

ISBN-13: 9781477841365
ISBN-10: 1477841369

Dedicated to the memory of Hazel Wilson

This title was previously published by Dorchester Publishing; this version has been reproduced from the Dorchester book archive files.

Chapter One

"Rider coming!" Delphinia called to her mother from die yard where she rinsed fresh-cut sprigs of basil in a small washtub. She snapped slender, purplish-green leaves at their stems with her thumbnail before swirling the herb under water. Delphinia sniffed the stems; their pungent aroma bit into the hot, desert air.

Amity Estes burst out the kitchen door, wiping her slender hands down the front of her white apron. "Rider! Where?" She squinted north, following the gesture of her daughter's hand toward Locust Cañon. Her pale eyes were fixed on the horseman moving fast, but still a dot in the distance.

"I bet it's Pa," Delphinia said.

"Think so? He's still too far to tell."

Delphinia shook out the wet basil, squeezing and bending it gendy into a bundle. "I can tell by all the dust that black horse of his kicks up...has feet big enough to fill a pie plate." She laughed, remembering how her father got annoyed whenever she made fun of his horse's big feet.

"I don't care how big his damn' feet are," Hawk Estes always told his teasing daughter, "as long as the bugger can cross rough country without coming up lame. Big feet keep a horse from sinking into sand."

Amity finished drying her hands and reached up to smooth her hair — a sure sign she knew by now it was her husband riding in. "It *is* your father!" She said it more to herself than to Delphinia, turning quickly back into the house, changing her dirty apron for a clean one.

Delphinia hung the wet basil, using twine, under the porch

roof at the side of the house. Shelves along the building were filled with dozens of small metal cans, glass jars, and odd bundles of herbs, spices, twigs, and dry leaves. Sewing thread had been carefully stitched through white tags and tied to each container with the name of each plant written for identification.

Running back to the front of the house, Delphinia met her father riding into the yard. He ran a suspicious glance about the place, an old habit born out of self-preservation, before turning his broad shoulders and dismounting with an easy step.

"Pa!" Delphinia reached for the bridle reins.

"Put my horse up, girl," he said casually, pulling his rifle from the saddle boot. His movements were easy — he was sure of himself. His smooth, square jaw caught sunlight slanting under his brown, felt cowboy hat.

She smiled, knowing better than to expect a hug from him — he had quit doing that on her thirteenth birthday, seven years ago. He just said when girls grow up they needed to be careful about squeezing. Of course, she knew that, but, still, he was her pa.

Lifting the hem of her blue calico dress out of the yard dust, she turned the big black toward the corral where her own horse, Slicker, and the bay team munched hay. Delphinia was anxious to join Hawk and her mother in the kitchen. Hawk usually had some little present for her, besides all the news from his latest adventures. People around here looked down on bounty hunters, but Delphinia considered her father's life style like that of a lawman — at least, that is the way he made it sound.

She shut the corral gate, wondering how long he would stay this time. She lugged his saddle and gear into the tiny saddle house, then charged up the house steps. She paused briefly to admire the beginnings of her rug stretched inside the frame loom on the porch where she had begun a new weaving project.

"Staying long?" she asked Hawk, dashing into the kitchen and plopping into a chair next to him.

He sat at the table, his hat and gun belt hung in the usual spot on a peg near the door. His rifle leaned in the corner. He sipped coffee while Amity fluttered around the wood stove, giddy like she always acted when her husband first rode in after a long absence. Amity poured grease into a pot before adding bits of onion. "We'll kill a chicken for supper," she said, brushing a stray blonde hair from her forehead.

"Don't go to any special fuss. I can't stay longer than tonight. I'm trailing four men who robbed a train."

"Robbed a train!" Delphinia sat at his elbow, waiting for the rest of the story.

He nodded, putting down the cup. "Southern Pacific run between Willcox and Cochise. Damn' dummies put a tree trunk across the tracks, then held up the engineer when the train stopped. They even managed to blow up the express car. Lot of good it did 'em."

Delphinia leaned closer to him. "Why? What happened?"

"Delphinia!" Amity scolded, "set the table. Never mind train robberies!"

Hawk continued his story as if he hadn't heard Amity. "They didn't get any money. The express box had nothing but a few papers. But robbing a train is robbing a train. Sheriff Hat ton and his posse are after them, figuring they'd make a run south for Mexico. But I found their tracks going north late yesterday, about ten miles from here. Thought I'd pay you ladies a visit while I was in the neighborhood."

"Do you know who they are, Pa?"

"Yes. Bate Thatcher, wanted for killing two men in El Paso. And the Rivera brothers, Raul and Lupe. A mean pair who would not think twice about doing anything you can imagine. I sent all of them to prison once before."

"Who is the fourth? You said there were four."

He ran his finger under his chin, switching his shoulders a little like he always did when he got nervous and did not want to talk about something. "Your mother is right, never mind train robbers. Tell me, what have you been doing, girl? You ever get off this place? Take a trip? How about Tucson? Just because your mother is happy living in these hills, never going to town, doesn't mean you can't ride into civilization once in a while."

She nodded, blushing. Her father's smooth hand patted her own across the table top, and she realized, as she studied her father's hands, that his were nicer, smoother than her own. Bounty hunters handled guns and played cards, maybe, but they did not dig post holes or chop wood or hoe in the garden. She curled her fingers so that he could not see the black walnut stains around the edges of her fingernails she'd gotten from harvesting wild walnuts. She drew her hands slowly under the table, folding them on her lap. "I'm all right, Pa. We drive to town for supplies once in a while. And people sometimes stop here for mother's herb remedies, and…I visit the Brubakers sometimes."

He winked at her. The Brubakers were the family on the next homestead east, their property bordering the Estes place. The Brubakers had a garden, a few cows, and lots of kids. "You're not still sweet on Jess Brubaker, are you? He's a handsome boy, good hearted, but you'll have nothing but a shack full of kids if you get hooked up with him, honey."

She blushed again, embarrassed that Hawk would talk to her about kids — her own kids. "Me and Jess are just friends, we ride and talk sometimes…that's all."

"Uhn-huh."

At the stove Amity continued to stir onions. "Delphinia, please go to the root cellar for a couple of jars of canned stew meat and potatoes. Some applesauce, too."

Walking out the door, Delphinia's glance caught a thin cloud of powdery dust in the draw. "Somebody coming up the arroyo," she called over her shoulder, hesitating at the door.

Hawk jumped to his feet, running for his holster.

"It must be old Cholla and his burro," Amity said. "He's the only one who comes up that way."

"He still snooping around here?" Hawk grumbled.

"Comes by every chance he gets for something to eat," Delphinia said, wrinkling her nose. "He likes Mother's cooking."

Pot-bellied Cholla erupted from the near side of the big gulch north of the house, dragging his shaggy, gray burro loaded with greasy sacks and bobbing shovel handles. Cholla shuffled across the yard, his broken boot heels making scraping noises. "Hawk Estes!" he yelled through his whiskers.

Hawk leaned against the porch railing, arms crossed, eyeing the old prospector. "Any gold in the hills?" His voice carried a hint of sarcasm.

Cholla laughed, wrapping the halter rope around the hitching post. "Only a mite here and there, just enough to keep me and poor Jitters here in a speck of grub. No thin' more." He wiped his pitted hands down the sides of his dirty blue jeans held up by wide brown suspenders. His shirt was old, red wool longjohns faded grayish-pink from many years in the sun rather than laundry water.

Amity squeezed nervously between Hawk and Delphinia. "Water your burro if you want, Cholla. You are welcome to share our noon meal. Delphinia was just going to the root cellar for stew meat. We have plenty."

He grinned at her, pressing the brim of his greasy, felt hat back against the crown. "Right, ma'am. That will surely be fine." He spoke with a slight Southern accent. Unwrapping the lead rope as nervously as he had tied it, he dragged his burro across the yard to the water trough.

Delphinia grinned up at her father. "You're making him nervous, Pa. He usually stomps right into the house making himself at home without Ma inviting him."

"Hush," Amity told her, turning back into the house.

Hawk scratched his ear. "You be careful around that old coot, honey. He acts poorly and pretends he's dimwitted and helpless, but I suspect it's all just a show with him. Most of these old prospectors are smarter than coyotes when it comes to taking care of themselves, and I'll bet he's not above petting a skirt if he gets a chance."

Delphinia laughed. "I figured that out for myself, Pa. He don't get to pet any skirts around here. But he puts on quite a show with his odd stories and old mule lore."

"Mule lore! Is that what you call it? Don't feel sorry for him, thinking he's poor, Delphinia. Like as not he's got a stash somewhere that could choke an ox."

Amity joined them in the doorway again, listening. "He has to be careful. I know he worries about somebody sneaking up on him and killing him…alone the way he is."

Hawk sighed. "Well, come on. Let's get this meal over with. I can't wait to hear some of his mule lore."

Delphinia carried a platter of beef stew and potatoes to the table where everybody took turns scooping their share onto their own plates. Cholla had a big laugh, telling about a stream above Locust Cañon where he claimed to have discovered a gold nugget in a trout pool.

"You got it with you?" Hawk asked. "I never heard of gold nuggets in Locust Cañon."

"No! I take everything right to town, where I buy fresh supplies. I don't carry anything with me. Nothing hidden, either. Everybody knows that. I had too many friends killed for keeping a stash." He dove into the stew and potatoes after placing a thick slice of fresh goat cheese on his plate. "Umm ...you make the best cheese, Miss Amity."

"Delphinia has taken over that job. She's made a pet out of the goat, so it seemed only right I let her make the cheese," Amity said.

Delphinia nodded, cutting into a small piece and sniffing before taking a bite. "Good. Cured longer than the last batch, I like it mixed with cow's milk, makes a good blend."

"You got a cow here now?" Cholla asked.

"No," she answered. "We trade things with the Brubakers ...they have cows."

Cholla nodded. "You got a right good life here. Plenty of peace and quiet. Always food on the table. You ladies are to be admired. I would not mind having a little place like this, 'cept I get the itchy foot and would not want to be tied down to feedin' stock or tendin' a garden."

"It looks to me like you have things going your way, Cholla. Not tied down to anything," Hawk said. "Free as a bird, yet stopping by here whenever you feel like it. My wife and daughter are quick to fill your plate."

Cholla glared up at him. "You sayin' I ain't welcome here no more?" He belched.

"Not at all. But it would be nice if you did a little trading like the Brubakers do. That way my wife and daughter could get something in return for all their hard work."

"I already told you I don't carry gold!"

"I'm not talking about gold. You spend your whole life up in the hills. Why don't you at least find out what Amity needs by way of herbs, and bring something down here that she could use?"

"Like what?"

"Mormon tea grows in the meadow near Locust Cañon,"

Amity said, breaking into the conversation. “A little handful would do me just fine.”

Cholla leered at her, taking another mouthful of stew. Delphinia hated the way he ate with his mouth open — chunks of food fell into his beard. She studied the scar running along his cheek to the edge of his nose that left a disgusting little flap at the corner of his nostril that was always dirty.

“I’ll bring you some Mormon tea. I surely will,” Cholla muttered, scraping the heel of his fork across his plate. He finished eating, stood abruptly, and muttered that he best be on his way. He barely nodded to Hawk at the door, thumping down the steps and disappearing a few moments later, dragging his burro by a rope.

The family stood on the porch. Amity looked up at Hawk. “You were kind of hard on him. I don’t mind sharing with the poor old man.”

Hawk shook his head at her. “I swear, Amity, you’d feel sorry for a sick skunk. That old fleabag has more tricks up his sleeves than a fox. Coming in here, mooching off you and Delphinia…that bothers me. It felt good letting him know about it. It doesn’t hurt to remind people I’m looking out for you.”

She smiled at him, anxious to change the subject. “Let’s take a stroll…how about a walk around the corrals? To that nice shady spot under the big mesquite behind the barn?”

Delphinia took the hint, pushing herself away from the porch railing, ambling around the corner of the house to the herb collection. The goldenrod stems tied under the roof were drying nicely. She tested the parchment-like leaves to see if they were ready yet for boiling that would make yellow dye for her wool. A box of last year’s walnut husks were on a shelf. She fished through them quickly, brushing the fine greasy residue away before it darkened her fingertips. She began working on removing the little black seeds from the centers of the prickly pear fruit. The dried seeds would be ground into powder for use in making red dye.

"What are you doing back here, Delphinia?"

She jumped at the sound of Hawk's voice. "Pa! I thought you and Mother took a walk."

"She decided she needs her shawl. Cool wind coming up. What have you got in these cans and jars?" He tipped a bottle, peering inside as if he were looking into a telescope.

"That's nettles, Pa, good for kidney ailments. And this jar"
___she picked up another and held it in her father's direction
___"is full of ground buckthorn."

"Buckthorn! That's the stuff your mother gave me one time when I was feeling all stopped up. Damn' buckthorn had me running to the outhouse for a week."

She laughed. "It's supposed to do that, Pa. Maybe she gave you a little too much."

"A little too much! By God, that stuff could loosen up a buffalo. What's this?" He pried off the top of a green metal can standing by itself, high above the others.

"Don't touch that, Pa. It's ground mushrooms, the poison kind."

"Poison kind! What the hell you keep it for?"

"We spread it along with ground corn when the mice get bad during winter. We keep it up high on that shelf, so it won't get mixed up with anything else."

He put it back on the shelf, quickly dusting off his hands, checking his fingertips.

Delphinia laughed. "You didn't get any on your hands."

He shrugged, reaching for another jar. "What's this?" He held the big blue bottle to his face, trying to read the label.

Delphinia flushed, stuttering: "Er…I don't know. Some things are Ma's…." She took it from his hand, placing it back behind the other bottles where the label wouldn't show. Amity had told her this herb was used when women did not want to have babies. Of course, living on a farm, Delphinia knew where babies came from, and how they arrived into the world. Once in a while neighbor women came to Amity for a delivery, and Delphinia got to help. Even so, Delphinia was not sure what the connection was between taking this herb and avoiding pregnancy, but she planned to keep it in mind.

"What's this stuff?" Hawk asked, poking through a bundle of dry eucalyptus twigs.

"You boil it, and breathing the steam helps a person with a stopped up nose...like when you have a cold."

He turned away, shaking his head. "You and your mother come up with the damnedest things."

"Hawk! Ready?" Amity peeked around the corner of the house, signaling him to join her for their walk. They disappeared, arm-in-arm.

Delphinia turned to her prickly-pear seeds, sifting them through a sieve, separating bits of dry pulp once more, before pouring the seeds into a mortar and smashing them with a pestle. She bore down, crushing the seeds into fine powder, grinding repeatedly until she was happy with the consistency, and then finally pouring everything into a glass jar marked RED DYE.

Brushing off her hands, she stepped around to the front of the house and sat in front of her loom. Picking up her weft beater, she began laying in new rows, all the while watching through the taut warp to the cut in the Cañon, keeping an eye out for visitors, while at the same time building layers into the rug. Opening the warp-shed, sliding in the batten, turning the batten on edge, laying in a row of wool. *Thump, thump.*

Somewhere behind the horse corral she knew Hawk and Amity strolled, enjoying their privacy. She sometimes felt in the way when Hawk came home, knowing her parents needed to be alone. She considered saddling Slicker and taking a ride, but decided against it tonight. She knew Hawk was worried about the outlaws. Sorting through her feelings about Hawk and Amity's life style, she came up with the same old answer. It was none of her business. Why Amity was satisfied to have her man ride in and out whenever he pleased was not a point discussed between her mother and herself when they were alone. Amity seemed to like it that way. And, after all. Hawk did come around from time to time, taking up life with Amity as if it was perfectly normal for a man to come and go as he pleased, unquestioned, all on his terms.

And yet Delphinia could not imagine having it any other way. She and Amity stayed on the homestead most of the time, but were totally independent. When she visited Jess Brubaker and his clan, she could not get used to the confusion of twelve boys carrying on, and Jess's father thrashing in and out of the house, tossing his shirts where they fell, shouting orders to Ma Brubaker, who shouted right back. The constant turmoil made Delphinia nervous. Her insides would quiver, and she would become anxious to bolt for home. In contrast, she and Amity spent their days in quiet solitude, tending stock, speaking quietly with one another, blending in with the land. Even their experiments with herbs seemed part of nature, like her spinning and weaving, like her quiet rides across the prairie on Slicker.

She sighed with contentment, glancing up toward Locust Cañon. A cactus wren chattered, giving off its raucous screeches like the busybody it was. A curved-bill thrasher whistled a sweet melody. Inca doves cooed. Delphinia worked on her rug until darkness finally made it impossible for her to see the pattern any more.

Chapter Two

Delphinia awoke early, too restless to fall back to sleep. Dressing quickly inside her bedroom, she tiptoed across the kitchen floor, past the big stove. Her mother's bedroom door was closed. Delphinia opened the outside door, thinking she might milk the goat and do her chores early, allowing her folks time to be left alone — Amity did not get up early when Hawk was home.

But Hawk was sitting on the porch in a chair, big boots resting on the porch railing, arms crossed in front of his chest, as his eyes traced the still-blackened hills above Locust Cañon.

"Pa! Up already?" She stood close to him, her arms wrapped in her shawl across her waist.

"Honey, I have to ride out early today. I'm worried about the Riveras and that bunch. I don't like the way they headed north...I figured they'd go south to Mexico. But they're up there some place, and I want to leave at daybreak. I'm just sitting here waiting for more light."

She inched closer to him. "Pa, do you ever think of quitting? I mean, just staying here with Mother and me, forgetting about risking your life?"

"All life is a risk, Delphinia. And no matter what people say or think, there is nothing wrong with bounty hunting. I've rid Arizona Territory of some of the worst outlaws."

"I know. I've never complained about your work. Sometimes...I think Ma doesn't like it."

"Your mother has never liked it, but she and I came to terms with it before you were born. She wants homesteading, and I like what I do. Sweating behind a team and a plowshare all day, or mending fences and messing with hogs is not what I call living."

"I understand, Pa."

"The only regret I have is not spending more time with you, honey."

"But the times we've had were good. You bought me Slicker, the best horse in the world. And you taught me how to ride, and shoot, and take care of myself. You don't have to worry about me when you're not here. I take care of Ma, too."

He grinned at her in the dark. "It's not only the people part of it, Delphinia. It's this desert that I love. I can't stand seeing it torn up and turned over. When I first came here with the Army thirty years ago, I learned the Apaches never expected anything more from the desert than what it had to offer. They were never disappointed. They lived on it the way it was meant to be lived on. It's a harsh land that never makes promises. You can't fight it. You have to go with it. It's a challenge every morning when that blistering sun comes up, reminding us each man is just one drop of sand in the total scheme of things."

"You knew when you met Mother that her folks were sodbusters."

"Honey, when the love bug bites, it doesn't make any difference where two people come from or what they do for a living. It's after the wedding day the trouble starts."

"Getting married is a lot for a person to think about."

"It should be. But don't get the idea I'm sorry." He repeated his old joke she'd heard many times. "I met Amity during a typhoid epidemic in Tucson, and I still have the fever." And then he added something new: "I reckon I'll die with it."

She caught a sadness in his voice. "Pa, what's wrong?"

He brought his shoulders up, shivering under his heavy coat. "It's these fellows I'm following…."

“Yes? The Riveras? And Bate Thatcher? And who is the other man? You never did finish talking about him yesterday.”

“It’s a long story, Delphinia. The fourth man...he’s somebody I’d rather not be chasing.”

“What did he do? You scared of him?”

“Me scared? No, not of his gun.”

She looked down at him, waiting for the rest of the story, but just then Amity opened the door, looking out, still wearing her long white nightgown. Her blonde hair swirled loosely around her thin shoulders. Her face reminded Delphinia of a delicate porcelain doll. It was a wonder she could keep her beautiful complexion so white and smooth in the desert wind and sun. Wearing bonnets and smearing her skin with plant oils she conjured up were the reason, Delphinia knew.

“Hawk...,” Amity began, but she did not finish her sentence because the first shots fired from the arroyo punched holes in the air with hollow cracks, fiery blasts in the darkness. Amity’s right arm shot up and back down as her hands flailed around her bloody neck, instinctively trying to cover the big, red spurt pumping down the front of her nightgown. She reeled back into the house with a cry.

Flinging Delphinia across the porch and back toward the door, Hawk hissed: “Inside!”

She flipped through the door behind her mother, stumbling across Amity’s body on the kitchen floor.

Hawk slammed the door behind himself, dropping the latch, grabbing his rifle from the corner of the room. He shoved his big pistol at Delphinia, yelling: “Your bedroom!” A crash had come from her room, telling her somebody had come through the window.

Shocked and staggering across the floor, Delphinia headed through the darkness toward her own room where a hulking figure, muttering in Spanish, lifted his hand. Orange fire spat from across the room. Delphinia fell backwards, hitting the doorjamb, firing Hawk's gun and missing as the man bolted past her, swatting her to the floor as if smashing a fly.

Rolling, gasping, she looked up at Hawk, turning from the door, yelling: "Lupe Rivera!" Hawk flew into Rivera, hitting him so hard in the throat that he rolled onto the floor with a groan, hugging his arms around his neck.

Delphinia struggled to her feet with her eyes riveted to the open bedroom window, expecting more trouble to come bursting through. The curtains only fluttered oddly in the stillness. Then, suddenly, a great golden flash lit the yard, throwing wavy red and yellow shadows throughout the house.

"They've set fire to the tool shed," Hawk yelled, hunched at the front window.

Delphinia turned to look outside. "And the haystack!"

"The bastards," Hawk said. "Likely they'll burn the barn next, and the house."

Delphinia inched past Lupe Rivera's body, scared to get too close, hoping he was dead, but not wanting to touch him. "He looks dead, Pa?"

"Check him! Make sure!" Hawk ordered. "You don't want the bastard shooting us in the back, do you?"

She gulped, reaching for the man's curly head. His hat slipped to the floor; dark eyes stared back at Delphinia. His mouth was slacked in a way that no person could possibly fake. She touched his throat, feeling for the vein that pulsed as Amity had showed her once. He was already turning cold. "Dead, Pa."

Hawk did not answer. He lifted Amity from the floor, hugging her to his chest, holding her gentle form, looking as small as a child. Her long, blonde hair hung from the back of her dangling head, swaying in the firelight, nearly reaching as far as Hawk's knees. He carried her into their bedroom and shut the door.

Delphinia did not have to be told her mother was dead. Her world was suddenly so full of terror she did not know how to respond. She crawled closer to the front window and held Hawk's big pistol across the windowsill, watching the yard light up as if it was daytime. The roar of the burning haystack sounded like a train in the yard; the tool shed crumbled into white-hot ash. Sparks and flames, white-gold heat, snapping and cracking, resounded against her ears and across the yard and high into the pre-dawn sky.

A crouched figure darted across the yard toward the house, and in the firelight Delphinia saw that the man resembled the dead one on the floor — dark-haired, big, wide shoulders, high Mexican boots. She shot once. Her bullet went wild. Billowing flames turned the yard into hell. She saw Hawk's black horse and the bay team and Slicker galloping around the corral in confusion, shaking their heads at the fire and gunshots. A movement near the porch brought Delphinia's attention back to the man dashing up the steps. He angled along the railing, running in the shadows toward the front door like a charging, but cautious, bull.

Her next shot brought Hawk out of the bedroom. Rifle in hand, Hawk yelled in hysterical tones like she had never heard from him before. The look on his face told her he had gone berserk over Amity. There was no stopping him now.

Yanking the door open, Hawk yelled once: "Come on you bastards!" He hefted the rifle across his arm and met the head-on gunfire roaring across the porch. Hawk staggered once, then pitched forward with a thud.

"No, Pa!" Delphinia screamed.

Raul Rivera stumbled over Hawk's body. Floundering for an instant, he regained his balance and rushed into the house.

"Lupe!" he shouted to his dead brother, and then hovered over the body. His eyes shifted to Delphinia, crouched against the wall.

"You!" he said.

She raised her pistol in what seemed like slow motion. The scene took on a dream-like quality, a nightmare. She watched in fascination as Raul Rivera slowly pointed his gun at her, too, taking his time, deadly serious, matching her movement finally, pulling the trigger and hearing only a sharp click from the spent bullet in the chamber. He pulled the trigger again — another click.

A tall, blond man rushed into the house, waving his arms, shouting: "Come on! We have to ride! We got the bastard, didn't we? Posse coming!" His screams filled the house. "I ain't going back to prison…never!" He ran out of the house, jerking Raul Rivera forward by his arms.

"I will be back!" Raul Rivera told Delphinia.

The two men paused in the doorway for an instant. "Posse?" Raul Rivera asked, confused.

"Come on!" Bate Thatcher said again, bounding off the steps. "They're coming fast!"

Both men bolted away across the yard as Delphinia listened to the thunderous rumbling of horses' hoofs and fast-moving wagons. Shouts and whisdes came from the road east — Brubakers!

Lowering Hawk's gun, Delphinia staggered to the front door in time to see the fleeing outlaws dash over the edge of the arroyo to the horses held by another rider. After they mounted, the three charged up the opposite side of the arroyo and spurred hard north in the direction of Locust Cañon. She went out onto the porch.

A dozen horses galloped wildly into the yard ridden by Brubaker boys. Ma Brubaker handled the reins of the big team, pulling hard into their collars, swirling the heavy freight wagon around the yard in a stone-tossing circle. "Halloo, Amity! We seen your fire!" the woman shouted above the plunging team.

Mr. Brubaker charged in behind his wife, slapping the reins against the back of a lathered horse pulling a buggy. He jumped out, dragging empty buckets that rattled and clanked from behind the buggy seat. "Fire! We've come to help!"

Ma Brubaker scrambled down from the wagon, pulling her long calico skirts up to her thick ankles so she could tromp faster. "Amity? Where's Amity? By gaw, what happened here?" She swung her head around so that her double chins hung like a dewlap. Delphinia let out an eerie, high-pitched laugh, like she was losing her mind.

Jess Brubaker arrived, jumped from his plunging horse, and dashed up the steps to take Delphinia in his arms, holding her tight against himself, looking at her like he had seen a ghost. "Del! You all right? What's going on here?" His eyes fell on the crumpled shape of Hawk Estes near their feet.

Mr. Brubaker clumped around the yard, heading for the well where he began hauling up water while his boys carried buckets. Some of the boys were so little they lugged the water in front of themselves, grunting and swinging the heavy buckets between their short legs. They sloshed across the yard, pitching water onto the smoldering remains of the tool shed and haystack.

Delphinia trembled against Jess who held her while his mother knelt over Hawk's body. Muttering, Ma Brubaker pressed her fingers across her mouth before creeping into the house. Her hesitant footsteps in the center of the kitchen told Delphinia she was hovering over Lupe Rivera's body. A loud gasp filled the room. And then Ma Brubaker walked into Amity's bedroom and screamed.

Chapter Three

Amity and Hawk were laid to rest at the edge of the garden. Jess helped Delphinia build a tight, barbed-wire fence around the graves. Delphinia decided that, while the coffins rested side by side, they should each face opposite directions. Amity faced the house, the garden, and the chicken coop. Hawk faced the high, wild hills of Locust Cañon. In death as in life, Delphinia knew, Hawk and Amity were happiest when allowed their own points of view.

"We lost 'em in the rocks at High Peak," Jess said, slumping in his saddle six days later. His tired horse stamped a hoof at a fly. The bay's dull expression showed he had covered many miles.

Delphinia sat at her loom, the way she had been each day since the funeral. "Any of them caught yet?"

Jess shook his head. "No. Pa went home, and the other posse members headed to town with Sheriff Hat ton. I'm sorry, Del. I'd hoped we'd catch up to them before they hurt anybody else."

"They won't get away, Jess," Delphinia said, giving the last row of yarn a hard thumping with the weft beater.

"Mind if I climb down for water?"

She smiled. "Since when do you have to ask permission for water around here?"

Jess dismounted stiffly, his hard heels thumping the ground. "You look kind of peaked. I just figured you might not want my company."

Her pale eyes searched the distant ridges, fine wrinkles

already showing on her young skin from harsh wind and hot weather and the last week of suffering. "Dry and cold up there. They'll be coming back here soon."

Jess's eyes followed the direction of her gaze. "I think they'll head over the slope before circling down south…likely go to Mexico." He walked his horse to the water trough, allowing the bay a long drink.

Delphinia shot one last stare at the distant mountains before putting her weft beater down. Then she got up slowly from the loom and walked into the house. Tossing a small log into the wood stove, she stoked up the fire.

Jess stomped noisily into the house, making his usual racket. He took his hat off, tossing it onto the peg that had always been reserved for Hawk's hat.

"Coffee?" she asked. "Not much else, sorry. I've not felt like cooking these past days."

He sat at the table, glancing around the room. "What are you going to do now, Del?"

"Do?" She placed the coffee cup in front of him, steam rising.

"I mean, you can't stay out here by yourself. Alone."

"Why not? I've lived here all of my life."

"That was different. You had your mother, and Hawk…. people taking care of you."

"The time has come for me to take care of myself."

"Six old sheep and a vegetable garden ain't much of a living."

"It's done us fine. The place is mine now. I don't need anything from anybody."

"Your mother used to trade and sell herbs, and Hawk was always coming around with bounty money."

"What are you driving at, Jess?"

He put the coffee cup down. "I know things happened fast,

Del, but I always figured you and I would get married. Don't we have an understanding?"

"Understanding?"

"Aw, come on, Del. I'm not one for beating around bushes. Your folks are gone now, and you can't stay here by yourself. It's time we got married. You can move in with me and the folks. And that's that."

"That's what? Jess, I don't want your charity."

He pushed the cup away. "I better go. We can talk about this when you are feeling better."

"I feel all right, Jess."

"You don't sound all right! It's crazy, you thinking of staying here alone."

"I like being alone. I'm twenty years old, Jess. Marrying you and moving in with your folks…I'd be having babies the rest of my life…like your mother."

His jaw fell. "Well, what's wrong with that?"

"Everything is wrong with it, Jess. You're taking too much for granted. This is my place now, and I'll run it the way I want. Amity and Hawk are buried here. I'm not leaving my life. Besides, I have to settle the score with those killers."

"Score! You crazy? I see something going on inside that head of yours, Del. You're up to something, ain't you? Thinking of going after them yourself? Like father, like daughter?" He shook his head with a snort.

Tight lipped, Delphinia turned back to the stove, lifting the coffee pot and shifting it from one place to another, unable to decide if she wanted to keep it hot.

Jess stood up. "I'll come by in a few days, and we'll talk about this again…see if you are all right."

"Thank you, Jess. That's kind of you."

Frowning, he grabbed his hat from the peg and stomped down the porch steps, jerking his bridle reins from the hitching post. “Come on, let’s go home,” he told his horse, spurring it into a trot out of the yard.

Night drifted through the house. Restless coyote howls, eerie as a child’s cry in the middle of the night, came to Delphinia’s ears as she boarded up her bedroom window from the inside. The scattered glass from the broken window crunched under the soles of her shoes. She stood back and examined her handiwork. It would do until she could replace the window glass. As she made her way to the kitchen, Delphinia stopped to run her fingers along the rough wood of the door that separated her bedroom from the kitchen. In order to make space for Delphinia’s furniture in the tiny bedroom, Hawk had hung the door so that it would open out into the kitchen. Amity had found pulling open a door to be a nuisance, but tonight, Delphinia realized, it could have its use.

Back in the bedroom, the door closed, and the chair positioned strategically, she rested the barrel of the sawed-off shotgun over the back of the chair, securing the gun stock to the foot rail of the bed with strong cord, gun barrels facing toward the bedroom door. After she had finished setting her trap, she checked that everything was in place — hammers cocked, gun loaded, string tied to triggers and crossed through the room to the doorknob, everything anchored back around the bedposts, string just loose enough so that the gun would not go off too quickly when the door was opened.

Satisfied, she climbed up the wooden loft ladder she had placed inside the bedroom earlier, pulling up the ladder behind herself and crossing the attic, ladder in tow, and sliding it through the ceiling hole above the kitchen. Before proceeding down, Delphinia glanced briefly around the loft used for storage, noticing the quilt bag and her mother’s old trunk. She climbed down.

Shivering, she placed several blankets on the kitchen floor near the stove, and, holding Hawk's pistol against her breast, she curled up in tense anticipation. She knew she was not ready to sleep in Amity's and Hawk's bed yet.

Daylight hung in a blanket of silver dew, morning shadows glowing pinkish across the far peaks. Ghost clouds hung in billowed white patches over the path winding its way from Locust Cañon. Delphinia squinted as she tried to locate the rider she knew was passing through the Cañon. She was confident because, since she had been a little girl watching for Hawk, she had come to recognize the signs of anyone traveling through that area. The minutes dragged by, and when no friendly rider presented himself in the yard, she knew it was time to act. Whoever stirred up there was coming in from behind the low hills that separated the house from the big arroyo where prickly pear grew as thick as a fence. A bunch of sparrows flew suddenly out of the cactus, causing Delphinia to smile to herself and think: *So, that is where you are.*

Milk bucket in hand, she crossed the yard slowly, weighted at the waist by Hawk's gun belt and the big pistol strapped under her shawl. Inside the pen she fed the goat, then waited for the frisky, white nanny to hop onto the wooden milking stand. Delphinia sat on a stool next to the squirmy creature's warm right flank, and, after placing the bucket under the goat's udders, she cleaned the long soft teats with a damp cloth before she began milking. She allowed the milk to flow into each teat, waiting for the swell before she clamped thumb and index finger and squeezed with her hand. Long warm streams of milk *pinged* into the enamel bucket, and slowly the liquid filled the container, frothy and white. Clamp. Squeeze. Clamp. Squeeze. She hummed to herself even though the hair stood up on the back of her neck. She felt the nanny flinch the way she always did when sensing the presence of a stranger.

Clamp…squeeze…*ping!* Clamp…squeeze…*ping!*

Delphinia kept her eyes on the foam. "Easy, girl, easy. Til be done in a few seconds." She wiped the goat's udders with the damp cloth, feeling they were flaccid from loss of milk. Delphinia stood up, released the goat from the wooden stocks, and patted the animal's smooth back before turning toward the house. She studied the horses in the corral. Their eyes, too, were drawn to the arroyo where the birds had flown up. Her gelding, Slicker, snuffled the air, testing. Hawk's big black watched the arroyo, perhaps sensing a strange horse.

Delphinia walked across the yard, aware of the pistol still heavy under her shawl, holding the milk bucket easy, legs heavy with the urge to run, but not daring — not yet. And then a bullet slammed, loud and sudden, piercing the enamel bucket so that it tipped like a child's swing, turning in an arc, bottom up, and causing the milk to spurt through two holes like a sieve, splashing down her ankle and onto her shoe. Delphinia froze for a few seconds then, letting go of the bucket, attempted a dash toward the porch as heavy boots thudded behind her. She was stopped by the crash of a body against her own, as strong hands grabbed her waist and spun her around. In a wild stumble both she and her attacker tripped over the milk bucket and fell to the ground.

Raul Rivera's bad breath, smelling like onions and tobacco, scalded her nostrils. "I told you I would be back," he sneered.

She cringed, stiffened, turning her face away from him. Breathing hard, she was pinned under his heavy body. She saw his wiry, black chest hair curling up from his open collar.

"Your father killed my brother, *puta!*"

She clenched her teeth. Being called a whore was the least of her problems.

"Get up!" he ordered as he pushed himself off of her. "I

do not roll in the dirt like a pig."

"Why not? You are a pig."

Yanked to her feet, she fought the urge to lash out at him. *Calm down, Delphinia, calm down.*

He laughed, reaching under her shawl and fingering Hawk's pistol. "So! You carry a gun. I don't blame you!" Still laughing, he tucked the gun into his belt and dragged Delphinia into the house.

Relax. Relax. The word buzzed around and around inside her head. She looked at Raul Rivera whose eyes roved around the room. "Nobody else here, eh?"

She shook her head. "Nobody."

He let out a laugh. "It is hard for me to believe you stay here alone. But that is good. We have plenty of time."

"Yes. Plenty of time. Where are your friends? Bate Thatcher, and the other man?"

"That posse killed Bate's horse. He and Blackjack wait for me in the mountains. This job is for me alone."

"Blackjack? Is he the other man who rides with you?"

He nodded. "Yeah, Blackjack Parry. I will give Bate my horse, now that I have the horse of Hawk Estes. The black is a strong animal. He will carry me far. I will ride him to death, knowing how Hawk Estes liked that horse...and I will enjoy every minute of it."

"I believe you," Delphinia said.

He cocked his head, his left eyebrow forming a question mark. "You are not afraid of me?"

"Of course, I'm afraid of you. How could I not be?"

He laughed. "I like that! A woman who is honest. Perhaps you are trying to fool me into liking you just a little so that I will not kill you. Eh?"

"You killed my parents. My father killed your brother. How could we like one another? You told me you would come back.

You must be full of revenge."

"Ah! So now we are going to talk, making up reasons why people do the things they do. You hope to distract me with talk. Eh?"

Before she could answer he grabbed her harder, pulling her against his body until she panted for breath, kissing her so hard her neck bent back until she feared it would break. His hot, wet lips repulsed her. His tongue found its way between her teeth. She gasped, choking and gagging.

He finally drew away. "So, I think perhaps you like this, eh? We will talk about the killing part later. Right now let us find out how much you want to live. It will be a game."

"Yes," she whispered. "A game. You should know…I never had a man before."

His eyes widened. "Ah! So you are curious? I promise you …daughter of Hawk Estes…you will die happy. You have my personal guarantee." He threw back his dust-streaked face and let out a roar.

"My bedroom is there," she said, pointing to the closed door with fingers cold as ice.

He nodded, still holding her wrist. "Now!"

"My hands are sticky with goat milk. They smell. Let me wash," she pointed to a water bucket near the stove with her free hand.

He eyed her. "You will try to run away?"

"Where will I run to?"

He dropped her wrist, keeping his eye on her, walking sideways toward her bedroom door, spurs softly ringing.

Delphinia reached the pail, slowly washing the sticky milk scum from her hands, listening to the slow creak of the bedroom door. Then a crash like thunder rolled through the house when both barrels erupted with flame and smoke, filling the place in a wave of sulphur fumes, blood, and urine.

Delphinia shivered but kept washing her hands. She braced herself before she dared to look over her shoulder at the torn body of Raul Rivera, quivering in death throes on the kitchen floor.

Then, suddenly, Jess appeared in the open doorway. "Del, are you...?" he stopped in mid-sentence. "You killed him!" Staring at the body, he rubbed his chin in wonder and amazement. "By God, you killed him!" he repeated, looking up at her. "What are you gonna do now?"

"Jess! Where'd you come from?"

"I just rode in and heard the shot. What happened?"

"He came back...tried to kill me."

"What are you going to do with him?"

"I'll take him to town," she whispered. Her body turned cold. She was shaking so hard she felt as if she would vomit. "Help me load him on his horse."

Chapter Four

Delphinia reined Slicker down the center of the dusty main street of town. Slicker's long, gray neck arched as he champed mildly on the bit. People stopped to look at the strange procession. Delphinia merely ignored them. She reined in at the sheriffs office, halting Slicker at the hitching rail and drawing the rope of the horse she led that carried the body of Raul Rivera tied, head down, across the saddle.

Delphinia unhooked her right knee from her sidesaddle and dropped lightly to the ground, careful not to bump Hawk's heavy pistol, retrieved from the body of Raul Rivera and hanging at her right hip.

"Who have you got there, Delphinia?" Sheriff Jim Hat ton asked, swaggering out the office door. He took long strides toward the corpse. Standing next to Rivera's horse, he lifted the dangling head. "Raul Rivera!" He looked sharply at Del phinia. "What happened?"

She tied Slicker to the hitching post, and, turning toward the sheriff, she lifted her long, black riding skirt so she would not trip while stepping up the edge of the board walk. "He rode into my place this morning. He wanted a horse." She peeled off her leather gloves as she walked into the sheriff's office, leaving the gaping crowd gathering around the body.

Jim Hat ton followed her inside, running his hand down his smooth-shaven face. "You killed him." His remark was more of a statement than a question. "How did you manage that?"

She faced him, shrugging. "I used Pa's shotgun on him."

"You sure did!"

"I brought him to you, along with everything he carried. A

pistol, that's still in his holster. His rifle is in the saddle boot. That's his horse. He told me Bate Thatcher and the other outlaw, Blackjack Parry, were waiting for him somewhere near Locust Cañon. They're out of food and supplies, and down to one horse. One of their horses was killed by your posse during the fight you had with the gang two days ago."

He sat, propped at the edge of his desk, still frowning at her. "Maybe you better stay in town until they're caught. They're liable to come looking for Raul at your place when he doesn't come back."

"I can't stay in town. I have chores to do."

"Yes. Chores...well, I expect you have neighbors to look in on you."

"I'll be all right. I can take care of myself."

"I can see that. There's a reward on Raul Rivera. Two hundred and fifty dollars. The same for Lupe, killed by your father. I have the voucher here for Lupe. You can cash it. I'll get a telegram sent out about Raul as soon as the body is positively identified."

"Two hundred and fifty dollars," Delphinia said. "Not much for a man's life, is it?"

"Were you expecting more?" His voice carried an edge.

"No. In fact, I'd forgotten about the bounty. I only meant, it seems strange how people put prices on one another."

"Your father made his living that way."

She nodded. "It was nothing my mother was proud of."

"And you?"

She shrugged. "I learned not to judge my parents' opposing opinions."

He smiled at her. "You have an interesting approach to life."

She noticed the way he crossed his arms, swaying a little at the edge of his desk, studying her with an expectant grin at the corners of his handsome mouth. She trembled under his scrutiny. "I have shopping to do. May I go now?"

"Go ahead. I'm not holding you for anything." He reached over the back of the desk and slid out a bounty voucher from the desk drawer. "Stop by in a couple of days, and I'll have the other for you."

Taking the voucher from his hand, she thanked him and let herself out of the office. She unhitched Slicker and made her way to the bank to cash her check, then continued on to the general store where she bought an enamel bucket to replace the one shot by Raul Rivera.

"How much longer you going to scrub that floor?" Jess asked, watching her from his position astride a kitchen chair. He rested his chin on his crossed arms.

Delphinia's hand worked methodically, back and forth, as on her knees she scrubbed the patch of floor between the bedroom and kitchen doorway. The first water she had squeezed from the scrub rag was dark brown, but it ran clear now. She arched her back, bearing down with her shoulders on the heavy, wooden-handled brush. "I want to get all the blood out of the wood," was all she said, brushing droplets of sweat off the corners of her mouth with her shoulder. Her hair was tied up in a gold-streaked bun at the nape of her neck. She had knotted the hem of her blue calico dress around the top of her knees.

"Hell, Del! I came over here to see you…talk to you… and the only thing I get to do is admire you scrubbing the dang-burned floor!"

"You wanted to marry me the last time you were here, Jess. Scrubbing floors and doing laundry is all women get to do. Married women, especially. Not very romantic, huh?"

"Scrubbing floors ain't any less romantic than shooting a

man and scrubbing up the blood. That's what you'd rather be doing? You are something, Del."

She got up off the floor, pressing her wet hands against the small of her back and letting out a sigh. "Here," she said, handing him the bucket. "Toss the water for me. You can pour it over the potato plants in the garden."

Grabbing the bucket from her hand, he swirled out the kitchen door. "Pour it over the plants! Good idea! We don't want to waste a drop of this water. A little fertilizer from Raul Rivera will be good for the potatoes, I reckon." He stomped away to the vegetable garden.

She poured herself a glass of water out of a clay jug on the sideboard and took a long drink. Staring out the window, she scanned the buttes where the afternoon sun lazed like a swirl of pink organdy. Dotted scrub oak slashed up hills that rose to the tops of the distant peaks. Purplish and quiet, lying in for another evening, the hills had rested this way for a million years before her and would likely rest another million after she had gone. She recalled her last conversation with Hawk about his love for the land.

Jess stomped back into the house, swinging the empty bucket. "Raul Rivera's resting quiet in the potato patch, Del."

She followed him. "There is nothing funny about it, Jess. I'm sorry you can't understand why I wanted to get this floor clean. Tomorrow I'll fix that shot-up bedroom door."

Jess stood in the bedroom doorway, eyeing the propped shotgun and the long strings that hung in loose loops around the bedposts and across the floor from the triggers. "You must have measured it just right, so's he'd get the door open before Old Betsy went off. How'd you think of it?"

"Hawk told me a story, once, about how he spent a week holed up in a shack with a fever so bad he kept passing out, and he knew the outlaw he was tracking would come looking for him. Pa wired up his gun so he could get some sleep."

Jess turned to her, making a face. "Is that all we get to talk about any more? Rigging up guns and shooting outlaws?"

"You asked me," she said by way of answering as she walked outside, resting against the porch railing. A strong breeze kicked up dusty wind devils across the yard, causing her skirt to flip around her knees and the horses inside the corral to snort. "Jess, remember when we were kids, playing over in the arroyo, where you tried to trap quail in that little wooden box you made?"

He stood close to her. "Sure, Del, I remember. I caught a few, too, after I finally figured out how to lay a trail of corn."

She nodded. "A trail of corn. It led them right into the trap. Those quail pecked along the ground, one kernel at a time, until they walked right into the box, and you had the very last kernel tied to the string that slammed the door on them."

He laughed. "It ain't hard to catch something, once you know how to set the trap."

She smiled at him. "I'm glad you remember, and understand."

He gave her a long, sad look. "I catch your drift, Del. You ain't going to be happy until you get the other two, are you?"

"They killed Hawk and Amity."

"Catching quail is one thing, Del. You got lucky with Raul Rivera. The other two might not fall for the same old trick. I don't want you out here alone. I lay awake all night, wondering what might be happening to you. It ain't fair, Del. You're making me sick with worry. Won't you please come over to our place, at least until Bate Thatcher and Blackjack Parry are caught?"

She shrugged. "Jess, after Bate and Blackjack, there might be others. Have you any idea how many men Hawk either killed or captured for reward money? How many want revenge?"

"Hawk's dead! Setting yourself up as bait won't solve anything. You have to get out of here."

"Where will I go? Bringing a trail of killers to your doorstep isn't what I want for you and your family, Jess. Always wondering, when you ride out in the morning, if you will be back at night? Wondering who will get you to get even with me? I don't want to live like that, Jess. I'd rather it stopped with me. I'm sorry."

He took her elbow, pressing his fingers gently into her flesh. "Does that mean you and I are through?"

She gulped, turning to face in the direction of the buttes where a heavy layer of dust told her that riders were coming.

His eyes followed her gaze when she stiffened. "Maybe Hat ton and the posse."

"Could be." She stepped back against the wall, sitting on the wooden bench and fanning her face with her hand.

The horses bobbed along in the evening dusk, anxious in their approach to the buildings for water. The posse entered the yard, and Sheriff Hat ton dismounted at the water trough. He tossed his reins to one of the riders crowding around the tank. He walked tiredly across the yard toward Jess and Delphinia.

"Any sign of them, Sheriff?" Jess asked, meeting the sheriff at the edge of the steps.

"They were south of Locust Cañon. We found their camp. The fire was still warm. They must have seen us coming."

"I was hoping you'd have them by now," Jess muttered.

"Delphinia," Sheriff Hat ton said, "I'd feel better if you rode into town with us tonight."

She shook her head in stubborn disagreement. "This is my home, and I won't be run out of it. I'll be fine. Anyway, they won't likely be back here again."

"The bad news is the other horse is dead," he told her.

"Blackjack and Thatcher are both on foot now, and this is the closest place to rustle mounts for themselves. You're looking for big trouble staying here by yourself, Delphinia."

"Thank you for the warning, Sheriff. But I can't spend the rest of my life jumping at shadows."

He reached for the bridle reins his deputy held extended toward him, having brought the horse up to the sheriff's side. "All right, have it your own way." He mounted his horse, looking down at Jess. "I'll count on you and your folks to keep an eye on her." Without saying anything else to Delphinia, he reined with the posse and headed out of the yard.

Chapter Five

It wasn't long after the posse rode away that Jess told Delphinia good bye. She watched him leave, a fine, powdery dust trail in the wind, heading east to the Brubaker place. Shivering, she clutched her shawl a little tighter to herself and then began her chores. When she was finished, she locked herself inside the house. In the glow of the kerosene lamp she had lit, she examined the floor where she had scrubbed away the pool of blood left by Raul Rivera. Satisfied that it was as clean as she would get it, she carried the ladder inside the bedroom, aligned it below the loft, and then reset the shotgun. She ascended to the attic through the ceiling hole.

As she made her way through the attic toward the kitchen side of the house, her attention was drawn by her mother's big trunk with the round top. She had been curious about it since she was a child. But she had long given up the idea of getting into it, Amity having insisted always it was full of nothing but old family clothing.

Now she gave into that childhood curiosity and found herself kneeling in front of the trunk. She examined it closely in the semi-darkness and found the big, rusted padlock secured as it had always been. Searching around the attic rafters for a key proved fruitless, so she let herself down the ladder into the kitchen and went into Amity's bedroom.

Delphinia looked around the cold room, flinching and remembering how Amity's body had looked. The room was still in disarray — bedclothes rumpled, a pair of leather, high-top shoes resting one against the other, left in the position Amity had slipped out of them the night before she was killed. She stared at the bloodied, white, cotton nightgown, draped where she had left it when changing Amity into her burial dress. Hawk's leather vest still hung over the back of a chair.

Lighting the kerosene lamp on the dresser, Delphinia gathered up the clothing and sheets. Tomorrow she would face a laundry tub. Tonight, she wanted to find the trunk key. She searched through the dresser drawers, across closet shelves, even inside a box of papers and old recipes, browned from age. Sitting at the foot of the bed, Delphinia read the papers and notes and determined there was nothing here of any consequence. Her mother had no secrets or surprises. A list on the dresser top was scrawled with reminders of what Amity needed to buy on her next trip to town — a bolt of cloth, salt, sugar.

Delphinia left the bedroom, closing the door behind her, and rummaged through the toolbox behind the wood stove until she found the screwdriver and hammer. Carefully she climbed back up the loft ladder with the tools tucked under her arm, a kerosene lamp in her hand. In the attic she lit the lamp and held it over her head to light the area. But her attempts to open the trunk were futile. She ended her efforts by smashing at the lock with the hammer and finally twisting the screwdriver into the keyhole, but the lock remained intact. Disappointed and tired, she gave up for the night, climbing back down the ladder, and falling into a fitful night's sleep on the blankets by the stove.

Hot morning sun choked the skyline to the east, yellow slashes against a slate sky heralding a hot, dry day. Delphinia hoed potatoes, carefully drawing up little sandy hills around each plant, pulling weeds with her hands. She interrupted her work at intervals to glance north toward Locust Cañon. Each time her eyes followed the ridges, waiting for dust layers to appear. It was during one of these moments that she noticed a wispy puff at the center of the place she had nicknamed Narrow Pass, where the air currents always carried dust in big, round puffs from men on horseback. But today the smaller, web-like layers told her a man was moving fast, on foot.

She stiffened. Calculating. *One man. On foot. Maybe two hours.* Hurrying to the chicken house door, she reached for the axe. Entering the little building, she pulled a red hen from a nesting box. "Sorry," Delphinia whispered, "you'd have laid a fine egg this morning, but I need you to help me with something more important."

Carrying the squalling hen out of the coop, she whacked its head off in one hard thump at the chopping block. She flinched when the head dropped, still spurting blood — round yellow eyes flickering, the red wrinkled eyelids closed in a half squint. No time to scald the feathers, she plucked them quickly and, reaching for a sharp knife, skinned the hen in wild jerks, finally gutting it over the fence at the pigsty. The pigs snuffled at her, eyeing the procedure before eating the warm chicken innards. A few quick chops dismembered the hen, and Delphinia was ready.

Biting her lower lip, she turned to the house. Inside, she quickly dropped several rough logs into the wood stove. Gathering her biggest stew pot and utensils, first she poured water into the pot and then cut up some vegetables. When all the ingredients were mixed into the pot along with a few spices, Delphinia hurried outside to the herb collection and chose the green metal can from the highest shelf. She returned to the kitchen and poured the finely ground, brown powder into the simmering chicken stew.

Having lost track of time, she stirred the pot and gazed out the window, watching for the dust to appear in a fine layer above the trail. A covey of quail rose in a big wing-fluttering cloud from behind the cover of prickly pear north of the arroyo.

Delphinia shook her head: *So there you are.*

She put a lid on the stew pot and then slowly dragged her spinning wheel and wool bag from the corner of the kitchen. Sitting in front of the wheel, she pulled sections of fleece from the bag and began tearing it slowly between her fingers. She scraped the strands across carders on her lap, then drafted the strands into yarn. Spinning — spinning. The wheel whirred and squeaked softly in unison with her rhythmic treadling.

When he spoke to her, his voice was so low and soft it did not startle her. Rather his voice somehow blended with the whirring of the wheel and the bubbling of the stew pot on the stove. "Ain't seen a spinning wheel since home."

She looked up from her spinning, noticing the long, dark shadow falling across the floor onto her lap from the doorway. She quit treadling. Her hands were stationary.

"Keep on spinning…don't let me stop you," Bate Thatcher said in an oily, rolling voice, colored by a deep Southern accent.

She watched him fill the doorway — a giant in tattered clothing. He held a rifle in his big, rough hand. There was no pistol in his holster. He wore a battered felt hat, and his blue jeans were too short. His jacket sleeves came halfway to his elbows, and he wore no shirt underneath. His sun-creased face was as lined as an old leather shoe.

"Where is Raul Rivera?" he asked, looking around the room.

"Who?" she said softly, nervous as a bird.

He squinted at her. "You know who he is. He was coming down here for guns and horses."

"All my horses are inside the corral. I haven't seen any-body."

"You lying to me, gal? Don't lie."

"You can look around, if you don't believe me. Is Blackjack

with you?" she asked, picking up more carded wool from her lap.

"No. He's waiting in the hills. Both of our horses are dead, but he's too lazy to walk down here. He sent me on ahead."

"I see," she answered, trying to stay calm.

He gulped, licking his lips. "I want guns and a horse, and then I'll go. I don't want trouble with you…unless you ask for it."

"You brought me plenty of trouble already. Both my folks are dead."

He nodded. "Your pa was on our trail, and ain't a one of us wanted to go back to prison. Your ma shouldn't have stood in the door that way, white nightgown and all…made me a good target. It was nothin' personal."

"May I stand up?" Delphinia asked.

"You set down there by yourself. Why do you need my permission to stand up?"

"You are pointing a gun at me. I have to stir the chicken stew before it burns."

He sniffed, licking his lips again. "Heap a plate for me, and some hot coffee, too. Hotter the better. Then I want your guns and horses. And then I'll decide what to do about you."

She nodded, standing up slowly from her chair, pushing the wool bundle away, and brushing off her lap.

"My mama used a spinning wheel," he said, walking across the floor in long, slow strides, towering over Delphinia like a tree. "Only she spun cotton into fine thread. Not heavy yarn like you are doing."

"My yarn is thick because I'm using it to make a rug."

"A rug? You weave, too? My folks were poor…picked cotton on a dirt-poor farm. My mama did spinning, making thread. One time I watched weavers in the town operatin' a big, smooth-running loom, weaving material to make fine shirts. But my folks wore homespun."

She walked carefully to the stove, reaching for a spoon, then stirring. Spicy aromas wafted through the room. "I learned to make rugs on a Navajo loom," she said. "My mother sent me to Tucson for three years where I went to school. A Navajo woman taught some of us girls how to weave."

He petted the spinning wheel with slow, gentle strokes. "If I had more time, I'd like to learn that myself. You could teach me. It would be something useful…weaving…being able to make a rug or a blanket. I don't mind telling you I like what you have here. All of it."

She stirred. "What I have here?"

He nodded out the door. "Them sheep…and the chickens. Good horses and a well. I wouldn't mind spending the rest of my days on a place like this, just poking in the garden and watching the days come and go. Quiet like. No folks nearby to bother me." His face saddened.

"Looks like you've taken a different road," she said, still stirring. The crash behind her brought her head around. She stared wild eyed, while he smashed the spinning wheel against the wall with vicious kicks. The wheel splintered in loud cracks under his huge, tromping feet.

"Don't tell me, and don't judge me!" He pointed the gun barrel at her chest as seconds dragged by, and the hatred drained from his red-rimmed eyes. "Pile up that stew, girl, and go sit down at the other side of the room where I can watch you. I'll have me a meal before I burn this place down."

Delphinia did as she was told.

Bate Thatcher hunched over the steaming bowl, grabbed a spoon, and shoveled the spicy chunks of chicken and carrots into his mouth. Wiping his lips on the edge of his threadbare sleeve, he gobbled more, washing down every couple of spoonfuls with hot coffee.

Shivers crept up the back of Delphinia's sweaty neck. Stay *calm, stay calm.* She was mesmerized by his thick fingers, how they wrapped around the spoon. His rifle was lying across the table, pointed at her. *How long will it take? A few minutes? An hour?* She gulped. The inside of her mouth felt dry and tasteless.

His head jerked up. His eyes bore into her. A surprised look crossed his face while he tried sucking in air through his nostrils. He dropped the spoon with a splash onto his plate. His mouth opened with a gasp. "What's in this stew? What…you put in here?" he demanded between ragged pulls for air. His mouth was open. His voice sounded like rasping accordion bellows.

"What?" she answered, tipping her head. Her hands were frozen in a knot on her lap, her fingernails cutting into her palms.

"You!" he raged, "you put something in this…?"

"Just chile and spices, that's all. Maybe you want more coffee?"

He staggered up, thrusting the bowl across the table so that it flipped onto the floor with a clatter. Stew splattered across the room. The spoon bounced with a clang. He reached for his rifle, struggling to find the trigger, rotating his head, blinking as if his sight were gone. He fought to get his fingers through the trigger guard, aiming the rifle shakily in Delphinia's direction.

"You're wrong," she said. "The stew is fine. I just put in spices…." Her look was serene and caring. *Calm down. Calm down.*

The rifle clattered to the floor as he whirled, wincing in pain, doubling over with both big fists clutched up under his breastbone, gagging. Blue, bubbling foam drooled from the edges of his mouth. Bate Thatcher sank to his knees, bumping his head on the table top, slipping to the floor, panting for air.

Delphinia rose slowly from the chair and walked the length

of the room until she reached his rifle. She picked it up. It hung heavily in her hands. She opened the chamber and saw that it was empty. Snapping the lever back in place with a metallic click, she looked at the outlaw who watched her with eyes full of pain and fear.

"I'd have killed you if I had a bullet left," he said.

Backing away from him, she went outside to saddle Slicker. By the time she got back to the house, he was dead. She looped a rope around Thatcher's ankles and, carrying one end in her hand, proceeded outside where she mounted Slicker. She dallied the rope around the saddle horn and dragged the heavy body out of the house and down to the barn, positioning the body underneath the pulley where she and her mother used to do the butchering. Next she slid the hay hook through Thatcher's belt. She remounted Slicker and rode the horse, drawing the body until it swung four feet off the ground. Finally, after harnessing the bays, she drove the buckboard underneath the swaying body and, releasing the hay rope, lowered the body onto the back of the rig.

Chapter Six

The buckboard bounced over the ruts, hitting rocks and stones and the hard-packed, clay ruts of old wheel tracks. By the late afternoon the sun blazed like a sizzling fry pan. Delphinia adjusted her bonnet strings — they chafed because she had tied them too tightly in her haste. Ahead the town could be seen — rooftops and adobe brown walls shimmering in the heat waves.

Sheriff Hatton's chestnut horse was tied in front of his office. Two small boys came out of the barber shop. People on the board walk stopped to stare.

"Frightful Delphinia got herself another bounty!" one of the boys yelled, and within seconds the street filled with curious townspeople, shaking their heads and whispering among themselves. Heads poked out of doorways; window shades were pulled back; faces looked out of the saloon.

"Frightful Delphinia!" the boys continued to chant, before somebody shushed them.

Delphinia ignored each and every face in the growing crowd, drawing the buckboard up in front of the sheriffs office. She climbed quietly down from the rig, tying the left bay to the hitching rack, and entered the office. "Sheriff? I have Bate Thatcher outside."

Grabbing his hat, Jim Hat ton hurried across the room from where he had been sipping coffee near the potbelly stove. "Bate Thatcher!" He gawked.

She followed him, readjusting her bonnet strings again, tired of their chafing. She finally loosened the strings completely so that they hung loosely down the front of her dress. The crowd now surrounded the buckboard. Amidst the nods and mumbles the people peeked under the saddle blanket Delphinia had placed over Bate's head.

"What's that blue stuff around his mouth?" Sheriff Hat ton asked.

"Looks like poison," somebody from the crowd answered.

Hat ton turned to Delphinia. "You know what this is?"

"Poison," she said.

Dark looks settled on Delphinia from the disapproving crowd.

"He rode in this morning, demanding guns, horses, and.... food," Delphinia said to the sheriff. "He told me he would never go back to prison."

Jim Hat ton looked at the crowd. "All right, you men. Get him out of the wagon and over to the undertaker."

The murmur coming from the crowd sounded like a swarm of bees. "You ought to arrest her, Sheriff," a woman cried. "Poisoning ain't right."

"Would you like it better if I shot him?" Delphinia said, stepping forward with her chin up. Heads turned away from her, embarrassed, shocked. Those willing to help took Thatcher's body, while others drifted away.

"You better come inside the office," Sheriff Hat ton said, picking up the saddle blanket that had slipped from Thatcher's body and tossing it back into the buckboard.

Delphinia walked inside the office and began pacing back and forth between the stove and the desk. "He didn't have a horse. He came walking into my place. His gun was empty, but I didn't know it. He had a knife. I found it in his coat pocket. He admitted killing my mother. He planned to burn my house down."

The sheriff gave her a stiff nod, going through his stack of wanted fliers. "There's a three-hundred-dollar reward on him. I'll get the papers processed. You can pick up your voucher in a couple of days. Meanwhile, here's the one for Raul Rivera." He handed it to her.

"Thank you. Can I go now? I have to do some shopping …kitchen things I need."

"Delphinia…are you feeling all right? I mean, you killed two men in four days, and the only thing you got on your mind is shopping for kitchen things?"

She noticed what a fine, straight nose he had, the intensity of his brown eyes, and the way he tipped his head a little when he looked at her. His voice was nice. "How am I supposed to act? Cry? Faint? When my father came in here with a wanted man, did he carry on?"

"Of course, he didn't. He was a man! But he didn't go around using poison! If you're not careful, this whole town will be turned against you."

"A killer brought in by a woman is what this town doesn't like. My methods are not really what is important. It's me. People don't like knowing a woman can take care of herself."

His jaw tightened. "There's truth in what you say, but it doesn't change the way you'll be treated around here from now on."

She adjusted the holster strapped across her calico dress. "Folks around here never treated me or my mother with too much affection. They gossiped because of my father's…. profession. They want dangerous criminals taken out of circulation, but the methods have to suit them. When there's a hanging, everybody in town shows up to gawk, and that's all right, as long as it's on their terms."

"You know, Delphinia, you are mighty sharp tongued and uppity for such a young lady. I'm not going to stand here and argue with you."

She gave him a cool smile. "I'll be back in a few days for my reward money." She stalked out of the office. After untying the team, she drove them to the bank and finally to the general store. She purchased a new stew pot, several plates, and a big spoon. She planned to throw the old ones away.

Delphinia was scrubbing the floor again when Jess rode in. She listened as he dismounted and tied his horse to the hitching rack. He clumped into the house. His face was distorted by a look of frustration. "Pa rode into town this afternoon and heard you poisoned that outlaw. The whole town is talking about it, Del."

"Really? I just did what that whole big posse couldn't do. Why the fuss?"

He flung himself into a kitchen chair. "You've given them enough to talk about for a year."

She brushed hard against the floor planks, dipping the stiff-bristled brush into a bucket of water after each round of circular motions.

"What are you scrubbing up from the floor this time?" he finally asked.

"It's where Bate Thatcher fell when he was coughing and choking on the poisoned stew. I want to make sure I get everything washed up."

"I reckon I won't be asking you for any stew for supper tonight," he chortled.

"It's not funny, Jess. I did what I had to do. Would people like it better if I didn't know how to defend myself? Would it be better if they found me dead out here…the victim…. all cut up and murdered? Then they could go around shaking their heads, saying what a shame how I got killed, and how my folks got killed. Everybody would feel good in their morbidity, glad it was me instead of them."

"If you'd agree to marry me, you could move to my place and be out of here. I told you that the other day. None of this would have happened."

"Moving away doesn't solve anything for me." She continued scrubbing.

He looked around the house. "All right, then, after we're married, I'll move in with you." He pointed around the room. "We can tell our kids how you killed two men in here.... poisoned one and shot one. That is, after Amity and Hawk got gunned down inside the house, too. We'll surround ourselves with all them good stories. Every time we look at the bullet holes in the door we can relive how it all happened."

"Why don't you go, Jess? Quit pestering me." She did not look up from her scrubbing.

He jumped out of the chair, storming across the room to fling open Amity's bedroom door. He walked around the room, looking at things and shouting over his shoulder. "This here's her shoes? And old Hawk's hat? We can sleep in their bed and keep their memories alive." He came back to the doorway, facing her.

"I haven't had time to clean up the room yet," she said. "I'll get everything out of there in time. I'm not creating a museum, so quit picking on me."

He lunged across the room, reaching for the doorknob of Delphinia's bedroom door. "How about this?"

She screamed. "Don't open the door, Jess!" She jumped up, grabbing his legs, knocking him back against the wall, as the gun exploded from inside the room. "Jess!"

Stunned, he lay crumpled under her. "You had that gun rigged up again!"

"Of course, stupid!"

"Del! I could have been killed just now. Or what if somebody came riding in here while you were gone today? That old prospector, Cholla, or somebody? Anybody could have been killed. Didn't you think about that?"

She stood up, scraping soap scum from her arms. "I forgot about it. I was so concerned over what had happened with Bate Thatcher. Jess, I'm only trying to save my own life and what's mine. I can't worry about everything and everybody else."

Obviously shaken, Jess pushed himself up to his feet. He put his hands on Delphinia's shoulders. "That ain't it, Del. I saw what was in your eyes the other day. You're after the men who killed your folks and making a game out of it. I think you like it."

"That's not true, Jess. I'm just doing what I have to do. I'm defending my house."

"Promise me you won't set that shotgun to go off again."

She nodded. "All right."

"Del, I don't know which way is up, or what to think about you any more."

"The trouble is you want me on your terms, Jess."

His expression was full of sadness. "I love you, Del." He kissed her, but her mouth was unresponsive.

She drew away. "I'm not feeling girlish right now, Jess."

He turned away. "I came over to invite you to Rosalind Sawyer's birthday party…a big shindig at the Town Hall Saturday night. It's her eighteenth birthday, and her father is going all out. It's going to be quite a dance."

"This Saturday night? I don't know. I have chores."

"To hell with chores. Our whole family is going, and we'll come by early and give you a hand."

"All right, I'll go if you don't mind being seen with me. A bunch of little boys in town today called me Frightful Delphinia."

"You don't scare me," he laughed, slapping his hat onto his head and walking out the door like a rooster. "Frightful Delphinia! Is that what they're calling you in town?"

★ ★ ★ ★ ★

Delphinia stood on her porch, scanning the hills one last time in an effort to see any telltale dust leveled in the last of the evening's glow. Her animals seemed content, no sign they sensed any approaching strangers. Walking back inside the house, she closed the door and bolted it. Her eyes traveled around the clean kitchen. The floor had not been scrubbed so hard in years. Now to put Amity's and Hawk's bedroom in order. She yanked the sheets and blankets from the bed. When added to the nightgown and other dirty clothing, she had a substantial pile of laundry stacked near the door. She had told Jess the truth when she had said that tomorrow she would have chores. She straightened Amity's shoes and tried them on. They fit her, as she knew Amity's few drEstes would.

Digging through the closet, she found two old pairs of pants belonging to Hawk, and one blue cotton shirt. She hugged the shirt to her face, embracing the scent of her father that still permeated the clothes — outdoor musk. She went through her mother's bureau, searching through the undergarments. The black straw hat with feathers and a veil that had been worn by Amity to funerals she found in the bottom drawer of the bureau. In a small wooden jewelry box Delphinia found a pair of black jet earrings, a cameo brooch, and a new gold wedding band. *A wedding band?* Amity had always worn her wedding band — she died wearing it — she was buried wearing it. Curious, Delphinia turned over the ring in her hand before placing it back inside the little box and closing the lid.

She looked around the room, sighing. Tomorrow she planned to clean and scrub the room, dust and change the curtains. Then she would move into her mother's room. She did not want to sleep in her own room again, fearful that she might wake suddenly in the night only to see the spot where Raul Rivera died in a fusillade of gunfire from the foot of her bed. Shivering, she walked into the kitchen, adjusting the revolver still hanging at her hip. One more task to do. She lifted the kerosene lamp over her head and slowly climbed up the ladder to the loft. Examining the locked trunk in the darkness, she was convinced there was no other way and slowly drew the pistol from the holster. Pointing the gun into the center of the lock, she pulled the trigger. One loud discharge followed by the odor of gunsmoke caused her to flinch and wrinkle her nose. She reached for the twisted lock that broke in her hand. Brownish glints bounced in the kerosene lamp-light. Delphinia slid the pistol back into her holster and lifted the ponderous trunk lid with a hard pull, allowing it to rest against the wall.

Books, a christening dress, a yellowed silk wedding gown — all Amity's parents' possessions, a lifetime of mementos from Missouri, from before the Civil War. She found an old Army Colt in its leather holster resting at the bottom of the trunk, still loaded. She fished through an envelope filled with papers. Among the papers she found a crumbling, brown news-paper article about the typhoid epidemic in Tucson in 1868. That was two years before Delphinia was born. It was the epidemic that took Amity's parents and little brother just shortly after they arrived in Tucson at the end of their long trek West. That year Amity had met and married Hawk, and they had moved here to the homestead land left to Amity by her dead parents. Sliding the newspaper article back into the envelope, Delphinia found another article beneath it, stuck so tightly with age and dryness that she had to peel the two papers apart. Bringing the article up to her nose in the poor light, she read the news item:

Amity Dwyer to wed Chauncy Kyd, Jr.,
wedding set for next Thursday, July 9, 1868 in Tucson.

Confused, she set aside the entire envelope of papers and poked briefly through the remaining contents of the trunk. The only other item of interest was a picture of her grandparents on their wedding day. Her grandfather looked handsome in his butternut gray Confederate uniform, his big handlebar mustache, his hair combed to one side, holding his cap on his knees. At his side, standing next to the chair, was his bride, a pretty girl with light brown hair combed up in soft waves around her face. Delphinia recognized the white dress as the same one inside the trunk. She looked closely at her grandmother's left hand, trying to determine if the ring she wore was the same as the one she had found in Amity's jewelry box. No, her grandmother's ring was much wider than the one in the box downstairs.

With the puzzle of Chauncy Kyd, Jr., bouncing around in her head, Delphinia closed the trunk lid and made her way slowly down the ladder from the loft, the envelope of papers tucked under her arm. It was too late now to read through them by kerosene light, so she placed the aged papers on the kitchen table. She sat on her blankets on the floor near the stove, her body yearning for the comfort of a featherbed. Only one more night of sleeping on the floor — tomorrow she planned to move into Amity's room. *Tomorrow.*

Restless winds blew across the yard, waking Delphinia from a nightmarish sleep. Had she imagined noises coming from the corral? She felt both trepidation and anger for being held hostage in her own house. She was too restless to fall back to sleep. Her head was pounding, throbbing, her mind full of disconnected and confusing thoughts over the happenings since the day of Hawk's return. Her emotions were pulled first one direction and then another. Was she going crazy? The loss of Amity and Hawk, the offer of marriage by Jess, the mystery of

Chauncy Kyd, the threat of Blackjack Parry — too many thoughts colliding, each important until driven away by the seeming importance of yet another thought.

Adjusting Hawk's holster at her side, she tiptoed to the door. Pausing for only an instant, she threw it open, feeling the sharpness of the night air. Without even thinking, she proceeded to the corral and saddled Slicker by the glow of the yellow moonbeams lighting the yard. Mounted, she reined north. Delphinia was resolved that if Blackjack was looking for her, she'd make it easy for him. Might as well get it over with. She'd not be trapped inside her own house again. She would settle with Blackjack and get on with her life.

Slicker's hoofs clicked on the hard-packed ground as she angled through the hills toward the high bluffs, leading up the Cañon. She guessed it was near midnight by the way the moon hung straight above when she reined into a small meadow where she had once picnicked with Hawk and Amity. She tied Slicker to a tree and then built a small campfire. She hunched near it, silent, until the embers burned down. The smoke from the fire circulated through the woods where night birds twittered and varmints scurried. The night noises were loud enough to keep a nervous person alert and cautious.

She trembled, clasping her cold arms around her knees. In her mind she heard Amity cry out when the bullet smashed into her body, and remembered Hawk's fatal burst of defiance. She imagined Bate Thatcher passing this way on his last walk to her place. And Raul Rivera riding through here, too, on his last trip. She gulped, remembering the aroma of her chicken stew and the roar of the double-barreled shotgun. She clutched at her throat, telling herself it was natural to feel what she was feeling — fear and shock, grief for her parents that at this moment threatened to engulf her if she would allow it. All the emotions she had kept in check were bubbling to the surface.

And huddled in the middle of the meadow, Delphinia let out a series of screams even she herself did not understand.

It was several minutes after she had exhausted herself that Delphinia instinctively kicked out the fire. She listened. There it was again, the sound of twigs snapping behind her, more clearly this time. She turned to face the empty night, Hawk's pistol pointing into nothingness. Assured that the embers were completely smothered by dirt, she ran for Slicker and yanked the bridle reins loose from the tree. As she scrambled to mount, she imagined hands grasping at her in the darkness. She let out a groan as she groped for the saddle horn and pulled herself up. Fear riding her back like wild wings, she reined Slicker down the trail, digging her spurs into his flanks so that the horse leveled into a long, hard run for home.

As phantom hoofbeats echoed all around her, she urged the horse into a harder gallop, flying over the hard-packed trail, skimming under low branches. Finally out of the rocks she plunged into a race that carried her thundering across the prairie in a desperate swoop. Neck stretched, legs reaching, long silver mane whipping, Slicker flew as if the devil himself were on his back.

Galloping into the yard, Delphinia drew her pistol, waiting for a shadow to leap from behind the fence or out of the barn. But the only movement came from the cold stir of night rustling about the buildings. Hawk's black horse and the bay team looked up from the corral with mild interest at Slicker's return, assuring Delphinia that nothing out of the ordinary stirred in the yard tonight.

Still trembling as she dismounted, she laughed at herself as she unsaddled the horse and turned him into the corral. *You're crazy,* she told herself. *Feel better now? Riding out there and scaring yourself half to death?* She dragged her father's saddle into the little saddle house and slammed the door. Surrounded by the saddles, exhausted, Delphinia leaned back against the wall and let herself slide down. There she remained for the rest of the night, hugging her knees, face buried in her calico skirts, sobbing out her loneliness, cradling Hawk's big pistol in her arms.

Chapter Seven

Brubakers' freight wagon rumbled into the yard at dusk on Saturday night. Before the wagon had come to a full stop, the Brubaker kids were spilling out over the side racks.

"Halloo, Delphinia!" Mrs. Brubaker bellowed while re-adjusting her white bonnet. "Ready for the dance?" Her big shout boomed around the yard.

Delphinia braced herself and stepped out from the house, closing the door behind her. The dark mauve traveling-suit with a bustle she wore had belonged to Amity.

"You look mighty prim in Amity's dress, darling," Mrs. Brubaker yelled, not one to miss anything. "It's a little old for you, though."

Delphinia looked up at Jess, sitting next to his mother who was wedged in on the wagon seat between the two men of the family. Hap Brubaker was on the left side, handling the reins of the big dun work team. A half dozen small boys ran around the yard in circles, chasing each other.

"Mighty gaw! Leonard! Charles! Elmo! Get back into the wagon before you dirty your shoes again!" Mrs. Brubaker's warning only caused the boys to run more wildly. "Ornery brats!"

Overwhelmed by the noise and commotion, Delphinia forced herself to step down from the porch. Three sets of Brubaker eyes stared as she advanced toward Jess who had jumped down from the wagon seat. He led her to the back of the wagon where he helped her up and positioned her on a wooden box, covered with a rolled blanket and placed directly behind the wagon seat. As soon as Jess sat down next to her, the herd of Brubaker boys clamored back into the wagon, surrounding Jess and Delphinia with giggles and taunts.

"Elmo!" Mrs. Brubaker yelled, grabbing the twelve-year-old

by the scruff of his neck and dragging him onto the wagon seat between herself and her husband. "You sit up here between me and your pa. Jess is attending Delphinia. We don't need any more of your horse play tonight!"

"Aw, Ma!"

The wagon swayed forward with a crack of the reins across the horses' backs. Delphinia wrapped her arms around her waist, wishing she had not agreed to go to Rosalind Sawyer's birthday party. Eleven Brubaker boys punching and hitting each other made her nervous. Jess, having noticed her uneasiness, tried joking her out of it, but she only glanced back toward the corrals, receding in the distance. She hoped her livestock would be all right till she returned home. Whenever she was around the Brubakers, she felt her life was no longer under her control — her solitude slipped away with each step of the team moving farther away from her familiar surroundings.

"You're mighty quiet, Del," Jess said, his arm still around her shoulders. He gave her a playful squeeze.

"I'm all right, Jess." She stiffened under his touch.

Jess batted one of his little brothers away. "You'll have a good time tonight. Have you thought any more about setting our wedding date?"

She shriveled up and glanced at the seat ahead to see if the Brubakers had heard. They had. Ma Brubaker turned her face with a wide grin, nodding as if giving Delphinia her approval.

"Jess…I…think we should talk in private," Delphinia mumbled under her breath.

"There ain't nothing private with the Brubakers, honey," Ma Brubaker shouted, while her husband frowned, pulling his old felt hat lower over his eyebrows.

Delphinia shivered. She felt trapped again, as though she were now being held hostage by all the Brubakers in the wagon, being taken to a party she did not want to attend. Jess and Ma Brubaker talked about the marriage as if it had already been settled, and she had nothing to say in the matter, that Ma Brubaker made the decisions.

"We plan a right nice wedding for you and Jess, Delphinia," Ma Brubaker continued. "We already talked about how your dress will look. I ain't much with a needle and thread, mind you, but we can fix up my old dress for you. After all I ain't got a daughter of my own who will ever wear it. Still packed away, but I expect it will be fine if the mice ain't got into it. 'Course, I ain't got the sewing fingers nor the fine touch your mother had, but we can get it to fit you all right. How's a month from now? November? You don't want to wait until Christmas. Weddings shouldn't get mixed up with holidays, I always say."

Delphinia cringed. A wedding was the furthest thing from her mind. Her gaze struck back toward her home, the outline of which had long disappeared in the evening dusk. Her thoughts were pulled in the direction of Blackjack Parry. *Will the horses be safe with him around?*

Jess's face was close to hers, and she drew back, embarrassed. The boys crowded around, laughing and sneering and chanting in sing-song rhythm: "Jess has a girl friend."

"Jess, please," Delphinia said, shrugging his arm away. "I can't breathe."

"Well, pardon me for living," he said, frowning.

She looked at his profile in the fading light. He was boyishly handsome. For the occasion, he'd slicked his hair back and wore a clean maroon wool shirt and leather vest. His boots were polished to a high shine — for her, she knew. In a way she felt guilty, but she could not. ignore the corralled feeling she got when in the midst of Jess's family.

"Eh?" Ma Brubaker called over her shoulder, tipping her head again toward Delphinia, waiting for an answer. "What did you say about the wedding date?"

"I didn't," Delphinia said softly.

"Well, you be thinking about it, because we have to make plans about where to put everybody once you move in. I'll be glad to finally have a female hand around the place. Thirteen men has about wore me to a frazzle."

"I don't want to leave my own house," Delphinia could not resist saying.

"What! I think you'd be more than anxious to get away from there, Delphinia. That place would spook me after what's happened there. Don't it bother you?"

"Every day," Delphinia said.

"Well, then, you have to move in at our place with Jess. Our homesteads border each other. It won't be nothing a-tall to dismantle your house and carry the lumber to our place. We'll use it to add a room onto our house for you and Jess. I understand how young people need their privacy. We'll do all that right after Christmas. Meanwhile, you can just bunk in with the rest of us."

"Dismantle my house?" Delphinia looked up at her.

"We got it all worked out, honey. You don't need to worry about a thing."

Delphinia turned toward Jess who seemed to cringe under her look. "They were just talking, Del, you know, in case you wouldn't mind."

"Wouldn't mind? Tearing down my house?"

"Nothing to it," Ma Brubaker threw over her shoulder, grabbing the side of the seat as the wagon hit a big rut and everybody bounced with a slam. Her double chins quivered.

"Your tool shed burned in the fire and your haystack is gone, so that ain't nothing to worry about any more. Your chicken house and the corrals can be taken apart in nothing flat.... the barn and the saddle house, too. We'll need your poles to extend our corrals and maybe build another lot, in case you keep the sheep. I won't mind having a few sheep around. I always liked mutton stew. And there's plenty of lumber for your new room, and with what's left over I'll build me a laundry shed. I always wanted a roofed-over place to do laundry, what with all I have to do! It will come in handy, you'll see."

Delphinia felt her jaws tighten. Her mouth went dry.

Jess leaned closer to her so that his nose touched her cheek. "How about it, Del, can we make the announcement tonight at Rosalind's party? Kind of one big celebration. Easy way to let the whole town know."

She turned to him. "It's Rosalind's party. She would not want anybody spoiling it with their own announcements. If I want to make an announcement like that, I'll have a party of my own."

"A party's a party," he mumbled. "How come all of a sudden you're so disagreeable?"

"I'm not disagreeable, Jess. I think I have the right to have my own engagement party, if that's what I want. I'll not ruin somebody else's doings."

"Who the heck has time to worry about who does this and who does that? You're mighty contrary all of a sudden, Del. Why can't you just go along with things and quit making a lot of bother?" He scowled at her.

The wagon jarred into town in silence, all conversation having ended some time back. Passing the sheriffs office, Delphinia took the opportunity to study Jess's profile in the glow of the lamplight coming from it. But then, without even thinking, she shifted her stare to the sheriffs office where she could make out the outline of Jim Hat ton slouched behind the desk, reading a newspaper. She felt her heart do a strange little hop.

Turning her attention back to Jess, she said: "I promise not to bother you any more, Jess. There will be no engagement."

Ignoring her remark, he stood up as the wagon came to a halt in front of the town hall where the crowd of party-goers had gathered. Pandemonium broke out as Jess's hoard of brothers vaulted over the sides and out the back of the wagon, yelling and snapping each other's suspenders. They disappeared in the tangle of people. Once they were out of sight, Delphinia stood up, allowing Jess to help her down from the wagon. She noticed cool glances from the people watching her. Arm in arm, she walked with Jess into the town hall where they were accosted by a blast of stifling air, carrying the smells of lavender water, apple cider, and cigar smoke.

Straining fiddles and plunking guitars struck up a lively waltz for couples circling the hardwood floor. Rosalind Sawyer swooped past in the arms of a young blond cowboy, her long lavender dress trailing rows of little pink velvet bows around the hemline and pleated edges of her short sleeves. Rosalind's red hair looked aflame, one section combed up high on her head in a twist, another allowed to hang down to her shoulders in springy, thick curls.

"There's Rosalind!" Jess told Delphinia, his eyes on the swaying girl.

"She looks very pretty, tonight," Delphinia said. "What a beautiful way to celebrate her eighteenth birthday." Delphinia thought of her own birthdays, quiet and secluded at the homestead. Amity had never mentioned parties for her. Birthdays and holidays were quiet times with home-made presents being exchanged, always appreciated, always practical. No big fuss.

"Come on, Del. I'll show you how to dance," Jess said,

sliding his arm around her waist and whirling her across the floor, stumbling in his haste. She knew he was teasing her because she had not attended dances. But he knew she could dance since she had once confessed to him that Hawk had taught her the basics, swinging her around the kitchen floor on a rare, playful evening or two. Back then — it seemed ages ago — Amity had laughed and clapped and hummed old Southern songs that had been popular when she was a girl. Hawk Estes had been big and strong, firm and sure of himself. When he encircled his daughter's slim waist with his hand and glided her effortlessly around the room, her heart raced, and she was filled with admiration for her father. She would close her eyes, confident in her steps, imagining herself to be the belle of the ball.

She would have liked to feel she was the belle of the ball now when she was with Jess, but in his arms his hesitancy mixed with the nervous pulls and pushes caused her only to be flustered. Her feet tangled with his, until she burst into embarrassed laughter. Jess finally gave up, leading her across the floor to the punch bowls and sandwiches.

Jess poured a cup of hot apple cider for her, and she took a long swallow, grateful for the chance get off the dance floor. Other couples whirled and turned in step with the fiddle music. Women's long skirts swirled and swayed.

A steady stream of people entered the town hall — friends, neighbors, and almost every young person for miles around. The cowboys from the Circle Diamond and Lazy B strolled in, spurs jingling, hair slicked back, carrying their hats in their hands. John Sawyer, a big, ruddy-faced man, stood at the door, shaking hands by way of greeting his daughter's guests. He had been a widower for several years. Rosalind was his only child.

"Dance again, Del?" Jess asked her, gulping the last of his apple cider.

She hesitated. “I’d like to just sit. Do you mind, Jess?”

He frowned at her. “I came to dance, Del. Just because you’re having a hard time of it, it don’t mean I’m going to hang around, leaning in doorways all night. Now come on, try again.” He managed to take the cider glass out of her hand, before pulling her across the floor.

Facing Jess once again, Delphinia sighed, determined to do better.

“It’s one two three, one two three…,” Jess told her. “You can count, can’t you, Del?” He pulled her waist toward his own, clutching her right hand in his own, head down, studying the floor and their feet. He concentrated, but once again his jerky movements confused her so she bumped against him, stepping on his toes.

Delphinia whispered: “Let me sit a minute, Jess. Catch my breath. I’m all fuddled and embarrassed.”

He brought them to such a sudden halt in the middle of the floor that another couple bumped into them, and Delphinia nearly lost her balance with an *“Oomph!”*

“Sorry,” Jess mumbled to the cowboy.

“Why don’t you do your practicing in the sheep pens?” the cowboy asked, giving a quick glance to both Jess and Delphinia before waltzing his partner away.

Self-conscious, Delphinia patted perspiration from her hot face. “What did he mean by that?”

Jess shrugged. “Everybody knows you raise sheep.”

She moved to the side of the room and found an empty chair. Jess sat next to her.

“I seem to be catching a lot of hostile looks here tonight, Jess.”

“Well, what do you expect? People don’t much like bounty hunters. And they ain’t used to spunky girls dragging dead outlaws in for a reward. Besides, your mother never did make much of an effort to mingle with townsfolk. You have to run with the herd if you want to be accepted, Del. Does that surprise you?"

"I never thought about it."

"When we announce our engagement tonight, all that will change. You'll be taken in under Brubaker wings. I told you that already. You'll be all right from now on."

She turned to him, feeling defiant. "I've always been all right, Jess. I like me. My mother was a fine lady, and Hawk may have been a bounty hunter, but I can live with that. If people around here hold that against him, I can live with that, too. But I don't need you Brubakers taking me under your wings. I've already told you there isn't going to be an engagement, Jess."

Jess's face showed he was crushed. Before he could say anything, John Sawyer strode to the center of the room, clapping his big hands, thus bringing the fiddling to a halt.

"Folks! I'm proud and happy you have attended my daughter's birthday party! Enjoy this fine evening. There's plenty of cider and birthday cake. Come on over here, honey, and blow out your candles!" He beckoned Rosalind, who emerged from the crowd smiling. Beaming at her father, she brushed her curls away from her shoulders before bending over the candles. With a big puff she blew out the candles, little spirals of white smoke dancing above the cake.

"Music!" John Sawyer commanded, gesturing in great circles with his arms as if cranking up the band. The dancers returned to the floor, whirling and circling again. Nearly all of Jess's eleven brothers were the first in line at the table for birthday cake, along with a dozen other children.

Delphinia pulled Amity's little rosewood fan from her reticule and fanned her flushed face. "Hot in here," she said.

"I'm getting cake," Jess muttered, standing up and storming

to the table, his neck and head held rigid.

Delphinia shook with frustration, sorry she had agreed to come here tonight, sorry she had snapped at Jess. Still, she would not acquiesce to the plans being made by the Brubakers about her future, not even if it was the right thing to do. Imagine the idea of dismantling her house! Obviously the Brubakers had discussed the matter before tonight as if her wishes were of no consequence. Hawk and Amity had taught her to be self-sufficient. Here she was feeling as though she were being swallowed up by Jess and his clan, and it was being taken for granted that she could not take care of herself. Amidst the crowd of merry-makers, she felt very much alone, and it dawned on her that she was not at all sure how she would make it by herself. Before, she at least had Amity.

"Delphinia? I'm so glad you came to my party," Rosalind said, standing over her. "You don't mind if I dance with Jess, do you?" The girl smiled, glancing over her shoulder at Jess who was leaning against the table, a plate with a big piece of cake balanced in one hand. He raised a forkful of cake to his mouth, stuffing it in while nodding at a cowboy who stood next to him. Delphinia could tell the cowboy was talking about roping by the way he made mock twirls over his head, snaking his wrist out like he was letting a rope go in a toss.

Delphinia looked up at Rosalind. "No, of course not. Go, enjoy yourself dancing with Jess. He'd like that."

Rosalind clasped her hands in excitement. "And Delphinia, I'm so sorry about your mother and father. I hope you will be all right."

Delphinia nodded at Rosalind, surprised at her sincere concern in the midst of the festivities. After all, she did not know Rosalind well, only that the Sawyers owned a big ranch, whose southeastern range bordered both the Brubaker and Estes homesteads.

Rosalind turned away, waving at Jess and hurrying to him. At his side, she became animated, her head tossing and wrist flipping in Delphinia's direction. With barely a glance at Delphinia, Jess put down his cake and took Rosalind in his arms. She had expected to see Rosalind's feet tangle and trip as her own had done, but Rosalind and Jess floated away in smooth rhythm to the music as if they had been dancing together for years. Delphinia let out a sigh, accepting the fact that she was the one who was out of step.

The absence of Jess signaled an invitation to the younger boys who began to taunt Delphinia, as she sat alone, avoided by everyone, the seats on either side remaining conspicuously empty. As the boys ran past in groups of twos, threes, and fours the words "Frightful Delphinia" rang out above the din from the music and merry-making of the crowd. None of the women were anxious to take up a conversation with her. Even Mrs. Brubaker kept her distance. At the moment she was busy holding court in a huddle of middle-aged women carrying infants near the door, no doubt catching up on gossip, exchanging recipes, and discussing gardening and baby-care tips. Delphinia trembled at the thought.

Fanning herself harder, she glanced across the floor where Sheriff Hat ton now lounged against a wall, arms crossed. He was watching her, a thoughtful frown on his face. She dropped her gaze immediately when their eyes made contact. Disgusted with herself, she gathered the courage to look up at him again only to find that he had moved away from the wall and was weaving his way between the couples on the dance floor, heading in her direction.

Feeling even hotter, Delphinia fanned harder. Then he was standing in front of her, looking down into her eyes. "You want to dance, Delphinia? I'm not much of a dancer, but I see your friend, Jess, is occupied with the birthday girl."

“I’m not great on the dance floor myself,” she said.

His laugh was easy. “That makes two of us. Come on, let’s try. Better than hanging around while everybody else is having fun. You really look like you’d rather be somewhere else.”

She stood up, looking into his eyes and noticing their color to be an unusual greenish-brown — hazel. “You’re right. I do feel stifled here.”

“Come on, I’ll waltz you to the door. If you want, we can get some fresh air.” He reached for her gently, barely touching her waist. His hands were clean and smooth.

Collapsing the fan in the palm of her hand, she placed her left hand on his shoulder while he took her right hand and moved her lightly across the floor. She expected to bump into him and make a fool of herself like she had when dancing with Jess, but he kept her at just the right distance, looking away across the floor instead of down at his feet. He turned her and held her so that she followed in a smooth turn without thinking about it.

Nearing the door, he said: “You still want some fresh air?”

“I’m all right. This is fun. Let’s finish the dance.”

He gave her a curious look, the hint of a grin playing at the corners of his mouth. “You’re full of surprises, Delphinia.”

“I don’t mean to be.”

“That’s the biggest surprise of all.”

While Delphinia was thinking about his remark, the music ended, and he guided her to the door. They slid past and between the groups of talking people and made it to the board walk. Here they leaned against the hitching rack, staring about the darkened street. Dozens of horses were saddled or hitched to wagons, dozing through the evening, waiting for the dance to end.

“I don’t suppose horses like dances as much as people do,” Delphinia said, not knowing what else to say.

Jim Hatton smiled and nodded in reply. He was at least ten years older than she. And for that reason Delphinia felt safe around him, like she had always felt around Hawk. Yet the two men were different. Hat ton was soft spoken and easy, not like the forceful, opinionated Hawk.

"I understand there is going to be an announcement tonight," he stated.

"Announcement?" She raised an eyebrow. "What do you mean?"

"Missus Brubaker has been buzzing around here all night long, passing the news that you and Jess are soon to be married."

Delphinia shook her head. "No! I have not agreed to marry Jess. In fact, we had a discussion about that coming over here tonight. I thought I made it clear to him that marriage is not what I want. At least, not now. The Brubakers keep trying to make plans for me, as if I don't have anything to say about it. I need time. I haven't made any promises. There've been too many changes in my life recently." She gulped, fighting an urge to cry, mad at herself for acting like a baby in front of the sheriff.

He grinned. "Don't let anybody railroad you into getting married, Delphinia."

"I won't."

"If you've had enough fresh air, we can take another turn around that dance floor."

She agreed, suppressing the desire to slip her arm through his. Instead, clasping her hands in front of her dress, she turned hesitantly in the direction of the town hall. Inside, Ma Brubaker
was shoving her husband to the center of the room where he raised his hands to quiet the crowd.

Hap Brubaker stuttered with nervousness, avoiding the watchful, eager eyes of his wife while scanning the room for

Jess. He finally found his son in the crowd and saw that he was holding hands with Rosalind Sawyer. His head snapped around toward the door only to be met with the image of Delphinia walking in with Sheriff Hat ton. "I...er...," Mr. Brubaker stammered, a befuddled look on his face.

"Go on! Make the announcement!" Ma Brubaker encouraged him from the sidelines.

He continued to look at Delphinia who returned his gaze with a cool stare.

Jim Hat ton strode suddenly across the floor, leading Delphinia by her hand. "What Hap Brubaker is trying to say is that he's wishing all the best to Rosalind Sawyer on her birthday, and, speaking for all the rest of us, he wants John Sawyer to know we are grateful for this fine evening!"

"Spoken like a true politician, Sheriff," one of the cowboys shouted, and the crowd burst into laughter.

Chuckling, Jim Hat ton gave a quick signal to the fiddlers who broke into another lively tune. Dozens of couples swirled around the floor. Delphinia moved comfortably back into the sheriffs arms. Together they circled the floor, lost among the other couples.

"I think you just saved me from a terrible misunderstanding," she told him.

"No misunderstanding. If I know Ma Brubaker, she was hoping to rope you into an engagement in front of the whole town, so you wouldn't be able to back out of it."

"I didn't know attending birthday parties could get a person into so much trouble," she said.

"Engagement parties lead to even more trouble," he said with a cynical laugh.

Chapter Eight

Fall coolness drifted out of the Cañon, causing Delphinia to accomplish a flurry of tasks in preparation for winter over the next several days. She chopped and stacked enough wood to last an average cold season. The canning of vegetables for the year had been done for some time. Now she eyed the pig and wondered how she would manage the slaughtering without Amity's help. She leaned against the pigsty gate, mulling the problem while thinking of the past month's events.

None of the Brubakers had been around since the night of Rosalind Sawyer's birthday party. The return trip had been different from the trip into town. Ma Brubaker had remained tight lipped all the way to Delphinia's home, and Mr. Brubaker had seemed grumpier than usual, snapping at the boys until, one by one, they began nodding off. Jess had brooded in his corner of the wagon, holding his arm lightly around her shoulder, but saying nothing.

Since that night, Jess had not ridden over for a visit. At first, Delphinia had fretted over the fact that the Brubakers were probably mad at her, but then she came to think that, for the present, it was for the best what with the push for a marriage. She was planning to ride over to their place around Thanksgiving and give them a basket of canned goods just as she and Amity had done every Thanksgiving, although this time it would represent a sort of peace offering. But that would be later in the month, for now she had the problem of butchering the biggest of the two pigs by herself.

She studied the yard. Shooting the pig was no problem. Dragging it over to the block and tackle with the team could be accomplished in the same manner she had used to handle Bate Thatcher's body. Bate Thatcher! She glanced quickly up the cañon across the cut in the trail, realizing she had grown lax lately, having been so busy with fall chores and getting supplies in for winter. She squinted, but nothing stirred up there. Sighing, she pondered the hog-butchering problem again. It had been always a big job for her and Amity together, and it would be twice the job by herself. The pig had to be scalded and then gutted and cut up. There was the lard rendering, sausage and headcheese making, and pickling of hocks and feet. She'd make liver sausage, too. It would take at least four days of work, doing it alone.

Hoofbeats from the east brought her attention around behind the house. She whirled, feeling stupid for being caught alone in the yard without her gun. Hawk's gun belt had been left resting across the back of a kitchen chair.

Then Jess and Rosalind Sawyer cantered their horses into the yard. Rosalind looked flushed and wind blown. Beneath her riding hat, her long red hair had come undone at one side, fluttering around the shoulder of her dark blue riding coat. She rode sidesaddle on a palomino horse whose elegant neck arched nervously under the girl's firm hand.

Jess reined his cow pony to the hitching post and dismounted. He reached up to Rosalind, easing her off the sidesaddle after she unhooked her right knee from the leaping head. She laughed quietly, resting her gloved hands on Jess's strong, young shoulders. Their lips nearly touched.

"I'm glad to see you, Rosalind...and Jess," Delphinia said. She wiped her hands on her apron, brushing back the wild hairs she knew dangled from an untidy chignon she'd carelessly rolled up that morning before chores. Rosalind's neat appearance made her feel dowdy.

Jess looked at Delphinia, anxiously biting his lower lip the way he did when something was on his mind. "Uh, Del.... me and Roz come over to talk to you. We have something important we want you to hear."

Delphinia faced Jess and Rosalind across the hitching rack. "Won't you come inside? Things are kind of untidy. I wasn't expecting company."

"I'm sorry," Jess blurted. "I reckon I should have come over earlier to warn you we were going to visit, but I thought it was better this way. Might as well get it over with."

"Over with?" Delphinia tipped her head, a little hurt by her suspicion that Jess had found a new girlfriend in Rosalind. She couldn't help notice the way Rosalind blushed, tucking her hand through the crook of Jess's arm. Actually, Delphinia was flattered by the fact that Jess appeared uncomfortable, but the awkward silence was making her nervous. She told herself to calm down. She walked up the steps and into the house. They followed.

Delphinia put cups on the table before pouring the rosehips tea that she had been brewing on the stove. She noticed Rosalind give the tea a hesitant look.

"Nothing for me, thank you," Rosalind mumbled.

"I don't reckon I'll have anything, either," Jess said. Delphinia noticed his eyes kept darting to the place on the floor where Bate Thatcher had died.

Delphinia placed the pot back on the edge of the stove after pouring herself a cup. She added a spoonful of honey from the brown clay honey pot on the table. She sat down. "What do you want to tell me?"

Jess and Rosalind exchanged nervous glances before Jess said: "We came to let you know we're getting married."

Delphinia choked. She had not meant to do it. But she had gasped a little at his words, and a few drops of tea went down the wrong way — she hacked and wheezed, patting her throat.

Rosalind rushed around the table, pounding Delphinia's back. "There! You all right? Oh, poor Delphinia! Don't be upset! Jess and I want to get everything all straightened out between us, so there won't be hard feelings."

Delphinia shook her head, pressing her fingers against her windpipe. "No hard feelings, Rosalind…honestly. I wish you all the best."

"Really?" Rosalind gushed. "I'm so glad you feel that way, Delphinia. I was so worried you would take the news hard."

"I'm happy for you," The tea cup rattled.

Jess looked at Rosalind. "Why don't you go outside and see how the horses are doing? I'd like to talk to Delphinia alone for a few minutes."

Rosalind smiled at him, lifting her head so that the blue feathers on her riding hat shimmered. "I don't think so, Jess. Anything said from now on to or about either of us is *our* business. Delphinia just said we have her blessing, so I don't think there is anything left to talk about, is there? We best be on our way."

Jess looked pained, but did not argue with her. "All right." He gave Delphinia one of his "I'll see you later" glances, and followed Rosalind out of the house. While Jess helped Rosalind into the sidesaddle, Delphinia slowly sipped the last of her tea.

After they rode out of the yard, she walked to the porch where she took a seat at her loom and, picking up the weft beater, began weaving because she did not know what else to do. She had to keep her hands busy, as thoughts bounced around in her head. This morning when she woke up her worst problem had been butchering a hog. Now she had to sort through her feelings about Jess's and Rosalind's sudden announcement.

She listened to Jess and Rosalind disappear at a crisp gallop. Shed stick, pull stick. *Thump, thump.* She passed the yarn, making her rows, building her pattern, tamping lightly with the weft beater. *Thump, thump.* The sound of hoofbeats finally dissolved away in the direction of the Brubakers' Delphinia smiled, wondering how Rosalind was going to like moving in with the Brubakers, doing chores for twelve people after life at her own big home where her father had hired servants. The most company Rosalind Sawyer ever put up with besides her father were cattle buyers and men of finance. Jess and Rosalind? The idea kept zipping through Delphinia's mind, changing by the second from funny to shocking. *Rosalind and Jess?* Well, why not? Jess was young, handsome, strong, clean, a hard worker. He did not drink or gamble or get into fights. He was a fine person with a future if somebody would give him a chance. A chance. The Sawyer ranch had a lot more going for it than the Estes homestead.

Delphinia was surprised when Jess rode back later that night, finally getting his opportunity to talk to her alone. She had not left her place in front of the rug even though darkness was coming on. It seemed perfectly natural to keep weaving, building carefully and sturdily with yarn, what she could not build in her life. The losses in her life were devastating. Hawk and Amity gone. Alienation from the townsfolk. And now Jess, whom she had always taken for granted, would not be around any more.

Jess sat on the top step, wringing his battered felt hat around in his rough, work-worn hands. "Delphinia, you sure you're going to be all right? I mean, no hard feelings? Me and Roz were concerned you'd be hurt."

"That why she insisted on riding out here with you? She wanted to see the look on my face?"

He shrugged. Female trouble was not something he dwelt on. "She thought it best we face up to you together. That's all."

“You and I were not engaged, Jess. There was nothing to face up to.”

“Aw, come on, Del. Everybody around here has known since we were kids that you and I would get married some day. That’s just the way it was.”

“Was it?”

“If Hawk and Amity hadn’t been killed…I mean, if your ma was still here and all, you’d be marrying me. Wouldn’t you?”

“I don’t know, Jess. So much has happened. I can’t change things.”

“I’ll always care about you, Del. But I can’t see riding over here, begging you to do something you don’t want any part of. I wasn’t meant to be a lonely old bachelor, picking eggshells out of my pancakes. I want to get on with my life.”

“I know, Jess. And, really, I’m happy for you. I hope you all get along together, and you get that new bedroom built. Roz’s daddy will be able to afford a pile of new lumber better than this old house would have offered.”

His look was full of embarrassment. “I’m sorry about that, Del…Ma letting on how she planned to move all your stuff over to our place. I wouldn’t have let her knock your house down…if you didn’t want it that way.”

“Knocking houses down isn’t what it’s about, Jess. It’s about talking first and making sure everybody is agreed on what’s to be done…not just a few people making all the decisions.”

He nodded. “Believe it or not, I’m beginning to understand what you mean by that. I have Roz and her daddy making big plans for me. I’m moving in with them at the ranch, and he says he’ll build us a house next year, when the kids start coming …he claims he ain’t used to having little ones underfoot.”

Delphinia burst out laughing. “Jess! Don’t let anybody make up your mind for you!”

He squirmed. "Roz and me will be fine. I'll work hard to earn my keep."

"I'm sure you will, Jess. Best of luck to you. When's the wedding?"

"Roz figured Christmas Eve."

"Christmas Eve! Didn't your mother say it wasn't good to mix weddings with Christmas?"

"That ain't the way Roz sees it." He stood, walked down the steps, and reached for his horse. "Guess I better be getting back before supper."

She thumped another row of yarn into the rug. "Hurry home, Jess. Wouldn't want folks…or Rosalind…accusing you of riding over here to see me." Her words were lost to him because he was already spurring east at a fast clip.

Holding her weft beater on her lap, her gaze shifted back toward the pigsty and the work before her.

Steam rose in the cold morning air above the cauldron. The pig hung by its hind legs from the hoist where Delphinia had gutted the brute, liver and heart tossed into a bucket of cold water for cooking later. The sound of her chopping and sawing cracked through the crisp morning air. In two days' time the lard had been rendered, headcheese made, feet pickled, and a batch of sausage stood cooling in enamel tubs ready to be stuffed into cleaned lengths of intestine. The hams were in the smokehouse.

The voice shocked her so she grabbed a knife before turning around only to face Jim Hat ton, leaning against the doorjamb in her kitchen. "Quite a job!" He eyed the buckets and vats, sniffing spices and curing vinegar.

"You scared me," she said, putting the knife back down on the table and reaching for her mixing spoon.

"I rode out to check up on you and give you some news."

She stirred the bubbling sausage over the stove. "If you came to tell me Jess and Rosalind Sawyer are getting married, I heard it already. They rode over four days ago. I wished them all the best."

He took his hat off, reaching for a kitchen chair. "That's not what I came to talk about. You should know Blackjack Parry has not been caught yet…in fact, he's been talking to that old prospector, Cholla."

She turned to face him. "How do you know that?"

"Cholla was in town yesterday, telling everybody how Blackjack came to his camp a week ago in Locust Cañon. Apparently Cholla was glad for the company, and Blackjack was glad for coffee and a plate of beans. At least, that's the way Cholla told it."

Delphinia frowned. "I had hoped Blackjack would be out of the country by now. Why is he hanging around?"

Jim Hat ton shrugged. "Why do outlaws do anything? You have extra coffee?"

She poured him a cup, laughing. "Sure you don't mind drinking my coffee? I offered a cup of tea to Rosalind and Jess the other day, and Rosalind acted as if I was trying to do away with her."

He took a sip, frowning. "Fact is, your friend, Jess, must have told her everything he knows about you. She's been talking to the ladies all around town. Everybody knows about the way you poisoned Bate Thatcher and about the shotgun trap you set for Raul Rivera. And old muscle-mouth Cholla is passing the news along to anybody he meets, so everybody…I mean everybody…knows what happened here. I imagine he told Blackjack, too."

She quit mixing the meat. "Thanks for the warning. I see I have lost the element of surprise."

"Worse. A kid down at the stable told me Cholla is spreading news about how you have a load of Hawk's bounty money stashed around here. I don't know what's got into Cholla. He'll have every drifter and saddle tramp riding in here after you. I thought he was a friend of yours."

"I appreciate the warning," she said, mostly to herself. "I'll be careful."

"I don't suppose you would consider coming into town for a while? I'm thinking of riding up to Locust Cañon in a day or two, maybe camp up there, alone. I'll likely catch Blackjack easier if he doesn't see a big posse kicking up a lot of dust."

"I appreciate your concern, but I don't want to stay in town. After Blackjack Parry, there will be somebody else, always somebody looking to get even with Hawk. Don't you think Mother and I knew that? Don't you think we lived careful, always watching, keeping an eye out for ourselves? I'm used to it, Sheriff."

He finished his coffee. "Why don't you quit calling me Sheriff? Jim will do."

"Oh, all right...Jim." She fought the sudden impulse to walk around the table and slide her arms around his body. And she fought a sadness, bursting with loneliness, that would have liked a human hug, just simple human contact, without leading to anything else. *Calm down, calm down.*

He wore a puzzled look on his face, as if trying to read her thoughts, but he did not say anything to give her an opening. "I'm riding to town now. Oh" — he reached into his pocket — "here's the voucher for Bate Thatcher."

She took it from his hand, stuffing it inside the blue clay jar on a shelf next to the kitchen door.

He hesitated for a second, looking at her, but, when she only turned away to her sausage-making, he walked slowly outside. "Be careful, Delphinia," he called out and then mounted his horse.

Chapter Nine

Riding astride in her calico dress, her skirts flying around her knees, Delphinia dug her heels into Slicker's sides, urging him harder down the road, leading to the Brubakers'. She clasped the small, metal milk can in her right hand, holding it over the horse's shoulder and allowing her arm to flow gently with his movements — the can was filled with eggs. She had placed a dozen big, brown hen's eggs inside the can that morning to trade Mrs. Brubaker for some cow's milk.

Slicker slowed at a dip in the road, then galloped ahead in a lurch up the gentle rise. Delphinia slowed him to a trot — no use tiring the horse just because her mind seethed with thoughts about Cholla. It bothered her to recall all the herbal remedies and meals she and Amity had doled out generously to the old prospector over the years, only to be repaid with his telling Blackjack Parry about her.

She had thought it over and decided to fix him good. She had set her plan in motion. As she rode Slicker through the gate of the Brubaker homestead, she saw Ma Brubaker sweeping the front porch. Scattered about the yard were a number of the boys doing chores — Leonard stacking wood, while Orville was greasing a wagon wheel. And all heads were up, watching Delphinia. A roan pup crawled out from under the porch, woofing, as Delphinia rode closer to the house.

"Good morning, Missus Brubaker," Delphinia said. "I've brought eggs for trading. A gallon of milk will do."

Mrs. Brubaker slowed her sweeping. "We don't have extra milk any more, Delphinia."

Delphinia rested the edge of the can on her knee, too

surprised to answer. She and Amity had traded eggs for cow's milk with the Brubakers for as long as she could remember.

Elmo piped: "We're buying chickens of our own, Delphinia. Ma says there ain't no need for you to be riding over here again."

"Hush up!" Ma Brubaker scolded, turning scarlet around her collar. "You boys get out of here…now!"

"That's what you said," Petey chimed in, pulling up his overalls by tugging at the shoulder straps.

"I don't want to bother you, Missus Brubaker," Delphinia said. "I just thought that…."

"No bother." Ma Brubaker gave the floor boards an especially hard whack with the side of her broom. "There ain't no extra milk. That's all. So don't be riding back over here. Save yourself the trip."

"Does this have something to do with Jess?" Delphinia asked.

"Jess ain't here! He's with Rosalind, making plans which ain't got nothing to do with you."

Delphinia nodded, understanding. "I didn't come here looking for Jess, Missus Brubaker. I'm happy for him and Rosalind.
They rode over to see me, and everything has been worked out."

Mrs. Brubaker raised an eyebrow. "I know better than that, Delphinia. No woman gives up that easy. You're just laying in some tricks."

"Tricks!"

Mr. Brubaker came up from the lean-to, leading a big dun horse. A scowl was etched deeply across his face as he looked at his wife. He tied the horse to the hitching rail. "If Delphinia brought eggs all the way from her house this morning, then we are going to be polite enough to accept them and give her the milk, Mother. Right now. If we have nothing to trade after today, that's another matter, but there will be no turning her away without notice."

Mrs. Brubaker turned on her heel, stomping into the house. Elmo reached for the egg bucket. "Ma's just all head-up over Jess and Rosalind gettin' hitched. Don't pay no never mind, Delphinia. The rest of us still likes you all right." His freckled grin was reassuring.

Delphinia let loose of the can as the boy took it from her hand, carrying it up the porch where he emptied it of the eggs so that it could be filled with milk.

Mr. Brubaker patted his tied horse. "Delphinia, you come around to the lean-to with me. Clem is just finished milking the cow." He took the empty bucket from Elmo, then turned toward the cow shed, leading with long strides. Delphinia rode behind him.

Clem poured milk into Delphinia's bucket without looking up at her, and Delphinia sensed the awkwardness that hung over everyone due to recent events. She knew things would never be the same between them any more. And that made her feel bad, as it obviously did many members of the Brubaker family. After all, she had been close to the Brubakers, and they all thought she might be part of the family one day. They had been the closest to kin folks she had had, next to Hawk and Amity. She looked around the yard, wishing Jess would show up and make everything right again, but there was no sign of him. His old brown horse was missing from the corral.

Mr. Brubaker handed the bucket up to her, the lid secured. "Delphinia, I am sorry about the way my wife just treated you. You did not deserve that. But you have to understand she is mighty excited about Jess and Rosalind Sawyer and the wedding plans. This is something really important to Jess and.... the rest of us. You know what I mean? We don't want it spoiled."

"I understand, Mister Brubaker. I didn't come over here to make trouble."

"I know, Delphinia. You have never been that kind of a girl. But the Sawyers got a big outfit, and Jess is going to do fine over there. We want the best for him, that's all."

Delphinia swallowed hard, smiled, and turned Slicker back in the direction of the house. She couldn't ask for straighter talk than that. She watched Ma Brubaker emerge from inside the house, picking up the sweeping where she had left off. Maybe Mrs. Brubaker's suspicions were not entirely unfounded. Maybe she had come looking for Jess this morning. Maybe she was just a tiny bit jealous. Jess had been her special friend since they had been children.

"I won't be back, Missus Brubaker. Thank you for the milk."

"Wait," the hesitant request came from the porch.

Delphinia stopped Slicker from leaving the yard and sat the horse, the glare of the sun in her eyes.

"This is how I feel, Delphinia," said Ma Brubaker. "You and your mother more than paid or traded for anything we ever did. And I ain't forgetting the powders and herbs your mother fixed up for this family whenever we had a sickness. I still got that colt she cured from the loco weed three summers ago. And I know we'd have lost that last baby if she had not come over here with her bitters and teas. I'm not forgetting any of that, Delphinia. You take care of yourself, and good luck to you. Any trouble over there, you just set a building afire, and I'll see the flames and come running…like the last time."

Delphinia smiled without answering, tapping her heels against Slicker who broke into a slow smooth trot across the yard and out the gate. Once out of sight from the house Delphinia urged the horse into a lope, hardly noticing the hills and shaggy brush around her. The morning sun sat hot and high. Her throat was so choked with tears she found herself gasping, biting her lips, and squeezing her eyelids to hold back her tears that gushed anyway. For the first time in her life she experienced a real sense of rejection, of being cut off with finality.

By the time she rode into her own yard, she had recovered from the crying by telling herself she had more important business to attend to. Looking around, she saw nothing out of place, nothing stirring. She unsaddled Slicker, put him into the corral with the other horses, and then carried the milk can across the yard and into the house. In the kitchen she began mixing the cow milk with the goat milk in a pot on the stove. After the mixture had come to a boil, she quickly took it off the heat to cool. Outside, she dug through her collection of herbs, finding the can of buckthorn.

As she poured the buckthorn into the milk, she smiled to herself, then stirred the finely ground powder into the milk mixture until she thought she had enough to…what had Hawk said…unplug a buffalo? When the milk had cooled completely, she dropped in a rennet pellet and waited for the milk to thicken. She next cut through the thickened mixture with a dull knife until the lumps of milk looked like slices of white pudding, then she took the bucket outside. She washed her hands before squeezing her fingers through the clabbered milk. When the whey finally rose to the surface, she poured it slowly into another container, repeating the process until the cheese was worked into a lump. She kneaded it like a small white loaf of bread, pressing and shaping it finally into a clean square of cheesecloth that she tied around the ball of cheese. Squeezing out the last drops of whey, she hung the round white ball under the shade of a big mesquite tree growing behind the house.

After that was done, Delphinia washed her hands and returned to her loom. Her gaze shifted between her work and the far reaches north toward Locust Cañon, west toward town, and south toward Mexico. She relaxed in the warmth of the porch, eyeing the distant, blue-gray hills teeming with thorny plants, wild birds, and quiet days.

She forced away thoughts of Mrs. Brubaker in a futile attempt to forget the unpleasant morning's encounter. Rudeness from a woman she had always trusted was new to Delphinia. She wondered why Amity had not instructed her better in the ways of people. Or had she tried? Four years of schooling in Tucson had brought her together with far more people than she encountered here, but all that seemed so long ago — school girl times. Nuns and discipline, that's all she remembered. And then back home to the ranch that she loved with the mother she knew and trusted. Here was security, something familiar. She could count on the loyalty of her animals; the seasons were simple to understand; and the vast stretches of lonely time and desert were part of her life, uncomplicated, without human interruptions, unless Hawk rode in.

Now that she thought about it, Jess and his clan had been a novelty for her. A break in the monotony, like the occasional visits from women living in the far-flung regions who needed Amity's advice about cures and birthing babies. Usually the women had taken Amity aside, alone, whispering, talking women things that Delphinia understood needed privacy.

Her mother had told her about various cures, and Delphinia had even helped through several birthings. It was not too much different than when her goats and sheep had their wobbly, wet kids and lambs. Delphinia had felt their suffering and sympathized, but she was ultimately more concerned with the curative and healing part of it than the actual deliveries. The thought of nesting with Jess Brubaker and having ten kids of her own did not appeal to her. At first she had scolded herself for not wanting a brood of children, but in time she had come to realize that she was who she was. Delphinia Estes.

Slicker's whinny brought her out of her reverie. The horse looked at her from inside the corral. It was time for supper. Sighing, Delphinia put the weft beater down, and, standing stiffly from her place in front of the rug, she arched and stretched her back. The whole day had passed. She had beaten on that rug until her mind had squeezed and sifted and wrung out every thought and idea she had ever had.

She limped across the yard, shaking stiffness from her ankles. After feeding the stock, she locked herself inside the house for the night. She ate her supper by lamplight, and, afterwards, she built a fire in the fireplace. It was then she remembered the big envelope full of papers that had been inside Amity's trunk. It still rested on the kitchen table under a stack of pans and dishes. She opened the package and then began scanning the news items again, pondering the little yellowed column about Amity Dwyer's engagement to Chauncy Kyd, Jr. That was all — nothing else. Dwyer was Amity's maiden name, yet Delphinia wondered if there might have been another girl with her mother's name? The mystery unsolved, she stuffed the papers back inside the envelope.

Tiptoeing around the kitchen, she strained her ears, alert to anything or anyone outside heralding trouble. Finally she was satisfied that all was well. She doused the kerosene lamp after she had poured hot water into the laundry tub standing near the stove. She undressed and hung Hawk's gun belt over the back of a chair within easy reach, then sank slowly into the washtub to take her bath. Splashing quietly in the semi-darkness, she resigned herself to the fact that from now on nothing in life would be simple again. Not even taking a bath.

★ ★ ★ ★ ★

Delphinia knew this was not a job to be done wearing skirts. Over the years, she had suggested to Amity often enough that certain duties around the homestead could be accomplished more easily in men's pants, but Amity would never hear of it. A lady wore her calico drEstes at home, her traveling suits when riding in a buggy, and her sidesaddle dress on horseback. And that was that. But Amity was gone now, and Delphinia knew some ladies had begun wearing pants for riding horseback astride. In fact, around home she rode astride, her calico skirts flapping annoyingly in the wind. Things were different now, and her mind was made up.

So at dawn Delphinia searched through Amity's closet until she found Hawk's pants, hanging from a hook at the back. When she tried on a pair, she was surprised to discover that, while her father had been tall and broad-shouldered, his waist was not that big. An ample tuck at each side of the waistband resulted in the pants fitting just fine, and it was an easy matter to shorten the legs, cutting off the extra length and hand-stitching a new cuff. Similarly, the sleeves of his duster were too long, but easily adjusted by rolling them back. By twisting up her long hair and making a pile of it on top of her head, she compensated for the fact that Hawk's hat was also too big. At the last minute she stuffed a chunk of paper inside the sweatband. Thus dressed in Hawk's clothing, hat pulled low to her eyes, gun belt strapped to her hip, she mounted Slicker and reined north toward Locust Cañon. In her saddlebags were packed three jars of pork stew meat and the homemade ball of cheese.

She kept her eyes on the trail, searching for eddies of dust or the swirl of birds. It was another hot day. The scalding sun dried her nose and mouth, and she reached for the canteen, tied on her saddle, on more than one occasion. She knew old

Cholla had his main camp at the head spring in Locust Cañon, nestled below a bluff so that he could spot anybody coming in from the south. She and Amity had visited the man's camp once, shortly after he had come by their homestead, coughing and red-eyed, for some "kneemonia" medicine. A few days later, Amity, worried about him, insisted they ride to his place to make sure he was all right. He was.

Delphinia was a little more than annoyed by his recent betrayal. She told herself the old coot needed a lesson. She did not want him telling every outlaw and drifter about her life and business. She would make it clear to him that she could and would take care of herself even though Hawk and Amity were gone, and that she wanted him to mind his own business.

Slicker's hoofs clicked sharply on the trail as he stepped forward into a hop up a low dip, coming out of a ravine. Delphinia leaned with the horse, her eyes studying the trail. They left the floor of the high desert and wound slowly into terrain covered with scrub and jagged brush indicating the beginning of the high country. Cholla's camp was still a way off. Delphinia looked for hoof prints in the sand when they crossed a wide gully. Only a startled squirrel chattered and bounced in long arched dives among some nearby bushes. Slicker snorted softly at the little animal, but he did not shy.

The sudden departure of a dozen turkey buzzards from the spot where they had been roosting in the branches of a leafless mesquite caused Delphinia to look up. Black feathered and red necked, the creatures made their ponderous way to another tree where they settled into the branches, watching with calm interest as Delphinia passed by. A brown chipmunk skittered across the trail; jays squawked and scolded amid musical trills of a curved-bill thrasher.

Approaching the first small stream, Delphinia allowed Slicker to stop and lower his mouth for a few swallows. She unscrewed the top of the canteen and drank, too, relishing the cool sweetness in her mouth. Catching sight of a young willow tree with wispy branches bending low over the water, Delphinia told herself she would stop here on the way back to cut some twigs. Boiled willow was good for infections and fever.

Once he finished drinking, Slicker began pawing the water with a forefoot as if he wanted to lie down, causing Delphinia to tap his flanks with her spurs, pull his head up, and urge him out of the stream. "Come on, you! No taking a bath with me in the saddle!" The horse scrambled up the opposite bank and made his way along the narrow trail covered with sharp little burro prints.

She found Cholla's camp in the same place it had been, only now he had added a canvas tarp stretched between poles to provide a bit of shade for outdoor activities. Delphinia called across the clearing before riding up, knowing she might startle the old man and run into a load of buckshot before he realized who she was. "Cholla! Hello the camp! Anybody here!"

He appeared suddenly from the doorway of his rude hut built out of rocks, pieces of tree trunks, and odd scraps of old wood. Rough-cut sapling poles, sagging under a layer of bear grass, were tied over the building for a roof. A ragged deerhide hung across the doorway. The building itself was little bigger than an outhouse. "Delphinia Estes?" was all he said, stomping through his camp.

She drew up, looking at the circle of charred rocks around a campfire where he did his cooking. A few embers still burned in their midst. Arched branches of ancient mesquites shaded his "kitchen." The burro was tethered nearby, munching twigs.

"How are you, Cholla?" she asked, crossing her hands over her saddle horn.

His eyes were wide with surprise. "By God! Dressed like that, I thought at first you was Hawk Estes!" He couldn't take his eyes off Hawk's hat and denim trousers. Nor the gun.

"Sorry I scared you, Cholla. I just came up for a visit. Can I step down?"

"Sure enough! You surprised me. I don't get no visitors up here."

She reined Slicker among the trees and dismounted. "I'm afraid I have some bad news." She thought it was best to act as if she thought he had not yet heard about Amity and Hawk.

"Bad news?" His look was suspicious.

"A gang Hawk was tracking rode into our place over a month back. Hawk and my mother were killed."

He choked, sputtering, and she could see he was mulling it over whether to let on that he already knew. "Er...*umph!* Bad news! Bad news!"

"You being such a good friend of ours, I knew you would want to hear it from me."

"Er...why sure. Sure!" He ruffled through his beard, eyeing the big sack she pulled from behind her saddle. His eyes still darting nervously over Hawk's holster and pistol she wore.

Delphinia sauntered to his campfire. "I have a couple jars of fresh pork sausage and scrapple for you. I butchered a hog a few days ago, and knew you'd like to share. It's an awful lot of food for me, now that I'm by myself." She drew out the cheese nesded at the bottom of the package, resting it on the lid of an old pot he had near the campfire.

He jumped forward with his eyes bugged. "It makes my mouth water just looking at it!" He stared at the jars, and she detected a wariness in his expression.

"I've been riding since early this morning, Cholla.... wouldn't mind having a bit of it myself. It ought to be nearly time for your noon meal."

He hesitated. "Er...noon meal?"

She stood up, brushing off her hands. "Let's get a few twigs thrown into these coals, and rest a pot. That all right with you, Cholla?"

He gulped. "Oh, sure. I'll get a pot." He stumped into the hut, returning with a pot sticky from past meals. Delphinia marched it down to the creek and scrubbed it out before returning to camp. She stood over the jars and said: "You pick, Cholla? Pork sausage? Scrapple? Vegetable stew and side meat?"

"I reckon that vegetable stew is as good as any."

She unscrewed the jar, pouring the contents into the old pot and resting it over the coals. "Got plates? Something to eat off?"

"I eat out of the pot," he answered.

"Oh, well, I don't suppose that's a problem. I'll just pour a dab for myself on the upturned cover when this is heated up. Got forks? Spoons?"

"Yep. One spoon. One fork." He bit his lower lip now that spicy pork and herb aromas wafted through the woods. "This has my poor, empty stomach rumbling, Delphinia. I don't mind telling you, you're as good a cook as your ma was. This is a mite better than burned squirrel which is my regular fare."

"Do you make biscuits in your Dutch oven?" She pointed at the heavily rusted, sharp-edged Dutch oven standing at the entrance of his hut.

"No. I'm out of flour. Got to ride to town one day. Can't keep too much out here, you know. Mice and varmints get into things. I reckon your mother had a way to poison varmints." He threw her a slit-eyed look.

She nodded, keeping a straight face. The stew was beginning to bubble, so she poured several big chunks onto the upturned pot cover. After pulling Hawk's big knife from the scabbard at her belt, she stabbed into the meat with the knife point. "Um ...good...dive in, Cholla. Don't be shy. This is your camp, after all." She gobbled the meat, making light smacks with her lips. "Just right, just right. That pig was mighty tender, milk fed the way he was on all our whey and corn." Without looking up at Cholla, she scraped everything off the upturned pot cover into her mouth, then dipped the point of her knife back into the bubbling pot. She stuck a chunk of potato into her mouth from the knife.

Satisfied the food was safe, Cholla grabbed for his spoon and yanked the pot away from the coals, slobbering happily over the stew. Delphinia smacked her lips, cleaning her knife blade off on some grass.

Satisfying his hunger, Cholla finally sat back on his haunches, throwing a queer look at Delphinia while muttering: "I can't get over you carrying Hawk's pistol and knife."

She nodded, sitting back on her heels. "He'd want me to have them."

"Oh sure, sure. I only meant it ain't common to see a gal packin' such a big iron. After all, women don't do much shooting with a pistol. I just thought he would have left it to his son."

"His son?" She couldn't keep her jaw from dropping.

"Oh! You mean he never told you about that? Well, I reckon I better keep my trap shut. Talking too much is a bad habit of the lonely." He sucked loudly on a piece of gristle, extracting the last sweet juices.

Delphinia could see he enjoyed her discomfort. Determined not to give him any further satisfaction, she allowed his remark about Hawk's having a son pass.

He continued to eat, chewing and swallowing as fast as the spoon would carry the stew to his mouth. Gravy dribbled down his gray-black beard. He scraped the bottom of the pot until the spoon shrieked.

"How about a slice of cheese?" Delphinia asked. "I could

go for a little bit myself." She sensed he would wait until she took the first bite. He seemed encouraged now that they'd polished off the stew, and neither of them was showing any sign of becoming ill. He nodded in agreement as she reached for the cheese and then cut into the soft white mass. She took one small nibble for herself before she handed him her knife. "Cut for yourself. It's your cheese now."

He cut a big piece, running it under his nose for a whiff before eating the whole thing in one chomp.

"Don't you like the way it smells?" she asked him. "I made it from goat milk mixed with cow milk I got from the Brubakers.
I like the mix, not overly strong, but still having a nice bite to it. You know, you've eaten my cheese before."

He nodded. "Oh, I ain't sniffin' for no particular reason, Delphinia. I just was enjoying the smell of it." He leaned back, patting his belly. "So, Amity and Hawk was kilt? I'm sorry to hear that. Who done it?"

"The Rivera gang. Robbed a train in Willcox. They'd all been put in jail by Hawk once before. They were determined they wouldn't go back to jail again."

Cholla eyed her. "That's the worry for a bounty hunter. I'm sorry to hear about your mother. She was a hard worker and a good cook. I just remember that the last time I come by your house, your pa jumped me about freeloadin'. I knowed what he meant. To show my good intentions, I'll surely rustle up a bag of Mormon tea for you like I promised. I'll come by your place the first chance I get."

Delphinia stood up, watching him finger the cheese. "Careful with the cheese, Cholla. Flies and ants will get into it unless you have a way of tying it up in the trees."

He looked above his head into the branches. "I'll think of something."

She nodded. "Of course, good smelly cheese like that, sometimes it attracts bears. We always keep our cheese closed up tight in crocks in the root cellar."

"Bears! Hell, honey, I'll eat it up today. No bear has to be coming around this camp."

"I have to go now, Cholla. You take care of yourself." She marched away to Slicker, pulling up on the girth.

Cholla followed her, still holding the cheese in his hand. "What you going to do now, Delphinia? Alone in the world? No ma or pa. Setting down there on that place with nobody to protect you." He grinned. "Maybe you wouldn't mind old Cholla coming in for a visit now and again? Keep you from getting too lonely? Little gal like you needs a man looking in on her once in a while." He winked at her, stepping close, patting his dirty, old claw on her back, his scratchy fingertips lingering at the base of her neck.

Easing away from his touch, she led Slicker far enough away from him so that she could mount quickly before Cholla had the chance to try for another pat. She gave him a straight look from atop her horse. "I'll do just fine, Cholla. Anybody coming by to check up on me unexpected is likely to find himself looking up the business end of Hawk Estes's Colt .45. Be sure you yell your name before you come to my door." She tipped Hawk's hat, pressing her spurs against Slicker until the horse moved off in a long, swinging lope across camp and into the timber. She stopped once to look back. Cholla was watching her while he bit into the ball of the cheese as if he were eating a big apple.

Chapter Ten

Light from the kerosene lamp flickered from inside Delphinia's house, warning her to approach slowly. She dismounted in the arroyo, and hand on her gun she smiled to herself, knowing now how it must feel for anybody sneaking up on her place. A startled rabbit darted in the bright moonlight of the night. In fact, so well illumined was the yard, that, only having taken several steps, Delphinia was able to recognize Jim Hatton's chestnut horse tied to the hitching rail. She was relieved.

She was unsaddling Slicker at the corral gate when Jim, hearing her sounds, stepped out of the house. "You all right, Delphinia?"

"Just putting my horse up," she called over her shoulder, pulling the saddle and wet blanket off Slicker's back. She released the horse into the corral.

Jim Hat ton came down the steps, settling his gun back into his holster. "Where have you been? I was worried."

She closed the gate and picked up her bridle, while Jim hefted the saddle to the saddle house for her. "I rode up in the hills to visit Cholla…took him some new canned meat."

He eyed her, placing the heavy saddle on its rack. "Why would you want to do that? He's made trouble for you, telling Blackjack all your business."

She just smiled, turning toward the house, feeling too tired to explain.

Jim walked along beside her. "I put the coffee pot on, and warmed up a little stew for myself. I hope you don't mind. Your door was open."

Once inside, she sat down wearily at the table. Immediately

she noticed that the envelope containing the wedding announcement between Amity Dwyer and Chauncy Kyd, Jr., had been opened. The papers were strewn about the table.

"Sorry I snooped through your papers, Delphinia, but it was a long afternoon, and I'm the sheriff. Prying is my job." He grinned guiltily at her.

"It's all right. I'm glad you came by. Kind of nice riding up to a warm house, with the light aglow. I always hate coming home to a dark place, cold and lonely…." Her voice trailed off.

"I know what you mean. My room over at the hotel is always dark when I get there." Then he changed the subject. "Some special reason you went up to see Cholla today?"

"Just brought him something to eat like I told you before." She didn't want to tell him she had loaded the cheese with buckthorn. It was merely a prank meant to teach Cholla a lesson, nothing more, but she did not want the story repeated. Frightful Delphinia did not need any new stories told about her.

He moved his hand across the table so that his fingers rested at the edges of the yellow newspaper clipping. "Do you know what Cholla's real name is?"

"No. Just Cholla. Like the cactus plant, all prickly and thorny…a prospector's name, like they all give themselves. A lot of these old men don't want people knowing their real names. All I know is that he's been coming around here mooching food and tools from us since as far back as I can remember."

He squinted at her. "I don't want to scare you, Delphinia, and maybe I'm way off track here, but Cholla's real name is Chauncy Kyd."

She put her cup down with a clatter. "Chauncy Kyd!"

He nodded, still tapping the edges of the yellowed news clipping with his fingertips.

She took the news item from his hand, reading it closely before looking back up at him. "I found this in my mother's trunk the other night. It surprised me. I didn't know she was engaged to marry a man named Chauncy Kyd. She never told me about it. You don't think my mother was really going to marry…Cholla?"

He shook his head. "I don't know. But that name is unusual. There can't be too many Chauncy Kyds in the world."

"How do you know Cholla's real name?"

"One time, a few years back when he came into town, he met some other old-timer at the blacksmith's. I just happened to be over there myself, and I recall the two of them hopping up and down, pounding each other's backs. They had not seen each other since the Civil War when they both lived in Missouri. I remember the other man calling Cholla, Chauncy…. Chauncy Kyd. I laughed because the name was so unusual, one you don't forget to easily. I thought no wonder he just wanted everybody to call him Cholla."

"Chauncy Kyd," Delphinia repeated it as if she could not believe it.

Jim Hatton leaned back into his chair. "This newspaper announcement indicates some connection with your family, Delphinia. Or at least with your mother."

She jumped up from the table, walking to the stove to fill a plate with stew. "Jim, my mother could not possibly have been engaged to marry Cholla! It's crazy…that smelly old goat! There must be some mistake. Maybe the Amity Dwyer in the newspaper article is somebody other than my mother."

Jim Hatton shrugged, then downed the last of his coffee. "Why don't you let me send a telegram to Tucson tomorrow? I'll wire the sheriff to see if he can find out something. Maybe there are some Kyds or Dwyers living over there who can throw some light on the subject."

"Would you? I'd really appreciate that. I'd like to find out what that wedding announcement is all about. You know, the news item is dated just a few weeks before Amity's family died in the typhoid epidemic and she married Hawk."

"I'll do it. Then why don't you ride to town the day after tomorrow? You still have that voucher to cash on Bate Thatcher, don't you?"

"Yes. I'd forgotten about it." Her eyes shifted toward the clay jar on the shelf near the door.

He got to his feet and reached for his hat. "Don't you worry about this matter. We'll clear it up. See you then, Delphinia."

"Jim. I wonder if you could help me with something else."

"Sure, what?"

"Today, when I was up there talking to Cholla, he indicated that Hawk has a son. Do you know anything about that?"

Jim Hat ton flinched. "What exactly did Cholla tell you?"

"He just passed a remark, kind of off-hand, like he assumed I already knew. He caught me off guard, and I just sat there with my mouth hanging open, so he knew it was a surprise to me. Then he refused to say anything more about it."

"Just like him," Jim muttered. "The first thing I'm going to do is find out who Cholla really is, then we'll worry about the rest."

"Jim, you didn't answer my question. Did Hawk have a son?"

He slapped his hat: onto his head. "You come into town day after tomorrow to see if I have any answers from the Tucson sheriff. We'll talk then." He turned away from her and left the house before she could ask any more questions.

Delphinia watched him ride out of the yard, his dark outline finally evaporating out of sight. She locked the door and went back to the table where she picked up the newspaper clipping again. Each word was read over and over in Delphinia's attempt to make sense of Amity Dwyer's engagement to a man named Chauncy Kyd, Jr. Stiff and tired, she cleaned up the dishes, scraping the plates and deciding to wash them in the morning.

After blowing out the kerosene lamp, Delphinia settled herself in the big rocker with her feet stretched out in front of her, a rifle in her lap. She dozed off, just as Hawk had done the night he positioned himself in the same manner when he suspected the outlaw, Clayton McAllister, would follow him home. He was right, and they wound up in a gun fight in the front yard the next morning. It wasn't long before she was wakened by the cooling night air. She shivered and pulled the knitted shawl that was draped over the back of the chair down across her shoulders. She wished she could settle into a hot bath, but she did not have the energy to stoke up the stove again to heat all that water. But the rifle felt good across her lap, comforting, something standing between her and anybody who threatened her life. It put her on equal terms. She fell asleep while wondering how Cholla was doing from the effects of the loaded buckthorn cheese.

A tap on the door brought her to her feet in one swoop, and she swung the rifle across her hips. Rubbing the sleep from her eyes, she realized that there were daggers of daylight stabbing through the window glass in hot shafts. Heat seeped through the house. Late morning! Somebody was at her door while restless, hungry livestock called from the corrals.

"Del! You in there? It's me, Jess!"

She opened the door, still swinging the rifle. "Jess! I overslept. I didn't hear you ride in."

"Been knocking on your door for an hour."

"You have not! Help me with firewood, and I'll make breakfast."

"No thanks, Del, I ate early at home. I just come over here to tell you I'm sorry you ran into trouble with my mother when you came over the other day. My brothers told me about it. Don't let anything Ma says get under your hide. She's just all excited about me gettin' hitched to Roz, is all. When women get to fighting, the whole thing turns out shitty."

Delphinia burst into laughter. "I couldn't have said it better myself!" She set down the rifle and approached the stove where she dug the poker under the coals from yesterday's fire. They came to life. "I've got fresh scrapple and pork sausage. How about a second breakfast?" She tossed new kindling into the fire.

He stood, sniffing at the stove. "I'll gather eggs and do chores for you, Del. I noticed your stock bellowing for morning feed. You surely have become a lady of leisure." He laughed, eyeing Hawk's pants she still wore from yesterday. "That's some getup."

Delphinia hurried around the room, gathering last night's plates and setting clean ones for breakfast, while Jess tromped outside, whistling. She watched Jess through the window, forking hay to the horses and sheep. He let the hens out of the chicken coop. In a few minutes he was back with a basket full of fresh, brown eggs.

When he handed her the basket, she realized how boyish he was, how fond of him she felt, and how she needed him like a brother. Not a husband. She realized how close she had come to marrying Jess for his friendship and companionship — nothing more. Her thoughts flashed to Jim Hat ton whose presence in the room last night seemed to linger on in the air.

"You're giving me funny looks, Del. What's wrong?"

She turned away, putting the egg basket on the sideboard, before choosing several large eggs that she then cracked on the edge of the black iron frying pan already sizzling with fresh pork sausage. "I'm thinking what a good friend you are, Jess, and how much I appreciate you. I'm thinking you probably shouldn't ride over here and take the chance of messing things up between you and Rosalind. Your mother is all excited about your wedding plans. Your family will be better off having Rosalind in it. All the doors are open to you now, Jess."

He came around the table, taking her in his arms, running his fingers along the back of her neck, trying to press her head to his shoulder, but she resisted. "Del? You're the only girl for me. Marrying into a big cattle family don't amount to a hill of beans to me. I'd trade that any day for just being here with you, like this, gathering eggs and helping you stoke up the stove. That's all I ever wanted."

"That's all we'd ever do, Jess. Gathering eggs and stoking up the stove. Running a few head of sheep on forty acres. Cutting hay. Trading vegetables with the neighbors. Would you want to hire out a couple times a year for much-needed cash money when we got into a bind? Would you trade riding for Mister Sawyer when you can own his place instead?"

He held her tighter, rocking her. "We'd make it all right, Del. Hawk and Amity did it all these years. My folks are just homesteaders. I never missed a meal."

"Amity made a living with her herbs, curing people and helping with sick babies. I'm not that good at it. I don't have her experience. And while she never accepted Hawk's bounty money, he kept us in supplies. I'm telling you, Jess, you can't throw away the opportunity the Sawyers are offering you. And Roz really cares about you, doesn't she? Besides, she's so pretty, half the cowboys in Cochise County would give an arm to marry her."

"You're sure trying your damnedest to discourage me, Del. Is that the way you really feel?"

She nodded. "I told you the night of the party in town, I'm not ready to make promises…to settle down the way you want me to. We grew up together. We're more like brother and sister."

"Brother and sister! God damn, Del! You think I don't know the difference?"

She pushed him gently away. "Simmer down and have your breakfast." She sat at the table, picked up her fork, and nibbled unhappily while he stomped out of the house, slamming the door behind him. Delphinia heard the mad clatter of his horse's hoofbeats on the hard-packed road winding like a ribbon north-east toward the Sawyer place.

Chapter Eleven

Gray drizzle enveloped the countryside, heavy clouds moved in from the distant mountain peaks. Delphinia rode astride Slicker, once again donned in Hawk's clothes. The canvas duster, hanging low on either side of Slicker and covering his steaming flanks, helped insulate her body against the rain.

Drawing up in front of Jim Hatton's office, Delphinia saw the sheriff inside, sitting behind his desk. He looked up at her through the window, quickly standing and opening the door. She dismounted, walking past him toward the stove. "Cold!" she said, flicking and rubbing her hands in front of the potbelly stove, creating a spray of water droplets on the floor nearby. The coffee steamed. "I rode in to see you like I promised. Any news from Tucson?"

Jim walked around the front of the his desk. "I got a telegram back from Tucson late yesterday afternoon. The sheriff said the date of your mother's engagement is long before his time, and, personally, he doesn't know of any Kyds or Dwyers living over there. But he said there is a young man named Kyd living in Douglas, so I wired the Douglas sheriff. This came back a few minutes ago." The sheriff extended a sheet of paper in Delphinia's direction.

"What does it say?" Delphinia asked, still warming her hands over the stove.

"A Missus Winslow Kyd lives on a little place east of town. She had a grandson, Obediah, killed in a horse stampede two years ago. Missus Kyd is a widow, originally from Missouri."

"Missouri! My mother and her folks were from Missouri. You suppose this Missus Kyd knows something?"

"It's worth a try," he said. "I haven't got any better ideas at the moment."

"I'll do it! But it's sixty miles to Douglas. I'd be gone at least a week. I haven't got anybody to take care of my stock."

"Why don't you cash in your bounty voucher, and buy a ticket on the stage to Douglas? Leave your horse with me. I'll put him up at the livery stable until you get back. I know a couple of teenage boys here in town who are always looking for work. They're good with animals...if you can pay them something." He handed her the bounty voucher.

"Of course."

"The Douglas stage leaves at noon. You have just enough time to cash your voucher and buy a ticket."

She thanked him and bolted for the door, hurrying in the direction of the bank.

The stage to Douglas was on time. Delphinia settled in among the rest of the passengers who eyed her odd clothing, but said nothing. She squirmed deep into the corner of the seat and hoped the bulge of Hawk's big gun inside her coat did not show too much. She pulled her hat down, thoroughly embarrassed by looking so much like a man. Why had she been so anxious to get the Chauncy Kyd business cleared up? She kept her eyes locked outside the stagecoach on the hazy ridges of the Chiricahua mountain range. It occurred to her that she had forgotten to ask Jim Hatton about Hawk's having a son. But she would worry about that later.

The driver blew his horn, alerting the stage hands at the next station that the coach was coming in and to ready a fresh teams of horses. The stage hit a rough stretch, rocking and thumping, while the. passengers groaned and hugged their waists with crossed arms and tried not to lean too heavily against one another. None of the passengers — three men across from Delphinia and a man and his wife next to her — spoke. The stage finally lumbered into the station yard as the driver bellowed: "Ten minutes! Git your coffee and grub. Hit the privy! No waiting for laggards...got a schedule to keep!"

Delphinia opened the door and got out stiffly, her legs cramped. She made her way to the privy and then to the station. The coffee smelled strong, but the food did not look appealing. At the cost of one dollar for rice and tortillas she finally settled on a hard biscuit for fifty cents. Back outside, she paced back and forth under the porch roof. It was still drizzling, and she wanted to stretch out her aching bones. She watched as fresh horses were backed into the traces — their ears back, steam rising from their quivering flanks where the cold rain ran down their sides in icy streams.

In a few minutes the driver yelled again: "Load 'em! We're leaving! Anybody not inside the coach in one minute gets left behind!"

Delphinia hurried across the yard with the other passengers. The stage groaned and creaked behind the bolting teams upon its departure. More bumps, more slams, more monotony until her spine felt like it had been driven into the base of her skull. She had a severe headache by the time they got to the next change station. She decided to eat a little more this time. Whatever it was that was served under the chile sauce was better left to the imagination, but the hot coffee tasted good. She ate hurriedly, still feeling uncomfortable under the stares of her fellow passengers. A woman traveling alone in man's clothing, carrying a gun, was not a common sight. Why hadn't she thought of that?

They arrived in Douglas well past midnight. The passengers, who were continuing on, were allowed one night of sleep before the stage left at dawn. Having arrived at her destination, Delphinia checked in at the Douglas Hotel, paying for her room with one of the twenty-dollar gold pieces she'd gotten from Bate Thatcher's bounty.

The man at the desk raised an eyebrow. "You be wanting water, ma'am?"

"No. Not tonight. I've had enough water for one day. But I want the room for two nights."

He kept looking up and down at her clothes. "May I ask your business? I mean, a lone woman taking a room more than one night…do you have means of support? We have rules about women staying here."

She caught the drift. "My name is Delphinia Estes. I'm Hawk Estes's daughter, and I am here on official business out of Sheriff Hatton's office in Willcox." She knew that was stretching things a little, but she did not like his insinuation.

"Hawk Estes! I heard he was killed."

"He was. I'm taking his place." She drew the edge of her coat back, exposing the handle of Hawk's big Colt .45.

The desk clerk's pale eyebrows shot up to his hairline, while Delphinia somehow kept a straight face. He handed her a key. "Number nine. Top of the stairs, to your left."

"I'll take my receipt, please. Two nights."

He nodded, scribbling. "Yes, of course." He handed it to her along with her change.

She walked, stiff legged, up the stairs, putting on a square-shouldered swagger, knowing he watched her every move.

In the morning Delphinia inquired at the desk about the location of Sheriff Benton's office. Although the rain had stopped, the moisture in the air combined with a westerly wind sent a dampness through Delphinia on the walk over that was hard to throw off. She found herself standing in front of the sheriffs stove no sooner than she had entered the office.

"You must be Hawk Estes's daughter," he said, eyeing her

from across his desk. He was a short man with gray hair and a long, drooping mustache. Pale, watery, blue eyes seemed to bore holes right through her.

"Yes, I'm Delphinia Estes. Sheriff Hatton sent you a telegram from Willcox two days ago, inquiring about a lady named Missus Winslow Kyd living here. Can you tell me how to find her house?"

He frowned. "What is your business with Missus Kyd? She's a fine, old widow woman who never bothers anybody."

"I'm not here to bother anybody. I just want to ask her some questions about my mother."

"Uhn huh. The clerk at the hotel told me you are staying two nights, and that you said you were here on Hawk Estes's business."

"Maybe I shouldn't have intimidated him. But he accused me of being a woman with no visible means of support, trying to stay at his hotel…I didn't like what he was suggesting."

"He's only following my orders. I asked him to let me know who comes and goes from the hotel. He helps me keep track of things around here."

She pulled her hands away from the warmth of the stove and walked toward the desk. "I'm staying two nights because I don't know if I can catch the afternoon stagecoach back to Willcox today, and I didn't want to be left without a room for the night. That's all. Sheriff, I understand you have your own way of running your town. Now, if you can tell me how to find Missus Kyd, I'll be on my way."

His eyes traveled to Hawk's gun and lingered there for several seconds. "Hawk Estes was no friend of mine. When I heard he got killed, it didn't surprise me. Wherever he went, there was trouble."

"Why does the Territory offer bounties? If you official peace officers were able to take care of outlaws by yourselves, you wouldn't need people like Hawk Estes doing your work."

"Don't you get smart with me, young lady! I can slap you in my jail for twenty-four hours on nothing more than loitering, if I want to."

She opened her mouth to respond, but his threatening look prompted her to save it for some other time. It was within his power to get even with Hawk Estes by hurting her. She would not give him the satisfaction. "You'll have no trouble from me, Sheriff. I appreciate all your help. You've been very kind." She turned to leave; she could get directions to Mrs. Kyd's house from somebody else.

"The Kyd place is a mile out on the road east. You passed it coming in on the stage. Little, old, battered wood house with a chicken coop and a sheep pasture. Red windmill."

Nodding, she closed the door.

Chapter Twelve

Delphinia Estes rented a sway-backed roan mare at the livery stable for two dollars and headed east on the road out of Douglas. Two men, riding in a freight wagon, passed her in the mist. Neither paid much attention. The Kyd place appeared right where the sheriff said it would, a mile east of town on a little rise, the buildings in need of repair. But a feminine touch was lent by a profusion of red and white flowers, growing along the sides of the house. A dozen sheep stood with stiff legs in a barren pasture that sprouted nothing but yellow flowers from the two-day rain.

Riding up to the house, Delphinia called out: "Missus Kyd? Anybody home?"

A fat, old, gray-haired lady, crippled at the waist so that she walked bent over, peeked out from the door. She dusted her hands on her white apron. Flour stuck to her fingers as if she had been rolling dough. "I'm Missus Kyd. What do you want?" Her dark little eyes darted over Delphinia's clothing.

Delphinia dismounted, tying the roan nag to the hitching post. "I need your help, Missus Kyd. My name is Delphinia Estes. My mother was Amity Dwyer Estes, and I wonder if you knew her family? Amity was killed about a month back, and I'm trying to find out about some family history." Delphinia took Hawk's big hat off, and her loose hair fell to her shoulders.

Mrs. Kyd opened the door, her eyes wide. "Amity Dwyer! You her girl? Of course! You look just like her! Come in, come in!"

Delphinia entered the warm little living room heated by a roaring, potbelly stove. A stack of firewood stood near the door.

The aroma of baking cornbread and apples emanated from the back of the house and pestered Delphinia's nostrils.

"Come into the kitchen and warm up," Mrs. Kyd said, signaling with a flour-covered hand. She made her way slowly across the room, bent over at the waist, the strategically placed furniture lending support to her bent body.

Delphinia followed her into the kitchen. After removing her father's duster, she took a seat at the table.

"Be right with you," Mrs. Kyd said as she rolled out the last batch of dough, spooning on an apple filling, then folding the dough triangles before pinching the corners. She placed them onto a pan and slid it into the big, black oven. Taking a chair for herself, she sighed. "We could go to the living room, but it's a long walk for me. Let's just set and wait for the dough to bake."

Delphinia smiled at her, warming to the friendly old lady. "You said you knew my mother? Amity Dwyer?"

"I knew her mother, Martha, and her pa, too. We traveled West together by wagon train from Missouri in 1868. We got to Prescott first, in Arizona Territory, and then some of us went south to Tucson. That's where Martha was to meet up with her husband, your grandfather. He came to Arizona Territory first, a couple years earlier, proved up on a homestead, and then sent for his wife and children. That would be Amity and her little brother, Charles."

Delphinia said: "Yes, I knew that much. My grandfather met everybody in Tucson, but they got caught in a typhoid epidemic, and the whole family, but my mother, died."

Mrs. Kyd nodded. "It was the worst. A terrible tragedy. We'd come so far, walked and struggled for months to cross the country, and then half of us died in Tucson."

"Missus Kyd, what was your relationship to Chauncy Kyd, Junior?"

She eyed Delphinia. "Why do you ask, darling?"

"I found an old newspaper item in my mother's trunk last week, and it said she was engaged to Chauncy Kyd. I never heard her mention him. Who was he?"

Mrs. Kyd reached for the teapot. "Tea, darling?"

Delphinia got the feeling Mrs. Kyd was evading her question. But she was wrong. The lady was only taking a breather, getting ready for the long story. Delphinia reached for her own cup, adding a spoonful of honey.

"Your mother, Amity, was a sweet, teenaged girl and engaged to marry Chauncy Kyd, Junior, who traveled West from Missouri with us on that first train. I don't believe Amity was in love with him, even though he was a bright young man, and a rather handsome rascal. But he had a vicious temper, and a bad drinking habit for one so young."

"How old was he?" Delphinia asked, still having trouble imagining Amity engaged to Cholla.

"About her age. Maybe a year or two older. You see, Amity's pa made arrangements for her to marry Chauncy Junior away back in Missouri before the war. It was a common practice ...people married off their children to combine properties in those days."

Delphinia nodded. "So what happened?"

Mrs. Kyd eyed her again. "Amity never told you these things?"

"No, never. I had no idea anybody named Chauncy Kyd existed until I found that newspaper item."

Mrs. Kyd hesitated. "Maybe I shouldn't go into this. Maybe Amity had her reasons for not telling you."

"Please, Missus Kyd. It's too late for that now. I've gotten this far. Won't you tell me the rest of the story so I can put it to rest?"

"You're right, darling. It's better to get things out in the open and be done with it. Besides, Amity was hardly to blame for what happened. The poor thing…not her fault."

"Her fault?"

"While we were camped in Tucson, Amity's father came to collect his family, but he got caught in the epidemic, and the place was sealed off. Nobody was allowed out. The village was quarantined. There was nothing any of us could do but just set and wait. But Chauncy Kyd was all anxious to marry your mother. After all, we'd trekked across the country six months, and he had worked himself into quite a fever."

Delphinia took another sip of tea, not interrupting for fear Mrs. Kyd would get distracted from her storytelling.

"A young man named Hawley Estes was in Tucson at the same time we were. He had not come West with us…I think he was a soldier just mustered out of the Army after some Indian fighting. Anyway, he noticed Amity, and she noticed him, and it did not take long before Chauncy noticed what was going on. Chauncy being so temperamental, he demanded Amity marry him right away, and the folks thought it was a good idea, kind of a way to take everybody's mind off the epidemic. They posted announcements in the paper and threw a party. The first trouble started that night, at the party."

"Trouble?" Delphinia finished her tea.

"It was obvious Amity and Hawley Estes had eyes for each other, so it did not take long for Chauncy to get his temper worked up. A fight broke out, and the two of them ruined the party. The very next day Chauncy called Hawley out at a saloon in Tucson, and there was a gun fight. Chauncy was killed. Of course, it was self-defense. Then the typhoid caught up to everybody. Amity's family died, and she and Hawley Estes married in Tucson and left. That was the last I ever saw of Amity."

Delphinia sighed, puzzled. "So Chauncy Kyd was killed? By my father?'

"Yes. But you know, Chauncy was not right for Amity. It was a shame the young man got killed, but he had a ferocious temper. I'm afraid Amity would have been very unhappy married to a man like that. I hope everything worked out for her and Hawley."

"It did, Missus Kyd. May I ask, how are you related to Chauncy Kyd?"

"My rolls!" she scrambled from her chair, reaching for the heavy oven door. "Having such a good time telling old stories, I nearly burned up the rolls!"

Delphinia laughed, helping Mrs. Kyd by pulling the tray out and resting it on the stove top. "*Umm,* smells good. You eat all this by yourself?"

"I love cooking. I never get tired of working in the kitchen, and I don't know why. Just in my blood, I guess. Only wish I had a family to cook for. My only son and his wife died, and my grandson, Obediah, got killed in a horse roundup. He never married. If only I had some young ones around to cook for, I'd have everything. I give most of what I cook away to needy folks in the community."

Delphinia helped put the rolls on a rack to cool. "My mother and I lived alone most of the time. We did a lot of cooking, too. She liked working with herbs and healing remedies."

Mrs. Kyd slapped her knee. "Just like her ma! Those women could look at a root or a sprout and tell you exactly what it was, and what time of year to cook it so it would heal some ailment or other. Those are special talents I never had."

"My mother was a special lady," Delphinia said, sitting down.

Mrs. Kyd plopped across from her, red faced and anxious to continue the story. "Now, about my relationship to young Chauncy Kyd. He was my husband's nephew. My husband, Winslow Kyd...we was married back in Missouri...had a brother, Chauncy Kyd, Senior, whose son was named after him."

Delphinia frowned, trying to sort it out. "Then the Chauncy Kyd who was engaged to my mother had a father with the same name."

"That's the way it usually goes…with a junior you've got a senior."

"Was Chauncy Kyd's father in Tucson when his son was killed?"

"No. He came West about a year after that. He was in jail in Missouri for riding with raiders after the war, so he was unable to come with the rest of us in the first wagon train."

"In jail?" Delphinia asked.

"Many things happened during the war, and lots of people got caught up in serious trouble they didn't ask for. And Chauncy Senior had a vile temper. My, he was a suspicious man. Always seemed to be in trouble. Got into a knife fight once that left him with an awful scar on his face, almost took his nose off."

"What happened to him?" Delphinia asked softly, feeling goose bumps crawling up her arms as she thought of Cholla's torn nostril.

"I don't know. Haven't heard about him in years. He went crazy when he got to Tucson and learned his son had been killed by a man who wound up marrying Amity. He went berserk, vowed terrible revenge. Left our family, and last we knew he had become a prospector somewhere east of here, in the Chiricahuas. But I couldn't tell you any more about him."

"A prospector? In the mountains east of here?"

"I never liked him even back in Missouri, a squirrelly man, eager to get into shooting scrapes. Rode with a bad bunch. I think he was hoping to settle in with the Dwyers once his son married into the family. He wasn't anything like his brother, my Winslow. Once he left this family, I did not miss him."

Delphinia locked the fingers of her cold hands together under the table. "What happened to Chauncy Senior's wife?"

"She died back in Missouri long before the war, in fact, shortly after Chauncy Junior was born. That's why there was only one child, and old Chauncy set quite a store by that boy. Raised him up alone, taught him everything. The only reason Chauncy Junior headed West without his father is because the old man was in jail." Mrs. Kyd sighed, talked out. "It was a long time ago, honey. I'm afraid that's all I remember."

"Thank you," Delphinia said, "you've answered all my questions." Her mind raced, thinking of Cholla…the father of Amity's dead beau. A father bent on revenge. Harboring feelings of hatred for Amity and Hawk. Amity, kind Amity, always trying to be nice to Cholla for what happened to his son. Feeling sorry. Guilty.

Mrs. Kyd reached for the cooled apple tarts and extended her arm toward Delphinia, offering her one. "Have a treat, darling, while they're still warm."

Delphinia smiled, reaching, mind racing. *Did Hawk know who Cholla really was? Did Amity ever tell him?* Delphinia's icy chill persisted. For years Cholla had been an enemy, criss-crossing the range, pretending to look for gold. Coming around, snooping, using excuses he needed food and medicine.

"You all right, dear?" Mrs. Kyd asked. "You look a little pale and distracted. I hope I have not said something to upset you."

"I'm fine, really. I just have a lot to think about. You've helped me more than you know. Is there anything I can do to help you here? Chores? I've got the day."

Mrs. Kyd clapped her hands, laughing. "If you don't mind

gathering eggs and tossing hay to my sheep! It would save a crippled old lady a walk to the barn in the rain. Meanwhile, I'll rustle up lunch for us. How's scrambled eggs? And corn-bread?"

Chapter Thirteen

"My! That rain is coming down hard again!" Mrs. Kyd said to Delphinia as she held the door open for her.

Delphinia walked out onto the porch, shivered, and pulled her hat to her eyes. "Looks like you have some sick sheep out there, Missus Kyd."

The old woman squinted, sticking her neck as far out the door as she could without opening it so wide as to let in the cold.

"I'll have a look." Delphinia told her. "When I first rode in this morning, I noticed several moving slow and stiff like."

Mrs. Kyd grunted. "They were all right yesterday."

Delphinia braced herself against the cold. Rainy wind beat against her face as she slopped across the muddy yard. Climbing the fence, she walked across the sheep pasture, eyeing a downed ewe and another spinning in slow circles, head twisted at an odd angle, gasping in watery spurts. "Here, girl, easy, girl," Delphinia crooned. She put her hand under the ewe's chin. The quaking animal rolled its yellow eyes, too sick to move away.

Looking around at the pasture, Delphinia walked across the soggy land. She found two dead sheep. Others were moving with aching difficulty, bleating in soft gasps. She followed the fence line and came back up along the slow-rolling hill, shouldering the rain, checking the new growth of little yellow flowers some of the sheep had nibbled. Kneeling near a big patch of new plants, she plucked the small bright petals, brought them to her nose, crushed the leaves, and tasted the pulverized droplets in her hand. Satisfied, she rose to her feet and hurried back to the house.

"Are they all right?" Mrs. Kyd asked.

"I'm afraid they've been eating those new yellow flowers out there."

"But the sheep have been in that pasture all year."

"Maybe so, but this rain is bringing up a fast growth of plants that are giving those sheep a belly full of poison. I've seen it happen. We've had the problem with our own sheep. My mother always said that you have to watch out for new yellow flowers when it comes to sheep."

"Oh, Lordy! What's to do?"

"Get the whole flock moved up to the corral, and we'll give them a big dose of warm water and molasses if you have it. I'll feed it to the sheep. You get the molasses cooking. Afterwards, they'll need hay for a few days, until those yellow flowers reach a point that they won't bother the sheep. It's probably just the new bloom."

"Oh, honey! You are talking a big job. There's thirty sheep out there. I hate to bother you."

"No bother, Missus Kyd. I'll see if this old horse knows how to push sheep into a corral. Then I'll need a bottle to get the molasses water down their throats?"

"I have one I use to feed bum lambs, a long-necked bottle."

"Good! Put a lot of water on to heat."

Nodding, Mrs. Kyd disappeared into the house without a backward glance while Delphinia rode the old horse into the pasture, driving sheep. They were staggering now, too ill to move or even care, paying no attention to the rider on horseback. Dismounting, she waved her arms and walked among them, pushing and prodding, but it did no good. She finally tied up the horse and got a lariat from Mrs. Kyd's shed. With a loop tied around a woolly rump, Delphinia led and pulled the stiff sheep, one at a time, into the corral.

Her arms aching as if they might disengage from the sockets at any moment, Delphinia barely noticed the rider approaching through the cold afternoon fog into Mrs. Kyd's yard. Hat pulled low to his eyes, the rider stopped his horse in front of the porch just as Mrs. Kyd emerged out the door, lugging a steaming bucket of molasses water.

"What's going on? Hauling water on a day like this?" Sheriff Benton shouted as he braced himself against the rain.

Mrs. Kyd struggled down the steps. "Sick sheep. Delphinia Estes is helping me. Don't just sit there, give us a hand! You're the sheriff, ain't you?"

"Herding sheep ain't part of my job."

"Pshaw! You ain't got anything else to do today, have you? What's a man for?"

He dismounted, running his horse under the roof alongside Delphinia's old stable nag, and slogged his way across the yard. He scooped the bucket out of Mrs. Kyd's hands. "Here, let me do this. You get inside the house before you get sick."

Mrs. Kyd turned back without protesting. "Here, take this bottle to her. And come inside as soon as you need more. I got every pot in the house bubbling."

Sheriff Benton took the pail of molasses water to Delphinia and helped her fill the long-necked bottle he had stuffed into his pocket.

"Were you looking for me, Sheriff?"

"I wondered why you didn't come back to town."

"Did you think I brought harm to Missus Kyd?"

"The thought crossed my mind."

She chuckled. "Well, you certainly got here just on time. There's thirty sheep in this corral, and I've still got twenty to bring in. You want to drench or catch?"

He eyed her. "Sheep! You do the drenching. I'll drag the damn' critters in. What's wrong with them anyway?"

"Got their bellies full of poison weed. Most of them'll be all right if they get a big dose of warm molasses water and out of that pasture."

"Damn' sheep critters," he mumbled, squishing away through the mud with a shoulder turned against the wind.

Delphinia watched him scuff out like an ornery kid. It wasn't long before he returned, dragging a ewe who pulled back, bleating and bracing against his arms. "Work the loop around her rump," Delphinia told him. "Pull her along easy. They can't take too much stress."

"Neither can I!" He roared, holding up his arm from behind the sheep's rump. "This damn' shitter has diarrhea!"

Delphinia grabbed the sheep, holding its woolly neck while lifting the chin, stuffing the neck of the long glass bottle between the ewe's lips.

"Sheep are more lousy trouble than they're worth!" the sheriff grumbled, while wiping his dirty arm against the sopped mass of soggy wool of the sheep's back.

"I disagree. They may not be entirely suited to the desert like some other livestock, but the wool is worth it. They're lovely, gentle animals, needing help and protection, that's all."

He snorted, running the accumulated dampness away from the edges of his mustache with his clean hand. "You done preaching? I'll go for another."

She nodded, slipping the rope off and handing it back to him. "Missus Kyd is a generous old lady. Anything I can do to help her is worth whatever trouble is going on here today."

Chastised, he turned away from her for another trip to the pasture. "Isn't there some way of doing this faster? Driving them in at once on horseback?"

"I tried that. They're too sick and confused, and they shouldn't be forced. This is the only thing we can do."

Swearing, he disappeared in the mist. The two of them set

about the work, gaining a natural rhythm as the time passed quickly.

Several hours later, forking hay into the manger, Delphinia smiled and admired the flock now contentedly eating hay under the lean-to. Out of the cold rain, some rested with legs curled underneath, chewing their cud, watching Delphinia and the sheriff with disinterest.

"Sheep!" Benton grumbled one more time, shaking his head. "I smell like the devil."

Delphinia put the pitchfork down and gave one last glance to their handiwork before turning tiredly back to the house. "I'll see what Missus Kyd wants done with the two dead ones."

He followed her. "I hope she has hot coffee in that kitchen."

Tramping up the steps, Delphinia shook the rain off her duster. "Not only coffee, she has hot cornbread and apple turnovers."

They stamped their feet, flicking water and mud about the porch.

"Come into the kitchen!" Mrs. Kyd yelled above the sound of slamming pots and rattling dishes. "It's a treat to have company, somebody to eat all this cooking!"

"Just as long as it ain't lamb stew," Benton muttered.

"What do you want done with those dead sheep, Missus Kyd?" Delphinia asked. "I think the others will be all right. Keep them out of the pasture for a couple of days. Feed them hay and corn if you have it. They need time to get the poison out of their systems."

"I lost two?" Mrs. Kyd said softly. "They are such beautiful creatures, I'm sorry I didn't notice them getting sick. Maybe I'm too old and stupid to be handling livestock any more. I should sell the flock."

"I'll send somebody from town to bury your sheep tomorrow," Benton said. "And never mind about getting rid of the flock. I know how much store you put by those critters. We'll figure how to get somebody out here to lend you a hand, at least a couple days a week."

"Will you? That is kind of you, Sheriff. I promise plenty of coffee and cornbread to the helpers. And whatever else I have to share."

"I know you will, ma'am."

They sat together, drinking coffee and listening to the rain lighten on the roof until it was only a soft drizzle. Heavy fog rolled across the land, darkening the land with layers of frothy mist.

"Cold and quiet out there now," Benton said finally. The women were both very tired.

Delphinia nodded. "I have to get back to town. The man at the stable will think I stole his horse. Thank you, Missus Kyd, for your kindness. I'll try to come back for another visit one day."

"Don't thank me, darling. It was wonderful talking old times. I had not thought of those things for many years. I'm sorry about your dear mother."

The sheriff looked at the women with curiosity, but not enough to ask what they were talking about. His expression told Delphinia that he assumed it was female things they had been gossiping about, and that he was not really interested. He and Delphinia made their way out of the house, mounted the horses, and waved at Mrs. Kyd who stood in the doorway. Her dark, bent shadow was framed in the light from the kerosene lamp on the living-room table.

"She's a wonderful lady," Delphinia said.

"The best. It was a hard loss when her grandson was killed. I didn't realize until tonight just how old and alone she is out here. She's always doing something nice for folks. I'm going to have to remember to keep a closer check on her, see that people ride out now and again to give her a hand."

"That will be nice. It's hard being alone…I know."

He eyed her, drawing his horse up closer to hers. "You see, I had you pegged wrong. Figured you were up to no good, bringing me trouble. Hawk Estes usually meant trouble."

"You changed your mind about me?"

"Frankly, yes. The way you helped Missus Kyd, and all. Not many people would have bothered."

"Missus Kyd was a friend of my grandmother's a long time ago. They traveled by wagon train together from Missouri to Arizona. She helped me today with some family information I needed, and, anyway, I'd have helped her with the sheep even if she hadn't been able to tell me anything. I live alone, too, now, and maybe a good deed I do will bring one back to me someday."

"Like I said, I had you figured wrong. I hope whatever it was you were looking for from Missus Kyd got worked out."

"It did."

The desk clerk at the hotel peered over the counter, eyeing Delphinia's wet boots and attire when she asked for the key to her room. His glance shot back up to her straggled hair. He sniffed. "Been working…livestock?" He dangled the key in front of her nose.

"May I have some hot water tonight, please?" she requested, and then started for the stairs.

"The water will be sent to the washroom at the end of the hall. We don't allow bathing in the rooms. And it will cost you a dollar. And, by the way, there was a man here, looking for you. He came twice, in fact."

"A man? Who?"

"Didn't leave his name. Sort of a cowboy, carried a gun, dark mustache. Just said he had old family business to settle with the daughter of Hawk Estes. He asked me what room you were in, but I told him we do not allow single lady guests to entertain visitors in the rooms."

She hesitated on the second step, looking back at him over her shoulder. "Forget about the hot water."

He rolled his eyes as if he were not surprised. "Very well, no water."

She trudged up the steps, flinging the duster across her shoulder and feeling the weight of Hawk's pistol against her hip. She wondered who the stranger could be. Cautiously, she let herself into her room, checked behind the door and under the bed. Then she threw the rolled duster onto the center of the bed. She peeled off her clothes and wrapped herself in a white bed sheet she pulled from the bed. Shivering, she was glad to be rid of the wet clothes. Her hair hung like sopped rope. She rubbed her hands over the red welts running along the edges of both shin bones where protesting sheep had stomped her while she had forced warm molasses water down their throats.

In the darkness she sat in a chair placed between the bed and the window. She could only think of the long stagecoach ride home. Home! She longed to ease her aching body into a tub of hot water, surrounded by her own possessions, inside her own house. Nodding with sleep and shivering again, she clutched the white sheet around herself and dozed lightly, her dry feet resting on the threadbare carpet. She groaned tiredly, in a half sleep, listening. A creak at the window brought her head up. She watched as a shadow grew in length across the floor of the room — a soft, black, creeping blotch. Then a shatter of smashed glass was followed by two quick gunshots, cracking in metallic reports. Gunsmoke filled the air. Delphinia came to her feet abruptly and moved nearer the window's ledge, an apparition in a long white sheet, blue-lipped, hollow-eyed, hair hanging wildly around a colorless face, holding Hawk's pistol in her hand.

The gunman's head turned suddenly in her direction. His eyes bugged out, and his mouth opened with a gasp. He teetered for a frantic second and then clawed at the window pane, before he flipped with a long howl off the ledge and onto the board walk two floors below with a hollow thump.

Still clutching the sheet, Delphinia peered out from the window and caught sight of a couple of people gathering around the body. Somebody ran, yelling for the sheriff.

It wasn't long before, having examined the corpse, Sheriff Benton marched into the hotel. Delphinia soon heard his loud knock at her door. Pulling the sheet more tightly about her, she peeped out at him, opening the door only a crack.

"I'm not dressed, Sheriff."

"Oh to hell with that, let me in."

She stepped back, opening the door just enough so that Sheriff Benton could enter without giving an eyeful to the group of onlookers who had followed him up the stairs.

"Go back, all of you!" Sheriff Benton ordered and slammed the door. He studied Delphinia before he asked the obvious question. "What do you know about the man who just fell from your window?"

"Nothing! I was resting in the chair by the window. My clothing was so wet...and I wasn't sure I could sleep because the desk clerk had told me someone had been asking for me. So I was in the chair, and the next thing I knew somebody broke the window and shot at the bed. I was startled. I jumped up and...and whoever it was fell off the ledge."

He walked to the window and looked down to the street below. He turned back to her, eyeing the white sheet. "You must have given that fellow quite a scare."

"He did the same for me."

The sheriff sighed, shaking his head. "His name was Boyl Simon. He heard you were in town and did some bragging at the saloon this afternoon. Apparently he felt he had some unfinished business with Hawk Estes, and you came close to finding out about it."

"I never heard of anybody named Boyl Simon."

"He spent two years in Yuma, after getting caught by Hawk for bounty. I expect he planned to settle a score here tonight."

She gulped. "He nearly accomplished his plan."

He studied the bed and then squinted at Delphinia. "The way you rolled up that duster on the bed…I don't suppose you were waiting for him?"

"Me? Waiting for him?"

He walked to the door to let himself out. "Miss Estes, I want you to do three things for me."

"Yes, sir?"

"Lock this door. Get a good night's sleep. And be on that stagecoach in the morning."

Chapter Fourteen

Delphinia Estes looked west over her shoulder at the cherry-red sundown glowing from behind purple clouds. The long, rugged ride on the stagecoach back from Douglas had been dreary — rocking, bumping, slumping into soggy wagon ruts, listening to the driver crack his whip. Delphinia's traveling companions had included a lady with two squirmy children and a whiskey salesman who let it be known right away he did not like kids. He had assessed Delphinia, too, eyeing her rumpled clothing and the bulging pistol at her hip. Otherwise the ride had been uneventful.

Jim Hatton lowered the newspaper he had been reading when Delphinia walked into his office. She looked at him and was filled with gladness, comparing him to the grouchy sheriff of Douglas. When he offered her a cup of coffee, his gentle expression told her he was glad to see her.

"How was the trip? Find Missus Kyd?" he asked.

"Yes. She's a wonderful lady. She remembered my mother."

"Did she know anything about Cholla?"

"Not as we know him. But she told me Chauncy Kyd, Junior, was engaged to marry my mother. They all came West together by wagon train. In Tucson, my mother met Hawk, and, before it was over, Chauncy and Hawk got into a gun fight. Chauncy was killed."

"Huh!" Jim sat back down behind his desk. "So how does old Cholla figure into this?"

"Cholla is Chauncy Kyd, Senior. He was back in a Missouri jail when the trouble happened here. He finally arrived in Arizona Territory about six months later and went crazy when he found out his only son had been killed. Then he dropped out of sight. Missus Kyd didn't know what happened to him after that. But she seemed relieved that he wasn't around any more. Apparently he was a bad character in his younger days. I didn't tell her I thought he was the old prospector who hangs around here going by the name of Cholla."

"You really think old Cholla is Chauncy Senior?"

"I'm sure. Missus Kyd even described his scar. There couldn't be two like that."

Jim Hatton's eyes squinted toward the street. The growing darkness was opaque, and rain had begun to spatter against the window glass. "Don't you wonder what's been going on in his head all these years?"

Delphinia sighed, stepping closer to the stove, her hands cupped around the coffee cup for its heat. "No wonder my mother was always so kind to him. She must have felt guilty about what happened to Chauncy Junior."

"Do you think Hawk knew who old Cholla really is? The father of the man he killed over Amity?"

"I doubt it. Knowing my mother, she would have kept quiet to avoid any more trouble. Maybe she wanted Cholla to live out his life in peace and leave everybody alone. My mother was such a gentle person, always willing to help people. She wouldn't have wanted Hawk and Cholla to fight."

Jim looked at her closely. "Your mother's good intentions are to be appreciated. But now you've got old Cholla telling every drifter in the territory that Hawk Estes is dead and his daughter lives alone in the hills. You best be careful with him, Delphinia."

She finished her coffee. "Do you think he's been waiting all these years to get even? Hawk's child for his?"

"I don't mean to scare you." There was a mixture of torment and concern in his eyes. "I just want you to be careful."

She walked over to the desk and put down the cup. "Has Blackjack been caught yet?"

"No. The Buckners think they saw him two nights ago.... that homestead northwest of your place. Somebody tried rustling a colt from their corral, but the horse kicked up a fuss and made so much noise that old man Buckner heard it and came out of the house, shooting. He thinks it was Blackjack, even found a hat the next morning in the brush that might be his."

"So, he's still out there without a horse...?"

"Or anything else, for that matter. I keep thinking he'll make a run south when he gets ready, and your place is a likely spot for him to grab a mount and supplies."

She nodded, changing the subject. "Is this the right time to ask you about my brother?"

He squirmed. "I'm still waiting for a telegram. I'll let you know in a day or two."

"Fair enough. Oh, before I forget, you should know I killed a man in Douglas last night. I wanted you to hear it from me before you got it from somebody else."

His jaw dropped. "You killed somebody? How?"

"I scared him to death."

A grin flashed across his face. "I think I'll wire the sheriff of Douglas to get the particulars on that one."

She laughed, reaching for the door. "Thanks for seeing to my stock."

"No trouble. The deputy's sons, Benny and Tuck, were glad to earn the money. I think you can count on them.... should the need arise again, even though they don't like milking goats. You should find them still out at the place."

She waved at him, got Slicker out of the livery stable, and headed toward home.

It felt good to be on horseback, even if it was raining. Hawk's wet duster weighed cold and heavy against Delphinia's back, and water streamed down on her lap from the brim of his hat. She had to hold Slicker, who did a dancing side-step, on a tight rein. Three days in a stall at the livery stable in town had him munching on the bit and tossing his head for a run. Delphinia talked to the horse, easing him back, not willing to let him run for home.

Slicker pulled against the bit, stepping lightly, closing in on the last five hundred yards to her homestead where the gate stood gaping against the black yard. A kerosene lamp inside the house threw long waves of orange light across the corral fence making blurred, spiked shadows in the rain. She rode up to the house. "Benny? Tuck? It's Delphinia Estes. I'm home."

The teenagers unlocked the door and peeked out through the crack. Benny reached for his jacket and placed it over his bony shoulders. "You need help with your horse, Miss Delphinia? I'd be glad to put him up."

She dismounted, not realizing until then how stiff her bones were as she stepped onto the ground, feeling a numbness run up through her ankles. "Thanks, boys, I'd appreciate that."

The boys tramped down the steps and led Slicker to the corral, while Delphinia walked into the house and, after shedding the duster and her father's hat, sank into the nearest chair, absorbing the friendly surroundings. She sniffed toward the hot stove where the boys had dirty pots and plates stacked up. The food was obviously scorched but smelled good just the same. She smiled at the mess they had made of her kitchen. In just three days' time the place had suffered from her absence. Her thoughts drifted to Mrs. Brubaker having to put up with thirteen men in the house. She quivered with the thought of it.

Benny and Tuck came back inside as she was tugging off her wet boots.

"Reckon we'll be riding home, Miss Delphinia," Benny said, standing over her with his thumbs hooked in his belt.

She awkwardly reached into her pocket for the money she had gotten from Bate Thatcher's bounty, handing him a twenty-dollar gold piece. "Is this enough for you and your brother's time?"

He brought it up close to his nose, his eyes wide. "I never had this much before, Miss Delphinia. I reckon we ate enough of your canned food and drank enough goat's milk to make up for any work we did. We wasn't expecting this much in cash money from you."

She smiled at him, now dropping one wet boot to the floor. "I want to be fair with you boys, so I know you'll come back if I ever need you again. Can you do one more thing for me? Could you bring in a couple of buckets of water from the well?"

They grinned, grabbed the empty water buckets, standing near the stove, and ran with them to the well, the prospect of earning more money in the future spurring them on. They returned in a few minutes. Both of them were wet from the rain.

"One other thing, Miss Delphinia," Tuck said, "we think somebody was around here last night."

"Why? What happened?"

"The horses were kind of restless after dark, the way horses are when somebody strange comes around. We only peeked out, but we couldn't see nothing. We didn't go walking in the yard, you know, because our pa told us to be careful...on account of that fellow, Blackjack, is still on the loose."

"So what happened?"

"This morning we checked the stock and all, but nothing seemed out of place, except them two coyote traps are missing."

"Coyote traps?"

The boys looked guiltily at each other. "That first day we

come here, we looked around the place, you know, just checking things. We noticed two fine coyote traps hanging over your work bench on the side of the house, where you have all those herbs stored. We sure admired them traps. And this morning, when we took a look around the place, we noticed they was gone."

"Traps gone?" she murmured.

The boys appeared nervous. "We don't want you to think we took them, Miss Delphinia," Benny said.

She crossed her arms. "I'm sure you didn't do it, and thank you for telling me."

They nodded, not sure they had convinced her. Benny clucked his tongue and grinned, showing the big gap between his front teeth. "Any time you need us, we'll be glad to help." They scooped up their belongings from the floor and chairs, anxious to be off.

She smiled at them, held the door open, and watched as they ran down to the corral and bridled their old pinto mare. Riding double, they kicked her into a stiff trot toward town. The rain seemed to be letting up a little.

Moonbeams seeped into the room, illuminating the edges of chairs, the table top, and the surfaces of the hot iron stove as if someone had dabbed along the edges with a yellow paint brush. Delphinia sank to her neck in the laundry tub, soaking in the hot water, swirling soap around her tired limbs. She vowed not to climb out of the tub until the water got cold. She rolled her eyes at the gun hanging on the chair back, her clothing folded carefully nearby.

The silent house enveloped her with its familiarity, and she found much comfort in her surroundings. But, she told herself, it was a big world out there, and she would have to explore it from time to time. Besides, living on this homestead had never been free from worry even when Hawk and Amity were alive, although they had acted as bulwarks against the world for her. She splashed again, watching the soap bubble rings bob in the pale light. She fought back a sudden rush of loneliness caused by the fact that the two best people she had known and loved now rested in the cold ground not far from her window. Never could they comfort or advise her again. They would not be there when she needed help. They would never again rise up in her defense. And in the midst of her pain she felt a flash of anger stab through her as she remembered the words of Bate Thatcher: *Your ma shouldn't have stood in the door that way, white nightgown and all...made me a good target.* She realized she would still have to sort out a whole gamut of conflicting emotions in the days ahead.

Chapter Fifteen

The rainy days were over, the weather warm and dry again. As Delphinia worked on her morning chores, she planned the dying process for the wool with which she would finish her rug. After doing a load of laundry, she saved the laundry rinse water to mix the batch of walnut dye. She filled the pot with walnut hulls and a rusty horseshoe — the iron residue acting as a mordant that caused the color to stick. When the dark brown froth was bubbling, she placed the clean wool in the pot and watched as it absorbed the coloring. She stirred gently with a long, wooden spoon so that the wool would pick up the color evenly.

With the wool simmering, Delphinia returned to her weaving at the loom. Her eyes followed the deep, rugged lines of Locust Cañon, looking for the telltale signs of dust drifting up from the ridges, but there was none. She shifted her gaze down the road toward town, and then south to the low brown hills slanting between her land and Mexico. Nothing. Just a gentle wind and a red hawk banking high to the south on silent wind currents.

Thump, thump went the loom. It had been a week since her return from Douglas, and still Jim Hat ton had not ridden out to see her. She resolved not to bother him. Whatever news he had for her regarding a supposed brother would come to her in due time. Besides, riding back and forth to town, seeking the sheriff, seemed like a forward thing to do. She did not want him to think she was a pest. No one else had ridden out to see her. It seemed as though the whole territory knew Amity was gone. When she was alive, visitors had shown up routinely, seeking herbal remedies and exchanging garden produce for health secrets. But not any more.

Delphinia felt how temporary human beings really were and their frivolous houses and fences and personal possessions. Everything was called back to the earth sooner or later. If she were to disappear, evidence that the Estes family ever existed would vanish. She sighed and glanced at Hawk's gun where it rested at her side under the little stool on which she sat, somewhat reassured.

Thump, thump. She pushed her thoughts away from Amity and Hawk and tried to concentrate on other problems, starting with the coyote traps. Who had taken them? And why? Could Benny and Tuck have been the culprits? Covering up for themselves by telling her someone had been prowling about? After all, they admitted discovering the traps because they were snooping. On the other hand, Benny and Tuck were not the sort to steal things, and, had they asked, she would have given them the traps gladly for helping her by doing the chores. The traps were not important. She herself had never used them. Amity had not liked them, either. They were Hawk's, and, because they belonged to him, they remained on the property. He used them from time to time to trap coyotes when they raided Amity's chicken coop.

Who else might want the coyote traps? She ran through the list again in her mind as she had so many times since the deputy's boys had left the night she'd gotten back. The Brubak ers knew about the traps. Was it possible some of Jess's little brothers, knowing Delphinia was alone, had chanced a raid for something they wanted? But the Brubakers were not the sort of people who stole things. A more sinister answer was Black-jack. Did he take them to test her? To see how close he could get, and what he could steal without resistance from the house? Or, perhaps, to torment her? To remind her he was out there.

And finally she had to consider Cholla. After all, she had played a mean trick on him with that buckthorn cheese. Maybe this had been his way of evening up the score.

She sighed with weariness. Over this past week she had treaded warily around the place, watching her step, hesitating before she reached into the wood pile. She had tiptoed carefully through the garden rows, poking the earth with a long stick to make sure the traps were not set for her in the worked earth. If Cholla wanted to get even with her for the cheese, the traps might be the answer.

Thump, thump. The isolation and vast stretches of time were weighing heavily upon her. She hated to admit she was lonely. She thought of Jim Hatton, and she even found herself missing Jess's comforting visits of old. Her eyes flickered at the sight of movement, her weft beater poised in mid-air. Dust hung beyond the line of trees to the west — the road from town. Slight, gray streaks rose enough to tell her one rider was coming at a slow trot. She checked for the gun even though she knew it was there, then continued thumping lightly. No sense slowing down her work just because a visitor was on the way. Yet her heart raced. *Company!* She self-consciously brushed a strand of hair away from her cheek.

The form of Jim Hat ton, riding easily across her yard, was, indeed, a welcome sight. She stood up then, placing her weft beater in the basket at her feet near the loom.

"How are you, Delphinia?" he asked, smiling. He dismounted, tying his horse at the hitching post. "I thought I'd ride out and deliver a couple of messages."

She fought a quickness squeezing her heart. "Come inside? Coffee? Tea?" She motioned him toward the house and turned to enter herself, hoping he would linger at her kitchen table instead of leaning at the hitching post anxious to ride away. He followed her into the house. She put the coffee pot on.

"Glad to see everything is under control here," he told her, taking off his hat.

"Yes! Thank you. Benny and Tuck did a fine job, taking care of the stock for me."

"They told me you paid them a lot of money, but they were sorry a couple of coyote traps were stolen. What do you think about that?" he asked from a chair at the table where he had taken a seat.

She sat down across from him. "I don't know what to think. They belonged to Hawk. They've been hanging under the porch roof where Amity and I tied our herbs. I don't know who would want to take them. And, for heaven's sake, there are other things around here more valuable to steal."

"It does sound odd, but if those boys said the traps were stolen, I believe them."

"I do, too," she said, standing and reaching for the hot coffee. She placed cups and saucers on the table. "I made cornbread yesterday. Missus Kyd, down in Douglas, gave some to me when I was there, and I liked it so much it inspired me to make some of my own." She cut a piece and handed it to him on a plate.

"I got a telegram from the sheriff of Douglas, telling me you have been cleared of any wrongdoing in that incident at the hotel."

"I didn't know I was suspected of wrongdoing! The sheriff of Douglas is a suspicious and unreasonable man, if you don't mind me saying so. He didn't like Hawk, and made no bones about having ill feelings toward me."

"You can't blame the man, Delphinia."

She shrugged, forking into a piece of cornbread. "What other news do you have for me?"

He licked the end of his fork. "There's a family in Lordsburg. Name of Parry. A woman with two sons, and they run a big cattle outfit called the Crown P. I understand they have good horses, but mostly cattle…old Spanish family from ‘way back. I’ve never met them. The woman’s oldest son, Bartholomew, is Blackjack Parry.”

“Blackjack Parry? The outlaw? Related to a big cattle family?”

“I know, it sounds kind of funny, him going bad, but apparently that’s the way it is.”

She frowned. “Oh, well, no way of telling how people will turn out, I guess.”

He nodded, finishing the cornbread and taking another sip of coffee. “Delphinia, this Blackjack Parry is likely your half-brother.”

She choked, putting her fork down and reaching for her coffee to wash down the crumbs stuck in her throat. “Blackjack Parry! My…brother!”

“The information from Lordsburg says Hawk took up with that Missus Parry, years ago…before he met Amity. She had a son. For some reason she and Hawk never married, and Blackjack was raised by a stepfather.”

She looked at him, shocked, trying to make sense of it. “Did Hawk know? Did Amity know?”

He shrugged. “I don’t think Hawk knew about the boy until years later, and all the details are kind of scrambled. If you really want to find out about that old stuff, Delphinia, maybe you’d better go to Lordsburg and meet with Missus Parry.”

She gulped. “But, Jim, I…does she know about me?”

“Look, Delphinia, there’ve been rumors for years. But you’re not hearing them isn’t hard to understand. It was Hawk’s old personal business. Considering who he was, nobody around here was going to gossip on such a touchy matter while he was still alive. You’re likely to stir up trouble, digging into the past on this one. I think you’ll knock loose a hornet’s nest, but you're on your own."

She ignored his warning. "Blackjack! My brother? He was here when Hawk and Amity were killed!"

"I told you, Delphinia, you're likely to stir up trouble."

"But how can I ignore this? I have to know the truth."

He sighed. "You've lived just fine so far. Maybe now you'll understand why I wasn't anxious to get into this. Family secrets can be dangerous business. Maybe it's best if you leave it alone."

"But, Jim, what if Blackjack comes riding back here? How will I face him? How will I handle things, knowing he's my own brother? Do I help him? Do we talk? What?"

"Whoa, girl. You're getting 'way ahead of yourself here. The man is an outlaw, a horse thief. Kin or not, you don't know him, and it's not up to you to sacrifice yourself because of some confused feeling of family responsibility you have. I say forget it. Stay out of it. So Hawk had an affair a long time ago before he met your mother. What business is it of yours now? You can't run the world, or save people from problems they made for themselves before you were born."

"I can't imagine he would want to hurt me...if he's really my half-brother."

"Hawk was responsible for catching him a couple of years ago for the bounty. Blackjack was thrown into the New Mexico Territorial Prison for horse stealing. He had plenty of reasons for hating his own father, aside from any personal grudges he may have harbored from when he was a kid."

Delphinia gulped the last of her coffee. "There is only one way to find out. Do you think Benny and Tuck will keep an eye on the place for me while I go to Lordsburg?"

"I'm sure they will." He stood up, reaching for his hat. "When do you want me to send them out?"

"First thing in the morning."

She watched him ride away without a backward glance, but she was too distracted to be disappointed. Then she hurried into the bedroom and pulled Amity's mauve traveling suit out of the closet, along with the black shawl. She got out the high button shoes and the pretty little hat covered with pink tulle and feathers. She would not go traveling looking like a man this time, drawing undue attention to herself. Lastly, she found Amity's black leather doctor's satchel that was small enough to carry easily, and yet big enough to hold a few personal items along with Hawk's gun belt and pistol.

Chapter Sixteen

Jim Hatton saw her off in the morning. At the stagecoach, he gripped her elbow and lifted her inside while she held her skirts with one hand like a lady and tipped her head so the little hat tilted, its fluttery feathers just skimming the coach doorway. In her other hand she held her satchel. She did not want to let it out of her sight by stowing it in the luggage boot.

"Thank you, Jim. I'll be back in a few days."

He shut the door, looking up at her with that odd, concerned expression crossing his face. She had an urge to reach out the window and caress his cheek, but she did not dare. Instead, she smiled, chin up, letting him know she had one more hurdle in front of her.

The driver let out a shout, cracking his whip overhead while the six big bay mules leaped forward, jerking the Concord stage with squeaks and rattles. Delphinia groaned softly, remembering her recent jarring stagecoach ride. *Give me a horse any day,* she thought. She distracted herself by looking out the window, catching a glimpse of store fronts and saloon windows, the open doors of the livery stable where a boy was still unhooking her team from the buckboard she'd driven to town. She'd need it to carry supplies home on the way back, and it was Slicker's turn to stay home instead of being tied up inside a livery stable again.

Two men sat across from her inside the coach, talking quietly between themselves — a businessman and a rancher. They discussed cattle and the possibility of Arizona Territory achieving statehood. Delphinia listened with little interest. Statehood and cattle prices were far from her mind right now.

A saloon woman, wearing a green silk traveling suit, sat next to Delphinia. Her high lace collar held an elaborate cameo, and her wildly decorated hat was pinned over her forehead at a saucy angle. Her red lips, face powder, and harsh perfume intrigued Delphinia. She and the woman eyed each other only briefly. Of course, Delphinia did not know who she was, but, when the woman opened her reticule to draw out a slender mirror to dab more rouge on her cheeks, Delphinia noticed the pearl handle of a Derringer. She smiled to herself, thinking she and the woman had something in common, even though her own gun was far bigger.

Delphinia watched the desert moving by outside the coach window. Dry, sandy earth erupted under sharp mounds of yucca and scrub mesquite. A sandy mound here, a faraway ridge there, all melting away into the hot sky where low, harsh hills angled away south into Mexico. Distant, purple swells staggered into clumps of rugged buttes and hidden places that Delphinia wondered about. She had not been east before; entering New Mexico Territory was new to her.

At noon they reached the first swing station at Steins Pass. Twenty miles beyond they met darkness and were told they'd rest through the night to avoid traveling over the rough country before daylight. The stage station consisted of a rustic common room that supplied boiled coffee and mule steak at a dollar a meal to the customers. Delphinia satisfied herself with leftover cornbread she had wrapped inside a small package and tucked into her satchel before leaving home. She nibbled while sitting in a chair on the station porch.

In the morning, just as the sun topped the low eastern buttes, the driver called for the passengers. The four of them boarded in the coolness of the beginning day. More bumps, more lurching, more swaying. Delphinia dozed restlessly in the corner of the coach. Mercifully they reached Lordsburg by noon. Delphinia stepped down from the coach, dizzy and tired, nodding to her fellow passengers as they drifted off on their separate ways.

Looking around the hot, dusty main street, she shaded her eyes and tried to determine the location of the livery stable. Horses and riders moved up and down past her; people tramped over the board walk. She heard voices coming from inside the general merchandise store where the air, wafting out, was scented with tobacco and pickling spices.

"You Miss Delphinia Estes?" a man's deep voice drawled behind her.

She twirled around and faced a tall, middle-aged cowboy who had walked up so quietly she had not heard his approach. His weathered face was like that of peeling tree bark. His hair was gray as ashes, curling in stray ends to his collar from under a battered, brown cowboy hat.

"Yes, I am Delphinia Estes," she said.

"My name's Buck. I've been sent by Missus Parry to pick you up and take you to the ranch." He tipped his hat with politeness, but his cool gray eyes told her he was not pleased by the order.

"How...did Missus Parry know I was coming?"

He shrugged. "The sheriff your way sent a telegram."

"Oh," was all she could think to say. Jim Hatton was taking care of her again.

Buck helped her into the buggy. She hung on as the vehicle bumped and lurched across the rutted road leading north toward the Parry ranch. Buck was not sparing the horse, nor did he seem happy driving the hard-bouncing buggy. He clucked, rapping the reins across the chestnut's croup and thus coaxing the mare. The mare was a pacer, moving her legs laterally — left side, right side, left side, right side — unlike the trotting horses Delphinia was used to seeing. Well bred, long, and lean, the mare's rasping breath came through nostrils that were blowing and fluttering like she could continue pacing all day and hardly show a sweat.

Now holding her hat on her head, Delphinia looked up at Buck. "Hot day. Windy." She hoped to break his sullen silence.

"I never worry about the weather. Nothin' I can do about it." He clamped his jaw shut again.

She reached up with her hand, readjusting the hat pin under the crown so it caught under a clump of her hair. She wished she had tied up her hair tighter before they had left Lordsburg. But it was too late now, and she did not dare ask Buck to slow down for anything as frivolous as fixing her hat. "How far is the ranch from Lordsburg?"

"I never worry about distance," he said. "Nothin' I can do about it. Things are what they are."

Delphinia studied Buck's profile. For some reason Buck was enjoying her discomfort. "If I have caused you an inconvenience, Buck, I'm sorry. I did not ask to be picked up at the stagecoach station. I planned to ride out to the Parrys' on my own. I apologize to you. But I don't see any reason to make this drive unpleasant."

He grimaced, slapping the reins against the chestnut mare so hard she broke forward into an even faster clip, the buggy bouncing high when it hit a hard rut. "It has nothing to do with you. Missus Parry knows I don't like driving this god damn rattle-trap, and it pleasures her to make me mad. I hired on to break bronc's and work cattle. I don't like baby-sitting lady visitors with Eastern buggy hosses out on social calls."

Delphinia gripped the seat harder after another bounce. "Slamming me like a flapjack in a pan is all right, Buck, I can handle it. But you're going to kill this poor mare if you don't slow down."

"She's tough," he said, slapping the reins harder. "She's got the legs of a deer and the lungs of a braying mule. Don't go telling me how to handle a hoss."

Calm down, Delphinia. Calm down. She switched her gaze to the road ahead, mercifully catching sight of a high ranch gate with cross poles bound to wooden supports above the road. They bounced under the gate so fast Delphinia did not have time to look at the big carved brand on the sign. Gasping with another jarring bounce, she resigned herself to Buck's ill temper and concentrated on the buildings appearing ahead.

Corrals, outbuildings, storage sheds, bunkhouse, and barn all nestled in a circle around the big main two-story ranch house with white clapboard sides and shuttered windows. Delphinia blinked, not having expected such a house in the middle of no man's land. A group of cowboys were gathered in front of the first corral. Several clung to the top rail while others drifted back and forth in front of the gate, watching a gray horse pawing desperately against a water trough.

"Damn," Buck muttered under his breath, pulling the mare to a shaky halt in front of the corral gate. "I hoped he'd be better by the time I got back," he said to a young cowboy who took the mare's bridle reins. Buck jumped out of the rig, leaving Delphinia sitting there, not knowing if she ought to alight or remain where she was. Nobody paid attention to her, so engrossed were they in the gray horse. It staggered against the water trough, slime-white foam drooling from its mouth and nostrils, gagging, coughing, hollow eyed.

Buck joined the crowd at the gate. "Not getting better?"

"Aw come on, Buck," one of the cowboys answered. "He's got the dog-bite sickness. You know shooting him is the only thing to do."

"Best damn' horse I ever owned," Buck said, pulling on

the gloves that had been stuffed in his back pocket.

A tall, dark-haired cowboy wearing leather chaps hopped down from the fence, making his way to the buggy where he offered Delphinia his hand. "I am Jesús Parry. You may drive the buggy to the house. I'll join you as soon as we take care of this horse. My mother is waiting for you."

"Thank you," she answered, feeling his grip firm and friendly. "What's happened to that horse?"

"He belongs to Buck. He's been grazing in the mountains. We found him this way yesterday. It's unfortunate, but the animal appears to have rabies. It will have to be destroyed."

"Rabies! But this is the wrong time of year…it usually happens in the spring and summer. That horse hasn't got the look of rabies."

He gave her a patronizing smile. "The look? Have you seen a horse with rabies?"

"No. Not a horse with rabies, but one time I saw a skunk that had it."

"Skunk!"

The cowboys jeered. They'd been listening.

"The horse wants water, and yet he can't drink. Look at the way he's pawing that trough," she said.

"Hydrophobia causes victims to do crazy things," Jesús said. "Buck has to shoot him."

"I'd like to take a closer look at the horse," Delphinia said, jumping down from the buggy.

"Oh, for Chrissakes," Buck yelled. "We don't need some sop-eyed woman interfering in this business. Jesús, take her up to the house so we can get on with it."

The cowboys nodded in agreement.

Delphinia walked around outside the corral until she reached a point opposite the drooling horse. She climbed up on the wooden rail, clucking to the gray. He shook his head, his mouth open, his eyes rolling. Drool continued to foam and ooze from the corners of his mouth each time he gasped.

She reached her hand out to him, and he backed away, pawing and choking. Holding her skirts around her knees, she straddled the fence and walked straight at the horse, her arm stretched out as she talked to him. The horse kept retreating, snorting yellow foam, wobbling backwards on shaky legs.

"You get out of there!" Buck called.

By now all the ranch hands had clamored to the top rail on the opposite side of the corral, watching Delphinia and the rabid horse. Somebody yelled at her: "You'll get yourself killed in there, missy!"

She motioned to the cowboys, her eyes on the horse. "Throw me a rope, somebody." She kept her distance from the cowboys so that none could try to grab hold of her and pull her out of harm's way. So they watched nervously while the horse groaned and frothed. The horse backed away and then hit its hocks on the rails at the side of the corral opposite Delphinia. Then he sprang forward suddenly with a head-shaking cough.

Buck held a rifle at his shoulder, aiming it at the horse.

"Don't shoot!" Delphinia ordered, her hand extended, still waiting for a rope. One of the men finally obliged, and a rope sailed through the air in a hard coil.

"Don't shoot him unless he charges," Delphinia heard Jesús Parry say.

"I'll take him down in one pop," Buck answered.

Shaking out a loop, Delphinia inched her way across the corral. With every step she was made more aware of the inadequacy of her high-button shoes for this work as they squeaked and pinched her feet. "Whoa, boy, easy fellow," she said, whirling the rope once so that the loop settled in one neat slap around the gray's head. She pulled slightly, and he followed, unable to resist his training, hurting and coughing, but obeying.

Leading him across the corral, Delphinia tied her end of the rope around a post and then called for somebody to rope the horse's hind legs. "We'll put him down," she said. "I want to look at him off his feet."

Tied, the horse seemed less dangerous. Several of the cowboys hopped into the corral. One shot a low loop, catching the gray horse by it's hind legs, holding firm. Never taking his eye off Delphinia, Buck followed the others into the corral and roped the horse's front legs. Then in one joint effort the cowboys, together, pushed the horse off its feet, lowering him with a thud while staying clear of his slobbering mouth.

"I need a piece of wood here," Delphinia said. "Something thick enough to hold his mouth open. I want a broom handle, too."

"Oh, hell," Buck muttered, "you're going to get that slaver on you. What the hell do you think you're doing?"

One of the men ran for a piece of wood and a broom. When he returned, Delphinia worked the broom handle between the space in the horse's mouth where horses have no teeth, then rolled it to the back of his mouth. "Keep his head tipped up!" she ordered.

Several cowboys sat on the horse and held its neck, while several others inside the corral kept the ropes taut. She motioned for two men to hold the wooden wedge and the broom handle. The horse's mouth was a wide open gape, its teeth pressed against the wood between his jaws. "Don't let go of that wood, or he'll take my arm off," she said.

They watched dumbstruck as Delphinia pulled off her leather gloves, rolled back her sleeves as far as she was able, and reached quickly into the horse's mouth and down his throat. She probed with her fingers and then in one quick jerk pulled out from the horse's throat a foot-long length of agave, a ragged, pulpy leaf. A single gasp came from the cowboys who stared in disbelief, while Delphinia examined it, trying to determine whether any part of it might still be left behind inside the horse's throat. Brackish and ragged, the fanged leaf hung from her fingers in a gooey, leathery chunk surrounded by its own gelatin and dripping with saliva. Delphinia backed away, motioning the men to let the horse up. Loose, the animal shook his head and staggered to the water trough where he buried his nose in water, sucking loudly, swelling his gaunt rib cage.

"He shouldn't have too much water," Buck said, walking toward the horse with his lariat coiled around his shoulder.

"Walk him after he drinks," Delphinia advised.

"I know that," Buck scoffed, but Delphinia noticed that the gruff tone of his voice was belied by the expression on his face.

Chapter Seventeen

Delphinia fidgeted in a chair inside the Parrys' dark living room, knowing she must look a sight. She ran her hand around the edges of the long, slimy smudge running down the front of her dress. One sleeve of her suit all the way to her elbow was covered with horse saliva and agave juice. The stain was a dark greenish-white and sticky. Her shoes were covered with dust; one French heel gouged raw where she had scraped it in climbing the corral fence. Self-consciously, she took the hat from her head and placed it on her lap in an effort to cover, at least partially, the stain on her suit.

Across the room from her Sonia Parry stood in front of the stone fireplace, her hands laced together as she stared at Delphinia. The corner of her lower lip trembled. Her eyes were full of suspicion. Her straight, black hair was parted in the middle and twisted into a silky bun at the back of her long neck. Sonia Parry must have been quite a beauty in her day. She still was. Straight, tall, and slim waisted, she wore a black silk dress that rustled when she moved.

Delphinia, feeling nervous and out of place, was compelled to apologize for her appearance. "I'm sorry I'm so mussed, and that my dress isn't clean, but I…." She looked at Jesús Parry who lounged in a leather chair near a big wooden desk.

Sonia Parry's eyes swept Delphinia from head to toe one more time. "Please don't apologize about your appearance. Jesús told me you saved Buck's sick horse. I am only sorry that you ruined your suit…it must have been quite expensive."

"More sentimental than costly," Delphinia said. "It was my

mother's...she made it. She was a wonderful seamstress."

"Really?" Sonia Parry's expression suddenly changed from one of suspicion to one of deadly hate. "We received the telegram about your arrival yesterday and...," but she did not finish the sentence.

Jesús filled in the silence. "Meeting Hawk Estes's daughter is not an easy thing for my mother," he said. "You surprised us."

"Jesús!" Sonia said, looking back and forth between her son and Delphinia. "I...."

"Missus Parry," Delphinia said, "I'm sorry if I have done something wrong by coming here. But, you were...acquainted with Hawk Estes?"

Sonia Parry's agonizing look told Delphinia everything. "I knew Hawk Estes a long time ago."

"Do you know Blackjack Parry?"

"Blackjack! What about him?" Sonia Parry's arched eyebrow formed a question mark.

"Blackjack Parry and some other oulaws attacked our homestead three weeks ago. Hawk and my mother were killed."

"Hawk! Killed?" Sonia winced, and her olive-skinned complexion turned ashen. She brought her hands to her throat. "Impossible! No!"

"It's true," Delphinia said. "I understand Hawk captured Blackjack several years ago. He spent time in the New Mexico Territorial prison. He was released about a month ago and hooked up with a gang that robbed a train near Willcox. Hawk was on their trail, but they doubled back on him, and he and my mother were killed. I found out that Blackjack could be Hawk's own son, and I was told that you might be able to tell me if it's true."

Sonia Parry turned to face the fireplace. Her hands gripped the mantle while her sleek head bent forward until her brow rested on her knuckles. "Bartholomew Parry is my son. Hawk Estes is his father. Does that answer your question?"

"I see...I only...." Delphinia stumbled for the proper words, but did not finish her sentence because Sonia Parry hurried from the room, disappearing with a swish of black silk.

Jesús stirred in his chair. "My mother is shocked by your news."

"I'm sorry. I handled that badly, didn't I?"

He shrugged, crossing his long legs at his booted ankles. "Look, my mother has pined over Hawk Estes most of her life. Your showing up here and telling her Hawk is dead has come as a terrible shock. But I can tell you one thing. She is a strong woman. She will survive."

Delphinia could not help studying his black hair and olive-skinned features, his white teeth and green eyes. "Are you.... my...brother...too?"

He burst into laughter. "Not a chance! The only thing you and I have in common is a half-brother named Bartholomew. Blackjack!" He stood up, still laughing. "Forgive me if I find humor in all of this. You see, the business about my mother and Hawk Estes and Blackjack and myself...all of that has been a big family tragedy ever since I can remember. It's old now. You have revived it with this latest news of Hawk's death."

"I'm sorry. I'm just trying to find out the truth...whether or not I have a brother."

He nodded, rolling his hand at the wrist as if grinding out the story one more time. "My mother was young, beautiful, and madly in love with a handsome young gringo horse soldier. But her parents were strictly Spanish hacendados. They brought their old country traditions here to New Mexico Territory. They were determined their only child not marry a man with no money, no future, no family background, and especially no religion!"

Delphinia sighed, thinking he had certainly explained Hawk Estes.

Jesús paced between his chair and the big window. "To make a very long story short, Hawk Estes was ordered back East when the Civil War broke out, and my mother discovered she was...how can I say it? Embarrassed. Pregnant. The father of the child was two thousand miles away, and my horrified grandparents needed a husband for her *muy rapido!* There was an elderly Spanish gentleman named Jose Parry who worked for them, here at the ranch. He had no money, was thirty years older than she, but the situation demanded immediate action. She had nothing to say about it. Bartholomew Parry was born shortly thereafter, and, while my grandparents never adjusted to having a little *bastardo* in the house, at least he had a name. I was born two years later. My father was a good and kindly gendeman, and, while my mother was not in love with him, she would not have hurt him for the world."

"You mean, she would not leave him for Hawk."

He stood in front of her now, arms crossed. "That's right. I remember the day Hawk Estes came riding in here. I was maybe five or six years old...Bartholomew would have been seven or eight. My grandparents were dead by then, so my mother could have just walked away if she had wanted to. But she didn't."

Delphinia waited for the rest of the story, barely breathing and trying to imagine Hawk, riding in to discover he had a son and the woman he loved married to another man.

Jesús studied her. "Miss Estes, I have told you too much already. I think it is my mother's privilege to tell you those things she thinks you should know. After all, this is her private business. She dashed away so quickly she forget her good manners, but I can tell you we have a room at the end of the hall always reserved for guests. I will ask the maids to bring water to you or anything else you might need. Join us for dinner? Perhaps you ladies can talk then."

"Maybe I should leave now. My presence here must be a terrible annoyance to your mother. Seeing me…the daughter of Hawk's wife. I'm so dumb, I even mentioned wearing her dress! I'm sorry I brought trouble to you."

"No trouble, I respect your honesty. Sometimes it is better to get things over with quickly. Now that Hawk Estes is dead, perhaps my mother will get on with her life."

Delphinia nodded. "I could use a rest. It was a long journey, and I'm not used to traveling by stage. I do appreciate your kindness." She gathered up Amity's black bag and walked tiredly down the hall leading from the living room.

The big clock in the dining room ticked out the seconds softly, but in the palpable silence the rhythm of the ticking seemed to fill the room, exaggerated louder and louder. Delphinia sat across the table from Jesús. Neither of them spoke. Delphinia knew now that Sonia Parry would not join them for dinner.

Jesús looked up at the clock and finally snapped his fingers. "Lucita! Our meal, *por favor*" He pointed to his plate, and the maid turned on her heel, returning with platters of *enchiladas* and rice, refried beans and fresh *tortillas.* A bowl of steaming turkey broth laced with lemon wedges and a smattering of crumbled white cheese was placed in front of Delphinia. The aroma wafted up to her nose.

Reaching for a warm *tortilla,* Delphinia looked up at her host. His eyes lingered on her face a little too long, making her uncomfortable. "Thank you for dinner, Jesús. I seem to keep causing more trouble for you."

"Don't worry about it. This is very much unlike my mother. I assure you, she is a sterling hostess…prompt and considerate of our guests. The news of Hawk Estes must be harder for her to deal with than I thought."

"And I assure you, I do not intend to inconvenience your family any more than I already have," she said, and, not wanting to look at him so that he might see the embarrassment she was sure showed on her face, she concentrated on smearing warm beans and chili sauce on a corn tortilla. "Will it be possible for one of your men to give me a ride back to Lordsburg in the morning? Or I could ride a horse, if the buggy is not available. I could leave it at the livery."

Jesús brought a spoonful of turkey broth to his lips and then wiped the edges of his neat mustache with the tips of the white cloth napkin. "Of course, you are welcome to go any time. But I think it would be best if you have a talk with my mother. I know she will regret it if you leave here under these circumstances. After all, it is hardly your fault that Hawk Estes married another woman after he discovered there was no life for him with my mother. Delphinia, my mother understands these things, it is just that she needs time to mourn Hawk in her own way. You and I happen to be children of unions that we had no say in. She's known all these years that Hawk married. She knew there was a woman in his life, but seeing you in the flesh must have been a terrible thing for her to accept. Please don't think too harshly of her."

Delphinia poked into the rice. "Yes, I understand."

"Good! Now I have an idea. Why don't you stay a couple of days? Is there a reason you must hurry home?"

"No. Not exactly. Except that I left two boys in charge of my livestock. They won't want to stay at my place any longer than necessary."

"But two more days? Three at most?"

Delphinia looked around the room and frowned. She could not imagine remaining an unwanted guest in this big dark house while she waited for Sonia Parry to speak to her. The conspicuous ticking of the big clock unnerved her. She was used to running her own life, getting up at dawn, and busying herself with her animals and her garden. No empty minutes, but days filled with baking, washing, riding, and repairing. She thought of her rug waiting on silent warp that would not sing unless she put her hands to the task. "I don't know, Jesús. I'm not good at sitting around a house and doing nothing."

"Who said you will sit and do nothing? You were so good with that gray horse of Buck's, I want you to ride with us tomorrow. The *vaqueros* and I go into the hills on a horse roundup. We are after the two-year-olds ready for breaking. They run loose from the day they are born, strengthening their bones, coping with the wild country that gives them balance and good lungs. The mares are Thoroughbred-Arabian cross, and the stallion is a fine Quarter Horse from Texas stock. We breed for size, speed, and endurance. You will want to see our herd, Delphinia."

"It sounds wonderful, but I didn't bring along riding clothes. I have just this traveling suit."

"Pooh! I will find clothing for you. Blackjack's room is full of things from when he was a teenager. You can ride in pants, no? And our chuck wagon is driven by Lucita and Maribella, our maids, two of the toughest women you will ever meet. They handle the mules, cook our food, and keep the men in line. You can sleep with them in the wagon. What do you say?"

She finished her bowl of broth. "I say, let 'er buck!"

He threw back his head, laughing. "Buck! That reminds me, our old wrangler was very impressed by the way you saved his horse. He has repeated the episode to each of the men. He was especially impressed by the way you snaked your arm down that horse's throat. He admitted it was something he himself would not have done."

Delphinia blushed.

Jesùs's eyes roved across her mouth and throat. "Everybody here thinks you are some lady!"

With one exception, thought Delphinia.

Chapter Eighteen

The big bay she rode thundered across a rocky flat and down a steep embankment. The horse lurched up the other side and scrambled over the loose gravel, the brittle sagebrush scratching his legs. Considering the terrain, Delphinia was glad that Jesús had found for her a pair of Blackjack's old leather chaps. She swayed in the big stock saddle, ducking mesquite limbs and reining in behind four fast-moving mares and several two-year-olds. The yearlings had long since dropped back and disappeared — they were not what the Parry crew was after.

Jesús Parry suddenly appeared from a thicket, reining in close to Delphinia, his big rowels jammed into the sides of his puffing black horse. The animal groaned from the hot ride, his long, extended strides pounding like hammers alongside. "Turn them!" Jesús shouted to her and, swinging his right arm over his head, pointed at the steep embankment they galloped toward.

Delphinia leaned in and spurred hard, sitting deep in the saddle and wishing she were familiar with the terrain. New Mexico sand country differed from the high country grass and caliche flats she usually rode. Four Parry cowboys joined her at the top of the ridge. They yanked their horses to a grinding halt under spade bits. "They're heading for the Cañon!" one of the cowboys yelled to Delphinia, spurring straight over the cliff edge.

Delphinia looked to her left in time to see Jesús riding hard along the crest of the hill before plunging his horse straight over the slope. Reins steady, she spurred her horse down the precipice, keeping the animal's head straight between her knees, maintaining control over the horse's natural tendency to turn sideways. She knew that allowing a horse to turn sideways was a sure way to roll the animal head over heels, and so held her reins even, forcing the horse to straighten each time he swung to avoid the descent.

At the bottom of the Cañon, she reined in behind Jesús who was spurring hard behind the runaways trying to escape through the gulch. Then there was a crashing and kicking sound behind Delphinia. She glanced over her shoulder in time to see one of the cowboys rolling and skidding under his fallen horse. The two bodies somersaulted to the bottom of the hill. Thinking fast, Delphinia caught the loose horse as it struggled to its feet, the cowboy, on the ground, his left foot hung up in the stirrup.

"Whoa, boy, whoa," Delphinia soothed the scared horse and tightened her hold on the bridle reins so that he would not drag the fallen rider. She dismounted, holding the horse still.

Buck rode up and leaned over his horse's shoulder. "He all right?"

Delphinia handed him the bridle reins and then slid the downed cowboy's boot out of the stirrup. She knelt over him, looking at his bloodied face. His breathing was regular, but there was a gaping, bloody cut over one eye.

Two more cowboys rode up, staying their horses and awaiting Delphinia's assessment.

"Knocked out," she finally said.

Delphinia examined the wound and studied the face of the unconscious cowboy. Several minutes passed before the cowboy opened his eyes, took several hard breaths, and winced. "Hell of a steep hill," he muttered, trying to make a joke.

Buck let out a snort. "You got a busted bone or what?"

Delphinia reached for the cowboy's hat where it had fallen

nearby and gently slid it under the back of his head. "What hurts?" she asked.

"Everything," he said. "I'm feelin' kind of dizzy, but I reckon I'll get my second wind."

Jesús joined them now. "What happened here? You all right, Woody?"

"His horse rolled down the hill and took Woody along for the ride," Buck answered. "Damn' fool, I told him to ride straight."

Jesús sighed. "Well, the bunch got away. Let's get Woody back to camp and take a rest. It's too late now to do any more chasing." He dismounted so that he could help get Woody back in the saddle.

"Nothin's broke," Woody assured them. "I'm just a little roughed up around the edges." Even with assistance, he winced as he climbed into the saddle.

Delphinia mounted her horse, concerned about Woody's head and knowing that the best thing for him would be to rest. She reined across the wash and onto a trail, sticking close to Woody and following Jesús who led the group back to the chuck wagon in a clearing overlooking the vast and harsh brown prairie. Lucita and Maribella had built a fire, and several Dutch ovens were nestled among the coals. A big black enamel coffee pot sizzled and foamed at the side of an iron grill.

"!Caramba!" Lucita called out at the sight of the cowboys, as she wiped her floury hands down the side of the greasy apron that covered her baggy pants. With them she wore a blue cotton shirt and a tattered yellow straw hat, tilted back on her head. "Where are all thee horses you beeg cow-boys are supposed to round up?"

"Never mind that," Buck grumbled at her. "You just rustle the grub and leave the horse chasing to us."

She scoffed. "We are farther ahead with our food than you

are with thee beeg roundup you *hombres* brag about. Catching horses! Pun! They are not even wild horses! Just old mares running with a few potros! My grandmother catches more horses than that riding her burro!"

Delphinia put her horse on the picket line after unsaddling. That day's work finished, she hunkered down near the fire. She relaxed over a cup of coffee and realized it felt good to have her mind taken off recent events by the new surroundings.

It wasn't long before she was joined by Jesús. "You are a strange girl," he said.

"Strange? Is that a compliment?"

"But of course! You ride like a man. You know how to keep quiet. And yet you looked beautiful in a dress yesterday, a lady."

She laughed. "You're embarrassing me. You don't have to figure me out. I'm just being myself. You see, Amity taught me to be a lady, and Hawk taught me how to take care of myself. I just put it all together without thinking about it."

He watched her for several seconds and then a soft look came into his eyes, a look she had seen in other men's eyes before. In Jess, when he was talking marriage. The look she had caught from Jim Hat ton when he said good bye to her at the stage station the other day. She swallowed hard when she realized she had not thought of Jess in many days. Even Jim Hat ton had been out of her mind since arriving at the Parrys'.

"What are you thinking about?" Jesús asked, leaning closer to her. "Something very deep is running through that shapely head of yours."

She tried to ease her body away from Jesús, unaccustomed to having a person she hardly knew probe into her mind. "Oh, just things. You know…about my house and what's going on there. People I know back home."

"Ah…a boyfriend."

"No! I mean...not exactly."

"You do not have to be embarrassed. Everybody has thoughts about special people in their lives. Amorous thoughts are natural, no?"

"Come on!" Maribella shouted, clapping her hands at the men and pointing to the big bean pot. "We have been cooking for you all day, thee least you can do is enjoy thee feast!"

Grateful for the excuse to escape Jesús's questions, Delphinia found a place in the chuck line. She noticed Buck was watching her closely. The line moved quickly. Lucita and Maribella kept up a constant banter with the cowboys, joking and laughing with them. It was all very friendly, and Delphinia knew they meant no harm even if the remarks sometimes got rough. She filled her plate and took a seat on a nearby rock. Hunched over her meal, cross-legged, she felt a little out of place being the newcomer. Still the cowboys were impressed by her having saved the choking horse yesterday, and by her riding today. Yet, none was familiar enough with her to include her as part of their horseplay. At least not yet.

Jesús was nowhere to be found during the meal for which Delphinia was grateful. But, later, when the sun began to sink into wild, rose gashes against the western hills and one of the men took a guitar from the chuck wagon, he appeared out of nowhere and resumed his position by her side. His nearness made her nervous.

"You like the guitar music?" he asked. "Romantic, no?"

She changed the subject. "How many horses do you think you'll end up with?"

"Forty head. We will find them in the morning and drive part way back to the ranch before nightfall. That is, if we do not have any more accidents." He nodded at Woody who was already stretched out under a thin blanket, his head on his saddle. "He had a bad scare today. I think he is still a little mixed up in the head from getting kicked by his horse."

"He could have been killed," she said. "That horse rolled over him at least three times. He sure was lucky. He should take it easy for a couple of days."

"Do you like our New Mexico evenings?" It was his turn to change the subject.

She nodded and, glancing at the sunset, crossed her arms. "Beautiful. Peaceful. A little sandier and drier than I'm used to, but a wild, lovely land. The purples running back there along the ridges are as deep as I've seen."

"You like beautiful colors? Reds? Full of passion?"

"I don't know about passion. But as far as colors are concerned, I'm always interested in new plants."

"Plants?" He looked puzzled.

She laughed. "Yes. I'm a weaver. I dye wool for my rugs."

"A weaver! The Chamayos, north of here, are known for their beautiful rugs and saddle blankets. Perhaps you would like to visit them? I'll take you to Santa Fé!"

"Santa Fé. That's a week's ride north from here, isn't it?"

"Ah, sweet Delphinia. There is much of the world you have not seen. You will enjoy Santa Fé. Very Spanish, very romantic. The lovely old buildings and the churches! And weavers! I will be delighted to show it all to you. Let us plan a trip."

She smiled and tried to act as though she did not take him seriously. She wished he would stop flirting with her. She had enough trouble sorting out her feelings about Jess and Jim Hat ton. Not to mention all the things that had happened in the last month and a half. A handsome hacendado full of longing and smooth talk was not something she wanted to deal with right now. "Perhaps some day I will do some traveling," she blurted. "When I'm...older."

"Older! Sweet Delphinia, you are old enough! Even your name sounds like a beautiful flower, full of tenderness and fragrant surprises, whose petals linger in dewy anticipation to be opened to the world. A tender, exotic flower, just waiting to be plucked."

"Plucked! Sounds like you're describing a chicken."

He laughed. "I know when I am getting the brush-off," he said, jumping to his feet. "But I enjoy the chase. Tomorrow is another day."

A big bay stallion with four, white socks and blaring like a cavalry bugle through his open mouth, led the pounding herd across the sandy flats. The horse with his flying mares and young stock plunged through hard-rock draws under a full wind that had fine dust particles blowing sand from the south-west.

Delphinia turned her face away from the wind and closed her eyes against the dark billows that had her spitting brown grit from between her teeth. She leaned hard to her right and slammed her boot against her horse's left side, jumping him hard against the farthest mares and driving tight with the plunging herd. The cowboys raced hard on galloping horses that moved in closer, boxing the bunch along a draw, dipping low in and out of a boulder-strewn arroyo, scrambling wildly up the opposite bank and finally into a steep box Cañon where big timbers had been installed years ago by the Parrys for corralling range horses.

The stallion galloped into the corral and realized his mistake immediately. Caught, boxed in, he circled among the trapped mares, whinnying and nipping. The riders slammed the gate shut and then watched the two hundred lathered bodies of the horses circle the corral, milling and staring through the poles toward freedom lost.

Jesús joined the men and rolled a smoke as he gave out the orders. "Lorenzo, ride back to the chuck wagon and help Lucita and Maribella pack up. Tell them we camp here at the corral tonight. Bring the wagon. Chato, Sylvino, you go with him, help the women! In the morning we separate the two-year-olds from the rest of the herd, and we'll let the stallion and mares go. Then we begin the long drive home."

Caught up in the excitement, Delphinia edged in next to Jesús. "Isn't it going to be hard to keep the two-year-olds from breaking loose and joining the others in the morning?"

He shook his head, puffing slowly on his cigarette. "None of them will be allowed to drink water tonight. In the morning, we will cut out the stallion, the mares, and the yearlings. Some of the men will drive them back into the mountains to their own range and water. They won't come back after that. The stallion will want to stay with his mares for breeding. A natural thing, no?" He winked at her.

She turned away, letting the remark pass. "I'll ride back and help the women with the chuck wagon."

"What about resting here for the afternoon? You and I can enjoy the coolness of the trees. Perhaps the time has come for you to discover the pleasures of the world. We can discuss that ...trip to Santa Fé."

"I'm sorry, Jesús. I'm not planning any trips to Santa Fé. I want to help round up horses, not be badgered by you."

Delphinia sat up on the wagon seat between Lucita and Maribella. She had accepted their invitation to ride in the wagon in an effort to steer clear of Jesús for the time being.

Lucita handled the reins, rolling her fat shoulders with each bouncing lurch. "So! You are thee daughter of Hawk Estes! We guessed as much thee moment we saw your face."

Delphinia looked back and forth between the middle-aged sisters. "You knew Hawk Estes?"

"We have been in the Parry household since before

Bartholomew was born. We grew up with thee, family and know all of their secrets."

Delphinia was torn, thinking perhaps she should not encourage them to gossip but at the same time interested in what they could tell her. Jesús had promised her that his mother would tell her more about Hawk in time. But so far.... Besides, the sisters were not to be hushed.

"Hawk Estes was a handsome *hombre!* A young lieutenant in thee American Army. Riding a beeg horse, wearing a blue uniform, it was not hard to understand how Sonia fell in love." Maribella clicked her tongue and smiled knowingly.

Delphinia turned to her. "I'm sorry he broke Sonia's heart."

Lucita clucked to the mules. "Her parents would never have consented to a marriage between Sonia and thee young *gringo,* even if he had still been around. They would have sent her into seclusion at thee convent in Santa Fé."

Delphinia looked at Maribella this time. "Jesús told me some of the story already. He said Hawk was called back East at the outbreak of the Civil War. And when the family found out Sonia was pregnant, they married her off to Mister Parry who worked for them at the ranch."

"*Si*, that is the way it happened. Poor Sonia was crazy with a broken heart. She clung to that child, Bartholomew, when he was born as if he were her lost lover. She even threatened to commit suicide. She had to be tied to her bed for weeks. The doctor said it happens sometimes to women who give birth...acting crazy. But...I think...with her it was more than that."

Delphinia was deeply moved. "My God, no wonder she is so upset."

Lucita clucked again, slapping the reins against the mules' backs. "Thee family wanted to keep it a secret at first, and, perhaps, they would have succeeded, but two years later, when

Jesús was born, thee difference between the two children was shocking. *¡Madre mia!* Bartholomew with his white skin and yellow hair, blue eyes, freckles! And Jesús with thee black hair and dark skin...thee green eyes of *Señor* Parry. And later, when these boys were growing up, Bartholomew sensed he was not a welcome member of thee family, he rebelled every chance he got. Perhaps he wanted attention, who knows?"

"Was Mister Parry kind to him?" Delphinia asked.

"In thee beginning he tried to be a good father to the boy, but it was not to be. Sonia favored Bartholomew over Jesús, so thee old man became resentful. Everybody was fighting like roosters. Bartholomew began riding into Lordsburg by thee time he was fourteen, getting into trouble...gambling, drinking, chasing women, taking little interest in thee affairs of the ranch. And so young. It was as though thee devil was in him."

"Did Bartholomew ever meet Hawk? I mean, before Hawk caught him for horse stealing?"

Lucita nodded. *"Si,* it happened when Bartholomew was six years old. Hawk Estes rode in one day. He was surprised to discover Sonia married with two sons. It was very obvious who thee father of the oldest boy was! Luckily Señor Parry was not home that day! Sonia wanted to go with Hawk, but he told her it was best if he just ride on. Alone. It was a terrible scene. She begged him...would have given up everything to run away with him. But he left that day, and never came back. Soon her love for him turned to hate, spilling over onto poor Bartholomew."

"Jesús told me that Hawk had come back and discovered Sonia married, but he said Sonia was the one who sent Hawk away."

"*Si,* that is thee way the Parrys like to tell the story, and why not? For Soma's honor, no?" Maribella said.

Delphinia was beginning to understand the extent of Sonia Parry's bitterness even if fighting among family members who lived under the same roof was something she had not experienced. She and Amity were not only mother and daughter, but best friends. And Hawk's visits were full of surprises and fun, something to look forward to. She could not remember a single instance of harsh words among them.

"When did Bartholomew finally leave the ranch?" Delphinia asked Maribella.

"It was thee night he stole a horse! It was a stupid prank to shame thee family by bringing a posse to thee ranch after him. I think he was drunk, but can you imagine? A Parry stealing a horse? It angered his stepfather. There were terrible words. *Señor* Parry said Bartholomew was nothing but thee *bastardo* son of a *gringo* bounty hunter. He ordered him out of thee house. Ah, I remember thee yelling as if it happened yesterday."

Lucita interjected as Maribella stared off in the distance: "That is thee day Bartholomew changed his name to Blackjack. He rode away just one step ahead of thee posse, and never came back. Later, we heard he got caught and sent to prison."

Maribella sighed. "We heard he was arrested by his own father, Hawk Estes. Poor Bartholomew, how he must be full of hate against all of his relatives."

The wagon neared the horse corrals in the Cañon. Delphinia noticed the way Jesús watched the three of them, as if he suspected they were gossiping. "Please," Delphinia said to Maribella and Lucita, "I would prefer you not tell *anyone* we talked about these things. I did not come here to cause more family trouble."

"Si," Maribella answered, "Jesús has his mother's sudden temper."

Lucita hauled up on the reins, yelling: "Whoa!" To the men

she called: "*!Ayuda!* Help us unload."

Delphinia hopped down quickly, purposely avoiding the harsh glances coming from Jesús. She went to the back of the wagon where her horse had been tied and released him. She watched Jesús from the corner of her eye.

He turned his back toward the wagon and began giving orders to the men. The chuck wagon was unloaded, and a fire started on the flat near the corral gate. Trees sheltered them from the evening glare of sundown while everyone scurried about the camp circle doing their last chores before nightfall. By the time the sun had dipped below the mountain peaks, the crew had scraped the last of the supper from their tin plates and guzzled the last of the coffee. The cowboy with the guitar strummed a melancholy Mexican tune, and Delphinia sat close to the dying embers, humming along to fight her sleepiness.

Jesús stayed away from her this night. She wasn't sure if it was because he had not liked her talking with Maribella and Lucita, or if he had taken her rejection of his advances to heart. No matter, they would be back at the ranch tomorrow, and she planned to be on her way home as quickly as possible. She would not stay with the Parrys any longer. Her presence was obviously a torment for Sonia Parry who had disappeared virtually from sight since her arrival. Now that she understood more fully Sonia's feelings about Hawk, she decided it was best to get out of the woman's way.

"You are staring into the fire so hard your eyeballs are going to heat up," Buck told her, squatting close by with a squeak of his leather chaps.

She grinned at him. "I'm just watching the way fire colors move and blend. The really hot coals are blue and orange."

"If that is your way of telling me to mind my own business, that's all right. I ain't one to interfere in another's thoughts. I just wanted to let you know I'm sorry for actin' so ugly in the buggy the other day. And I want to thank you for savin' my gray horse. I would have shot him."

Before she could respond, Buck had stood up straight and ambled away with a swagger. She looked back at the fire, smiling. His rooster walk reminded her of Jess.

The long line of tired horses drifted through the cloudy dust like ghosts on a misty range. Forty-five head of two-year-olds — sore-footed from three days running with no shoes, heads lowered, necks stretched for weary balance.

"We'll be home in an hour," Jesús said to Delphinia, riding alongside of her after keeping a cool distance since yesterday afternoon. Last night had been uneventful, and dawn found the riders separating the horses in the Cañon corral. Jesús had selected those men who were to be in charge of driving the mares and stallion east into the hills. The rest of the riders had begun the long twenty mile drive back to the ranch.

She nodded at him. "Sounds good to me. I'm looking forward to a hot bath, especially since I'll be leaving tomorrow morning. I hope this won't inconvenience you…I mean one of the men will have to take me to Lordsburg."

He shrugged, showing her he did not care. "But of course." He reined his mount closer to the wagon, gave Lucita and Maribella some instructions Delphinia could not hear, try as she might, and finally rode back to the men where he remained, exchanging stories and smoking cigarettes.

Delphinia turned her attention back to the horses. It wasn't long before she saw the ranch buildings in the distance — the Parry house towering over the barn and sheds and horse corrals. The tall, square house did not seem right against the barren hills. Delphinia would have paid less attention to the house and more attention to the garden and corrals had she built the place.

As she rode into the yard, her assessment of the Parry land ceased when she saw a bay horse tied in front of the house and a heavy-set man, leaning against a porch support. A sheriffs badge glinted from his vest. Mrs. Parry stood next to him with a grim look on her face. A slight breeze ruffled the gauzy material of her long white dress. As Delphinia approached the porch, she saw her mother's black leather satchel resting on a bench, wide open. Then her eyes saw the mauve traveling suit, ripped to shreds and strewn across the porch floor. Her high button shoes stuck out of the leather bag; they, too, had been slashed.

"You Miss Delphinia Estes?" the sheriff asked, stepping off the porch and reaching for her bridle reins.

"Yes, I am." She looked inquiringly into the flat eyes of Mrs. Parry.

The sheriff had everyone's attention, and slowly the cowboys lined up behind Delphinia, including Buck and Jesús who reined in next to her.

"You are under arrest for stealing jewelry, miss. You'll have to come back to Lordsburg with me."

"Stealing!" Delphinia gaped at him. "What jewelry?"

The sheriff turned a weary face in the direction of Sonia Parry. "Missus Parry notified me a piece of her expensive jewelry was missing, so I rode out. We found it sewed up in the hem of this dress of yours." He pointed at what was left of Delphinia's mauve traveling suit. There was little left of Amity's handiwork.

"She's spent the last two days riding the hills with us, chasing horses." It was Buck defending Delphinia.

"She must have taken my jewels before she left," Sonia Parry said, glaring at Buck. "And, anyway, you keep out of this."

Delphinia looked at Jesús who glared sullenly at his mother, but said nothing.

"And there's three gold double eagles in that black case that Missus Parry claims are hers, too," the sheriff said.

"Those are mine!" Delphinia said. "I brought them with me to pay my traveling expenses."

"Where did you get this kind of money?" the sheriff asked. "Kindly step down from the horse, please."

Delphinia glared at him as she dismounted, unwilling to admit in front of everybody that it was bounty money.

"I want her off this property," Sonia Parry said, turning away and into the house.

"I have to take your gun, miss," the sheriff said, reaching carefully toward Delphinia. "Just slip it out of your holster and hand it to me."

Delphinia was too tired and confused to do anything but obey the sheriff. She handed him her gun.

"Now, the belt, unbuckle it. Slowly." The sheriff turned Hawk's revolver over in his hand, examining it, while Delphinia dropped the gun belt to the ground.

Shaking their heads in disbelief, Lucita and Maribella rumbled away in the chuck wagon and across the yard.

As the cowboys backed their horses away from the house, Delphinia waited to hear what the sheriff had to say next. His tanned face reminded her of a cracked moccasin that had been in the sun too long, but his blue eyes were bright in spite of the deeply etched wrinkles around them. "Well, we better gather up your things, here," he said, flipping his wrist in the direction of her ripped clothing.

"Sheriff," Delphinia said, "can you at least show me what I was supposed to have stolen?"

He shrugged, drawing a gold necklace out of his pocket. Red stones set in delicate filigree swirls caught the last glows of afternoon sun, splashing sparkles across the sheriffs hand. "This necklace belongs to Missus Parry. It was sewn into the hem of that purple dress. I found it myself. No use talking now. Save it for the judge."

At this point, Jesús Parry dismounted and handed his bridle reins to Buck. "Take care of the horses."

"I do not want her inside my house!" the voice of Sonia Parry snapped from inside the house entryway.

The sheriff looked at Jesús. "You got some place to hold the girl for a few hours? Your mother invited me to supper. And since I can see the presence of Miss Estes is causing some consternation…."

Jesús nodded, motioning two of the cowboys to his side. "Lock her inside the bodega." Then he turned and walked stiffly up the steps and disappeared into the house with the sheriff.

Delphinia, knowing it would be useless to argue as well as beneath her to cause a stir with the cowboys by resisting the sheriffs request to place her in the storage house, turned and followed the men across the yard to the little rock house. When the heavy wooden door closed behind her, she had to wait for her eyes to adjust to the darkness. It was a thick-walled room, full of grain and supplies — no windows. She felt her way around piles of wooden kegs and glass bottles. The room smelled like kerosene and garlic. She found a pile of gunnysacks and sat down heavily, resting her forehead against her arms. She braced herself against the tight, raw, burning sensation in her throat, refusing to cry.

Chapter Nineteen

The lump inside Delphinia's throat turned into a burning knot. She coughed, but it would not go away. She staggered to her feet, stumbling across bean sacks and kegs. Her groping hands served as eyes as she moved around the storage room, feeling her way in the dark, listening for outside sounds. Nothing stirred. She tripped over a large metal container and, standing still, listened to the glurging and dripping sounds at her feet. She pressed her fingers into the puddle on the floor and then brought them to her nose and sniffed. Cooking oil.

A soft tap at the door brought her head up. She listened to the sound of a key in the lock. *Scratch. Plink.*

"Miss? Can you hear me?" The key turned inside the lock.

Stumbling toward the door, hands outstretched, Delphinia tripped over the flour sacks and bundles of wire. "Who is it?" Her voice barely made a squeak. Her sore throat burned.

"Buck. We're riding." The door creaked open after another twist of the key. "Come on, and be quiet." His angular frame was outlined against the candle glow coming across the yard from the Parry house.

"Buck! Thank heaven. You can't imagine how glad I am to be getting out of this dark room."

"I ain't surprised. Now listen up. I got that little doctoring bag of yours and two good horses. We have to ride out of here. Right now."

Delphinia merely nodded as she followed him to the horses where she mounted a tall chestnut. Amity's black satchel was hooked around the saddle horn. She reached for the latches to look inside, but Buck's harsh whisper stopped her.

"No time for that! Come on." He reined his gray horse behind the house and across the yard toward the sharp outline of the distant hills without looking back. An hour later they had reached a stony slope covered with short brush that led to the entrance of a steep trail, angling west. Riding together in silence, Buck and Delphinia urged the horses at a fast climbing walk along the little-used path that was strewn with chunks of limestone. The trail rounded the shoulder of a craggy cliff and then dropped steeply into a small valley covered with grass that looked ghostly white against the upcoming winter moon.

Buck finally drew his horse to a halt at the other side of the meadow. For the first time he looked back at the trail they had left behind.

Delphinia wanted to ask Buck why he was taking such a risk by helping her, but she could see he was preoccupied and all business. Besides, she already knew he was a man who talked little. She contented herself by pulling up her coat collar tight against the soreness in her throat.

Buck's glance told her only that he was ready to ride on. Urging his gray with a light tap of his spurs, he allowed the horse to move back onto the narrow trail. Delphinia followed close behind him. They rode deep into the night, along paths that wound through rocky gorges and steep-sided cliffs covered with finger-like dry bushes clutching at the horse's legs. Delphinia nearly dozed in the saddle, but was brought back to life
by the sound of both horses pawing and sloshing in a fast-moving stream before they drank.

Buck looked at Delphinia, shoulders sagging with fatigue, hands across the saddle horn. "We can rest now."

She nodded gratefully. The burning in her throat was worse, and she had trouble swallowing.

Buck squinted at her, then lifted his horse's head with a

gentle tug on the bridle reins, moving out of the stream and up the opposite embankment to a clearing. They dismounted and started a fire.

Delphinia sat cross-legged on her saddle blanket in front of the snapping flames. She hugged her coat around her shoulders. "Thanks for helping me, Buck," she finally croaked.

"My pleasure, miss. We will be across the New Mexico territorial line by daylight, and you can skedaddle on home from there."

"Do you think there is a posse after us?"

He snorted a laugh. "I doubt the sheriff of Lordsburg will think you are important enough to rustle up a posse. A jewel snatcher is about as important as a chicken thief."

"I didn't steal any jewelry. Missus Parry lied."

"It don't come as a surprise. That woman has more tricks up her sleeve than a medicine show."

"You don't like her, do you?"

"Nope."

She looked at him across the yellowish fire, waiting for an explanation that did not come. Instead of talking, he pulled a package of jerky out of his bedroll and munched on a hard, dry piece. He handed one to Delphinia. "Here, eat up. It's all I got. We left in kind of a hurry, but you'll be home tomorrow. You can eat then."

She nodded, taking the jerky from his hand and crunching into it, squeezing the dry meat between her teeth for juice that was not there. The hard little chunks scratched her sore throat, causing her to cough. "I'm sorry, Buck, I'm coming down with a bad sore throat."

He shrugged, champing into another bite of his own. "Well, do the best you can. We've got nothin' better, and ain't no point frettin' about it."

"What will happen to you now, Buck? Helping me get away,

you're going to be in trouble. At least out of a job."

He wrinkled his nose so that his mustache twisted to one side. "I should have rode out of there a long time ago. The pay was all right, and Jesús Parry ain't a bad sort of fellow to work for, but that mother of his is somebody I won't miss."

"Her oldest son, Blackjack Parry, is my half-brother. I guess I had some foolish notion I could make friends with the family."

He swallowed the last of his jerky. "I don't know anything about that. I stay out of people's business. I just figured a straight-shooter like you wouldn't be mixed up in anything as low as snatching a piece of jewelry from a house where you were a guest. It's my way of thanking you for saving my horse."

A terrible fear gripped Delphinia. "Does the chestnut I'm riding belong to the Parrys? If it does…I'll be wanted for stealing a horse as well as the jewelry."

"Wait a minute, miss. He's mine. You ain't stealing no horse."

She nodded. Although relieved, she was acutely aware of the pain in her throat when she swallowed the last of her jerky.

They rode due west through a small mountain range humped in ragged slashes at a point dividing the New Mexico and Arizona Territories. The trail dipped quickly, staggering among broken rocks to the bottom of a slope and into a grove of oak trees, flagging their last russet leaves in the November morning wind. They reached a fork in the trail and pulled their horses to a halt while viewing the vast, salmon-colored valley that stretched into the flat lands that sat warm and glowing, pointing the way south into Arizona. Buck had wanted to stay with Delphinia until he knew she was safe across the New Mexico line in case there was a posse after them.

"You got about a forty-mile ride to home," Buck said, with a sweep of his arm. "If you stay south of the Peloncillo Mountains, you should find your way into your own back yard with no trouble. I'm leaving you now."

Delphinia felt that loneliness creeping up on her again, and she was still a long way from home. "Where will you go, Buck? You know you're welcome to ride home with me. I can pay you. I could maybe help you in some way, if you need anything."

He shook his head. "Going north. Figure I haven't seen the Utah country in a few years."

"But winter is coming on," she said.

"Winter is always coming on, miss. You take keer of yourself."

"Buck! What about this horse?"

"Keep him for me. He's getting old and stiff in the shoulders, ready for a shady corral." He reined away down the slope.

Delphinia stared until he and the gray horse disappeared in a bluish shadow against the jagged cliffs. Then she turned south, urging the chestnut to pick his way carefully through the shale littered across the path. Hitting the Cañon floor, she reined toward home, squinting against the back side of the familiar mountains she knew ringed her home valley. She sighed and braced herself for the long, solitary ride.

Shaking with fever, when the sun was high, she dismounted in the midst of a fit of coughing. She fought an impulse to fall asleep in a nearby bed of leaves, knowing she might not be able to wake up and all too aware that she could not spend another night out in the cold. Resting the horse briefly, she pulled herself back into the saddle, reining south...always south.

Occasionally she took small sips of water from the canteen Buck had left with her. The horse continued its slow, easy gait, stopping briefly to graze when she allowed. Now she stayed in the saddle, fearful of dismounting and not being able to climb back up again. Her skin turned hot and cold, her throat burning as if a chunk of charcoal was lodged across her windpipe. Nose stuffy, eyes burning, mouth dry, she whispered to the horse: "South, fella, south."

Late afternoon found her skirting the edges of a small homestead, but she did not linger. She eyed the weathered buildings briefly, imagining the comforts of a home, then reined the horse away. South. Even in her delirium she knew she rode a dangerous trail. It appeared that with a few exceptions people were either frightened by her or trying to settle some old score. *Stay away from homesteads...stay away.*

She kept her eyes on the hills. In the dusk her own familiar valley loomed ahead, and she kept in the saddle. She hoped the poor, tired horse would make it the last few miles and felt badly she could not give him a rest, but she could not stop now. She spotted another homestead. A little house nestled on the prairie among outbuildings and corrals. A barking dog. Slowly she recognized the Brubaker place. Brubakers. She considered riding in for help, but the coldness of Mrs. Brubaker
on her last visit discouraged her from seeking their help now. Besides, she was so close to home. *Almost home. Almost home.* Six miles through the last sloping hills, she followed the hard packed road south of the Brubaker pasture. She reined the chestnut easily because he was a good horse. *Home...home ...buzzing bees...Slicker...home.*

"Miss Delphinia!" The faces of Benny and Tuck peeked out the doorway. A yellow light from the kerosene lamp framed their young, bony bodies. The last thing Delphinia remembered was sliding off the horse with Amity's little black satchel held tightly across her chest.

Chapter Twenty

Her labored breathing erupted into a series of choked coughs, settling finally into a loose rumbling within her chest. Warm strong hands lifted her shoulders, turning her body, helping her hack out her lungs. Delphinia looked up at the gentle daylight that streamed through the bedroom window. The curtains were drawn back. She caught a glimpse of Amity's and Hawk's wooden crosses in the yard.

"Glad you're finally awake," Jim Hat ton said. He sat on the edge of the bed where he could lift Delphinia's torso upright whenever she was wracked by a coughing spell.

Slowly the sheriff came into focus as Delphinia, still shaking from the cough, studied the face above her. Her eyes traveled about the room — a litter of cups and glasses stood on the nearby table top. "Jim…what…what…happened?"

"Darned if I know," he said, loosening his grip so that she rested back against the pillow. "Last I knew you were in Lordsburg with the Parrys. Two nights ago Benny and Tuck came riding to town like they saw a ghost. Said you came riding home on a strange horse and fainted. They were so spooked they just left you laying there in the yard while they came to me for help. I rode out here, found you, and put you to bed. I brought your team and buckboard home."

"I'm sorry I've caused a big commotion." Her glance slid across the edges of her nightgown sleeves peeping from the covers. "Who…put me to bed?"

He frowned. "I saw you were in a bad way, fevered and sick. I carried you in here, and then I rode over to Brubakers, thinking Missus Brubaker could take care of you what with

Doc Pettigrew being gone on some emergency."

Delphinia watched his lips as he formed his words. "Oh? So, Missus Brubaker…was she here?"

"No. She said she had a sick child of her own to take care of. So I came back, and I've been here with you ever since. I couldn't leave you alone, Delphinia. I hope that doesn't upset you." He touched her forehead. "At least, the fever broke."

She managed a weak smile, slipping back against the pillow, and fell into a shallow sleep.

Hours later he was beside her again, helping her through another bout of coughing. "You feel better?"

She nodded, leaning over the side of the bed. "Thank you, Jim. I feel badly…about you having to see me like this. Embarrassed, you know? But I'm grateful to you, too."

"If it makes you feel any better, Delphinia, I was a married man. Once. You're not exactly in the hands of a roguish bachelor." He smiled.

She looked up at him, leaning deep into the pillows. "Married? You? I didn't know that."

He nodded. "It was a while back. We were both kids." He supplied the information in one long rush as if anxious to get it out, not lingering on any details. "We lived in a little shack north of town while I worked as a cowboy for the Chiricahua Cattle Company. We had big plans about saving money for a place of our own. She died the next winter having a baby. Took her three days to die. There wasn't nothing the damn' doctor could do…the old drunk…even after he got there. Both of them died. Her and the baby. She meant everything to me. I went crazy for a few years after that, gave up cowboying, got good with a gun. One thing for sure…I vowed I would never touch another woman again. Would never be responsible for hurting one like that. A three-minute roll in the hay is not worth the horrors of what that girl went through. I still hear those screams."

"I'm sorry," she whispered, closing her eyes, stifling another cough. Her forehead felt damp but cool. She dozed off again.

The window glass was black with night. A kerosene lamp glowed from the kitchen. Delphinia heard the crackle from the wood stove. Through the open bedroom door she could see Jim Hat ton sipping coffee at the kitchen table. "Jim?" she called.

He got up, striding quickly into the bedroom. "You called? How about something to eat?"

She nodded. "I am feeling a little hungry. What are all these cups and glasses doing in here?" She pointed feebly at the pile of empty vessels on the table.

"While you were in that fever, you kept calling for willow water. I figured you must know what you were talking about. I found a jar of willow stuff out in your herb collection.... some green dry leaves. I boiled some and made tea. Then you talked about some other herbs, too, so I just kept going back and looking for what I thought you wanted. You've had a slug of just about everything out there. I hope it was all right."

She leaned back, smiling. "It must have worked."

"You kept talking about buckthorn, but that jar was empty."

"Buckthorn! We're both lucky that jar was empty, Jim."

"Why?"

"Never mind. Do I smell stew?"

"Yep," he said and walked out of the room to the kitchen where he spooned stew from a pot on the stove onto a plate. Then he returned to the bedroom.

The food did wonders for Delphinia and seemed to restore her strength somewhat.

"How is everything here?" she asked between bites.

He pulled a chair over to the edge of the bed. "First off, Hawk's black gelding was stolen. That's one reason Benny and

Tuck were so nervous when you got home. They thought you'd be mad at them for losing the horse. They're still feeling bad about those missing coyote traps."

"Hawk's horse! Stolen?"

"I tried to pick up the tracks, but I couldn't find much. The horse, the saddle, the bridle, the whole outfit, gone. But, at least, nothing else is missing that I could see."

"Maybe Blackjack stole the horse. Has he been caught yet?"

"No. But what about you? What happened to you in New Mexico?"

She took another bite of stew. "I'm wanted by the sheriff of Lordsburg for stealing jewelry from Missus Parry."

"Stealing!"

She coughed, more easily now, so that she was able to bring it under control. Then she grinned. "Missus Parry is Blackjack's mother. And Hawk was his father. I'm afraid Missus Parry wasn't open to the idea of making friends with Hawk's daughter by another woman. I should have left the ranch right away, but I let her son, Jesús, talk me into staying a couple of days and helping on a horse roundup. He thought it would give his mother time to adjust to the news of Hawk's death...so that I might part with them under friendly circumstances. But by the time we got back from the roundup, she had the sheriff waiting for me. She said I stole some of her jewelry. The sheriff insisted he found it sewn into the hem of Amity's dress. They locked me in a storage building, but one of the cowboys let me out. We rode for Arizona Territory."

He looked at her in awe. "You get yourself into more trouble."

She leaned back against the pillow. Although she had only eaten half of the stew Jim had brought her, she was full. "At least I found out one thing for sure...Blackjack Parry is my half-brother. He was treated badly growing up. If Hawk's horse is all he wants, it's the least I can do for him."

"Now don't go jumping to conclusions. I'm not sure who took that horse, and you shouldn't assume Blackjack is harmless just because he's your brother. He rode with the Riveras and was here when Hawk and Amity were killed…."

His voice droned on, putting her to sleep.

At dawn she crawled out of bed and, with some difficulty, managed to slip into one of her calico drEstes. She made her way outdoors to the privy, going past Jim who slept in the rocker near the door. Next she gathered a few eggs and even considered forking hay to the horses, but decided against it, her energy being quickly depleted by the few tasks she had set for herself. She sighted Buck's chestnut and smiled with sadness when she thought of the kindly cowboy. She wondered what wooded ridge he was camped on this morning. She walked back to the house.

"Delphinia! You shouldn't be up prowling about in the cold," Jim fussed, brushing back his tousled hair. His eyes were still full of sleep. "In fact, you shouldn't be up at all."

"Oh, hush! This is my land, my kitchen, and my life. I feel much better today. You go on about your business, Jim Hat ton. If you want to help, go feed the horses. In the meantime, I'll work on breakfast and give you a call when it's ready. How do eggs and flapjacks, pork sausage, and the best coffee you've tasted in years sound?" She moved into the house and set down the eggs on the sideboard, fighting a wave of dizziness after her first exertion in days.

"Fine," Jim replied, shaking his head as he walked outside to the corral where he forked some hay to the horses before he disappeared inside the goat shed. Delphinia watched him through the window. It wasn't long before the pork sausage was sizzling. The aroma picked up her spirits as she worked on the flapjacks and added the eggs to the skillet. She hummed a tune, glad to be home, strangely content knowing Jim Hatton was close by. Out of habit, her eyes quickly scanned the sky above Locust Cañon, looking for those identifiable layers of rising dust.

Jim entered the house, swinging a bucket of goat milk from his hand. He set the pail near the stove. "It isn't just anybody I'd milk a goat for, Delphinia. That damn' little critter doesn't think much of me."

"I didn't know you could milk a goat," she laughed.

"I just learned." He sat at the table, pretending a pout. "I was raised on a homestead in Texas. My mother thought it was important for everybody in the family to know how to milk the cow. Goat's not much different...just a little smaller and a hell of a lot jumpier."

Still laughing, Delphinia put his breakfast plate in front of him. She became serious. "Jim, after breakfast I want you to be here when I go through Amity's satchel...the one I took to Lordsburg. The sheriff told me Missus Parry's jewelry was stitched up inside the hem of the dress I had been wearing."

He shrugged, forking through the layers of flapjacks. "All right, but you don't have to prove to me you didn't take the woman's jewelry."

Delphinia swirled a piece of pork sausage in a pool of syrup. "You know I had three double eagles, sixty dollars in gold from Bate Thatcher's bounty. The sheriff of Lordsburg found it in the satchel, and, of course, Missus Parry said the money belonged to her, too."

"Did you tell him it was yours?"

"No. When he asked me where I got that kind of money, I couldn't bring myself to say it was bounty money. Anyway, the sheriff wasn't in the mood to believe me. It was my impression he kind of liked Missus Parry, and this was an opportunity for him to shine in her eyes. Besides, the Parrys are big people over there. You should see the size of their house."

Finished with his breakfast, Jim said while dabbing his mouth with the back of his hand: "Well, come on. Let's have a look inside that satchel."

Delphinia rose from the table and retrieved the satchel. She set it between them and opened the metal clasp. She lifted out Hawk's gun and holster first and then what was left of Amity's mauve dress. It was rolled into a crumpled nest of shredded material with feathers and straw that had once been a hat.

"Oh, no, Amity's dress!" Delphinia said, plucking at the tattered fabric. "And her shoes. Look, the heels are carved up, the buttons are cut off. Everything's in ribbons."

Jim studied the mess. "Whoever was going through this stuff was doing more than hunting evidence. I'd say this stuff was slashed by somebody with a temper."

Delphinia sifted through the dress remains. As she examined the hem, she saw that the original thread had been removed and then resewn with purple thread of a darker shade. "Look! Here! This section has been restitched with different thread. See, it's a different color. I knew it. Missus Parry must have hidden the jewelry in the dress herself. She had plenty of time while I was on the roundup."

"Delphinia, I'd say you were lucky to get out of New Mexico Territory alive. Missus Parry might have gone after you next."

Delphinia gathered the remains of the dress, shoes, and straw hat into a pile. "I think I'll just burn all this. There's no use keeping it. I'm sorry Missus Parry is so full of hate. I had no idea. And you were right, Jim. You told me I might be stirring up a lot of trouble going over there. It appears I did."

Jim pushed his chair back and rose to his feet. "Look, you had to get it out of your system. Now, you've found out the truth. That's the important thing. It'd be best if you and Missus

Parry just got on with your separate lives."

Delphinia faced Jim, her hand stroking, unconsciously, the tattered fabric of Amity's dress. "Jim, will I spend the rest of my life dodging Amity's and Hawk's secrets?"

"You haven't dodged anything yet. I'd say you've been going at everything head on."

While she was frowning and mulling over Jim's words, she heard the sound of buggy wheels coming across the hard-packed yard. She looked hesitantly at Jim before walking to the door. He followed her. They stood in the doorway together, watching as Ma Brubaker brought the wagon to a halt. Two of the younger Brubaker boys sat in the buggy with her. Horace's blond hair was tousled, and he held a gallon glass jar of milk on his lap.

"I come to trade milk for eggs," Mrs. Brubaker stated, her eyes darting back and forth between Delphinia and Sheriff Hat ton. Next she scanned the yard, eyes hovering at Jim Hatton's horse pulling hay from the manger beside Delphinia's horses.

Delphinia walked to the porch railing, still holding a small remnant of Amity's dress against her chest. "You said you didn't want to trade milk for eggs with me any more."

"Changed my mind. We decided not to have chickens."

"Coyote got 'em the first night we brought 'em home," Horace piped in.

His mother elbowed him into silence. "Besides, the sheriff told me you were sick. I came to see if you need anything."

"I'm better now, thanks," Delphinia said.

"I can see that," Mrs. Brubaker answered, her little eyes darting over the sheriff from head to toe. "Who else is here with you two?"

"Nobody," Delphinia had to answer, and then flushed.

"Amity Estes taught you better than to take up with a man,

even if he is the sheriff. But I reckon it's your life, miss."

"Now look here," Jim Hat ton said, stepping off the porch. "I rode over to ask for your help the first night she got sick. You turned me down flat. I couldn't leave her alone out of her head with fever. Don't go jumping to a lot of wrong conclusions, Missus Brubaker."

"Wrong conclusions! Ha! Don't get smart with me, Jim Hat ton! There are other women in the locale you could have turned to. Plenty of others who owed a favor to Amity Estes for her help over the years. You don't fool me with your lame excuses."

"Riding all over the country in the middle of the night, looking for somebody to help, was not something I had time for."

"Oh, no? You got time now to hang around here alone with Miss Uppity. You think I ain't got sense enough to know what's going on around here?"

Delphinia felt dizzy, sick, and weak. She sagged against the porch railing while whispering: "Please, Jim, I have to go inside. Don't fight with her. She hates me enough as it is." She turned away and staggered back into the house, swaying and bracing herself against the doorjamb.

"Nosy old biddy," Jim Hat ton roared.

Mrs. Brubaker yanked the horse back, turning the buggy. With a slap of the reins she jolted furiously out of the yard in a hard clatter.

"Ma? Ain't we forgettin' the eggs?" Horace Brubaker asked in his high little voice.

Chapter Twenty-One

"And the worst of it is, she's right!" Jim Hat ton said, pulling up the cinch of his saddle.

Delphinia leaned against the corral post, hands braced on the top rail. "Jim, don't be upset. Missus Brubaker is worried that I'll try to break up Jess and Rosalind Sawyer. She needs time to understand I'm not a threat to her. She probably thinks I'm trying to make Jess jealous."

"That's not the point, Delphinia. The trouble is she'll be spreading the gossip all over the county that I've stayed here with you. Your reputation is ruined, and it's my fault." He grabbed his bridle, shoving the bit into his horse's mouth, sliding the horse's ears through the headstall.

"You helped me, Jim. You were here when I needed you. I might have died here alone."

"Yes, but she's right. I could have ridden for help elsewhere ...if not that first night, at least since then. But, believe me, I was too worried about you, Delphinia. Sick and alone. I couldn't help thinking you might be in danger while you were too ill to defend yourself. But I could have gone the next day to look for a woman." He led the horse out of the corral, closing the gate. "I'm going to town. I have to get back to work."

She thanked him, watching the lines of tension deepen in his face and feeling sorry that he was so angry with himself over her. Latching the gate, she turned slowly toward the house, coughing. Her nose was stuffy, and her head hurt.

"Take care of yourself, Delphinia," he said, reining out of the yard, and disappeared in a clatter of wild hoofbeats.

Knowing it might be dangerous, she fought the desire to sit on the porch, fall asleep in the sun, and let the whole world go by. Instead, she shuffled slowly back into the house and latched the door. Sitting in the big rocker near the stove where Jim Hat ton had spent the last three days nursing her, she looked through the doorway at the bed and realized he'd set the chair up so he could keep an eye on her sleeping figure. It dawned on her how much she owed him for his care.

Later, she brewed a cup of eucalyptus tea and then napped in the chair again, awoke, napped again, finally feeling stronger. Outside, she did the evening chores and noticed the new firewood stacked near the chopping block — another chore Jim Hat ton had done for her. The long-handled axe embedded deeply into the chopping block caught her eye. She tried pulling it out, thinking she might do some chopping herself, but she couldn't budge it an inch. Swaying with dizziness, she gave up that idea and made her way back to the house, casting a glance across the distant ranges bathed in purple haze. Everything was quiet. She locked herself in the house after dark and washed in the old laundry tub in front of the fireplace. She scrubbed a week's worth of dirt and fever from her skin, blotted her body and face, and toweled her hair dry. She felt better.

Just as she was ready to relax, she heard a board on the porch squeak, and then again. She reached for Hawk's gun and, hardly breathing, listened to the hollow silence outside. She was sure she had heard the board creak, the way it did when any weight was put on it. Moving slowly to the window, still wrapped in towels, Delphinia peeked through the curtain, scanning the yard half lit by moonlight. She blinked, making out the upright shadow of a man near the woodpile that melted into nothingness. She told herself she was weak and that she had not recovered from her illness yet. She was hearing and seeing things, jumpy as a cat.

Scurrying back to the stove, she finished drying herself and slipped back into her calico dress. A nightgown would not do tonight. She would sleep in the rocker near the stove with Hawk's gun on her lap.

Toward midnight, when the moon cast an eerie half light about the buildings, she awoke with a start at the sound of tinkling glass, coming from the side of the house. It was the clinking sound of jars and bottles bumping one another as if searching fingers moved them about in the darkness. *A mouse,* she told herself. Sometimes rodents crawled among the herbs on the work bench, sniffing drying goldenrod and batches of walnuts hanging in baskets. That's all it was…small creatures hunting for food. She sat tense for some time, but all remained quiet, and she drifted back to sleep.

In the morning Delphinia awoke with a start, recalling the disturbances of the night. It was my imagination, she told herself as she rubbed the back of her neck that had stiffened up over the course of the night. Hawk's gun still rested in her lap. The fire in the hearth had almost burned itself out. It took a major effort to push herself up from the rocker and walk over to the stove where she placed several small logs into the fire and stoked it with the poker, arousing orange and blue coals into renewed bursts of heat. Once the warmth of the fire had permeated her limbs, she strapped on her gun belt and put on her coat. She opened the door and looked outside. Everything seemed calm. "It was my imagination," she said out loud this time. Reaching for the milk bucket, she braced herself against the cold air and began her morning chores. Everything seemed normal as she went about her business. Her horses looked fine when she fed them. The goat hopped and scrambled about in its usual fashion. The red hens bolted out the door when she opened the chicken coop. But when she entered the lower corral behind the barn, she found a dead sheep. Its throat was slit from ear to ear. The animal was cold and stiff, its hind legs jutted out in rigor mortis. A pool of dried blood spilled out from under its head.

Delphinia's heart was racing. Here was the evidence that someone, indeed, had been in her yard last night. Her illness had not conjured up false fears. She slumped down by the dead sheep. "Poor thing," she consoled herself as much as the sheep. The gentle creature had harmed no one, just supplied wool. Delphinia looked around the pen, half expecting to see the killer, but nothing stirred. The rest of the sheep bunched quietly against the fence, chewing their cuds. She pushed herself up from the ground and opened the gate to let the other sheep out into the pasture. The dead sheep would have to be dragged away or buried to avoid attracting coyotes to the yard.

Delphinia walked to the shed for a shovel but then realized she was not yet strong enough to dig a deep hole. Instead, she caught Slicker, saddled up, and dragged the carcass from the pen with her rope, hauling it far into the Cañon south of the homestead. Let the coyotes have their meal, she thought. Riding back into the yard, she wondered how she could protect her sheep tonight, and the night after that, and the one after that. Too weary to dismount, she crossed her hands over the saddle horn and gazed across the yard, her eyes settling on the two crosses that marked her parents' graves. She stifled a flash of anger at them for having deserted her. She would have to see this through on her own.

She unsaddled Slicker and dragged her tack back to the saddle house and stopped suddenly in her tracks. The axe was missing from the chopping block. Driven by a surge of panic, she began searching the yard. On the side porch she discovered her herb jars opened and tipped upside down, their contents scattered across the work bench and onto the ground. Many years' worth of herb gathering, selecting, drying, cutting, and measuring was now ruined. She got a broom and furiously swept everything first into a pile and then into a pail that she took to the chicken coop. Maybe they'd find the bits of leaves, powders, and stems a tasty snack.

Delphinia next went to the garden. It was in a shambles. All the squashes had been slashed. Seeds and pulp sat in orange clumps and piles mixed with the squash skin. The roots and vines of the plants had been yanked from the soil. Almost everything in the garden had been cut and hacked. *Had it been this way yesterday?* She didn't think so. Or had she been too weak yesterday to notice? No. Jim would have noticed. In a rising fury, she began to look for tracks. If she found little footprints, she would know that it was the neighbor boys taunting Frightful Delphinia on a midnight foray. Larger footprints would indicate a man — old Cholla getting even with her for that buckthorn cheese or Blackjack Parry out for more revenge.

But she couldn't find any tracks, and in her anger she kicked at the remnants of the garden, stomping and screaming until she collapsed, gasping for air. No tracks, no clues. "What if you had found a footprint?" she asked herself out loud. Answers and more questions flashed through her mind. *I'd grab my gun and go riding off. Would you shoot up the neighbors because your squash and your herb collection have been ruined? But the sheep is dead and the axe stolen. But why? Why, why, why? Calm down, Delphinia. Calm down. You said you could take care of yourself. Now do it. Stop feeling sorry for yourself*

She got to her feet, and, as she made her way slowly through the garden, she saw that the potatoes had not been disturbed. Her eye traveled along the row, the neat bank of sandy soil from last summer's hoeing when the plants had been cultivated for watering. Then she noticed a dark rim, angling strangely from one mound, and she kicked at it, not thinking. *Snap!* The coyote trap's iron jaws bit into the fabric of Delphinia's calico dress, scraping along her foot as it snapped shut. Her heart beat so hard, she could hear its thump in her ears.

"My God," she whispered as she slumped to the ground. "So close…so close to my foot." As she sat staring into the teeth of the trap, images of her foot cut clean away from her leg flashed through her brain. She began the work of freeing the hem of her dress from the trap. "All my drEstes are going to be torn to shreds if this keeps up," she mumbled to herself, as she finally just tore the dress away from the trap's teeth. She stood and stared down at the gaping hole along the hemline of the dress.

"Miss Delphinia! Hey! You in there?" It was Cholla's voice that called out from the side of the house from where he was making his approach.

Delphinia walked toward the house as Cholla came into view, trailed by his burro loaded down with camp supplies. "Cholla! You surprised me."

"Yeah, didn't mean to," he said as he tied up the burro. "Wouldn't have some hot coffee for an old, wandering soul, would you? I brought down the Mormon tea I promised." He was at the side of burro now where he rummaged through the packs and finally pulled out a bundle wrapped in paper. A big grin on his face, Cholla ambled up the porch steps, stopping several feet short of where Delphinia now stood. His face registered his usual expression, a sort of brash and unconcerned look.

"Come on inside, Cholla," she said as she entered the house. "I've got some coffee from yesterday, but it's not hot. You'll have to give me a few minutes." She busied herself, while Cholla took a seat at the table. When the coffee was heated, she placed two cups on the table, studying Cholla's face, trying to determine if his showing up today was merely a coincidence or something else.

He slurped his coffee. "I'm going away. And I'm not planning on comin' back."

"Going away?"

"I'm not a man given to long speeches, but I'll tell you this. I've spent more than twenty years in these hills, and I'm too old to hunt for gold any more. On top of that, my innards are protestin'. I've been awful sick since I saw you last. I have the skitters worse than a chicken. I've made more trips to the bushes these past days than a man ought to put up with. I think the water in the hills has turned bad. Maybe the mining up farther in the cañons has brought leaching down to contaminate the whole valley."

"Well, Cholla…I'm not familiar with mining procedures. Do you really think the water's gone bad?" She took a sip of her own coffee, trying hard to keep a straight face.

He continued after his eyes scanned the room. "Worse yet, Locust Cañon has been ruined by the presence of that Blackjack fellow."

"Blackjack!"

"Yup. I'm sorry to have to tell you this, Miss Delphinia, but he's riding Hawk's horse. I seen him up there in the draws a couple of times now, and he's the worst possible man to have criss-crossing my trail. He's a thief and a mean killer. Come into my camp twice already, demanding food and threatening to slit my throat. You should see his knife! I am too old to put up with men like that. I'm afraid he thinks I've got a hoard a gold hid somewheres. He's been keeping a close eye on me."

"So, you're thinking of leaving Locust Cañon?"

"Not thinking, going. I'm on my way out now. Going into Willcox for a day or two, and then I figured I'd head up to Dos Cabezas. I know a fellow over there owns the livery stable,

Pete Boyer. He offered me a place to sleep and meals if I'd work around the stables for him. At least, I'll get away from Blackjack and the bad water around here."

"Cholla, I'm sorry to hear you're leaving. I'll be happy to share my stew meat with you. Would you like some canned food?"

"No food! I can't eat a thing. Goes right through me, faster'n a jack rabbit."

She thought his answer came a little too quickly, but she couldn't be sure. She watched him as his eyes darted around the room again. But he'd always been a wary soul.

Slurping the last of his coffee, Cholla pushed himself away from the table with a grunt. Clumping in his heavy boots, he walked over to the door. "I want to thank you for everything, Miss Delphinia. I appreciated what your mother did for me, her always sharing food and worrying about my health. Better than a doctor, she was."

Delphinia followed him outside, resting against the porch railing.

He turned to her, sweeping the greasy felt hat from his head, bowing with a flourish that showed his bald spot. "Good bye, Miss Estes."

"Good luck, Cholla. On your way through town, will you tell Jim Hat ton that Blackjack is around here riding Hawk's horse?"

"I surely will do that, Delphinia. I surely will."

Chapter Twenty-Two

It was two days before Delphinia felt strong enough to gather the broken squash and feed it to the pigs and chickens. After that, she carefully raked through the entire garden, searching for the other trap, but she found nothing. She stood in the middle of the garden, inspecting her work and stretching her weary muscles. The autumn air hung cool but sullen. A whistling thrasher landed on the fence, watching Delphinia with bright red eyes. Then the bird flitted away. Delphinia looked south and saw a circle of dust rising above the cut in the trail. One rider coming. Five minutes away. Delphinia adjusted Hawk's gun strapped across her waist and moved quickly toward the safety of the house.

As she watched from the window, she recognized Jim Hatton's lanky chestnut. Little puffs of yellow caliche dust rose from beneath its hoofs. Jim's tall, broad-shouldered body swayed slightly, alerting Delphinia that he was a man in a hurry. He drew up at her porch.

"Delphinia? You feeling better?"

"Yes, I am. Coffee?"

"No, thanks. I'm on my way to the Sawyers'. They had some trouble over there last night...a cow missing. How about here? Anything going on I should know about?" He scanned the yard.

"One of my sheep was killed. My axe was stolen. And one coyote trap was set in my garden. I nearly stepped into it. And most of my fall harvest as well as my herbs were destroyed... the herbs were dumped on the ground. Almost everything was spoiled."

"Any idea who did it?"

"No. I couldn't find any tracks. I don't know what to think about it, really."

"Could be pranks…well, maybe not the coyote trap."

"Pranks or not, I've become a lot more cautious. Haven't gotten much sleep lately."

He shook his head. "I'll stop here on my way back and have a look around."

"All right, Jim." She watched him leave the yard, glad to have seen him again, but disturbed by his curtness.

Inside the house she cleared the table and washed the dishes, and then found herself fussing over what to fix for supper and wondering if she had time enough to wash her hair before Jim's return. She didn't know why Jim Hat ton affected her this way. She wrestled with her confused feelings. Didn't he say no woman for him after what happened to his wife? Hadn't she told herself she could get along fine by herself?

Slicker whinnied once, loud and demanding, reminding Delphinia that her horse had been neglected lately. He'd been confined in the corral for far too long. She scolded herself for allowing her heart to get carried away over Jim Hat ton and, going in the bedroom, took off her calico dress and changed into an old shirt and Hawk's pants. Once she had the gun belt strapped on again, she remonstrated herself: *Jim Hat ton comes riding in here whenever he feels like it, and you start planning the rest of your day around the off chance he might return in time for supper! It's best you went for a ride, Delphinia!*

She hurried down the steps and across the yard, heading for the saddle house where she pulled her bridle from the hook and joined Slicker. Bridling the horse, she flipped the reins over his neck, led him out the gate, and swung up bareback. Once Slicker had cantered out of the yard, she reined south across the caliche flats past the arroyo where she had left the dead sheep. Here and there she saw a scattered bone or a tuft of wool clinging to a low greasewood or mesquite branch.

Slicker, enjoying his freedom, cantered across the uneven ground, snorting and tossing his head in flight. Delphinia leaned close to his neck, laughing, rolling with the strength of his long warm strides, pounding, gliding, thundering over the hard prairie. Reining farther south, they reached the line of hills that rolled sharply. The land was dotted with more greasewood and clumps of staggered yucca that horse and rider were careful to avoid.

"Easy, boy…easy," Delphinia soothed, drawing the horse up for a breather. At a trot she rode back east, finding herself close to the Brubaker homestead. Their land was outlined by bent mesquite fence posts and strands of barbed wire. Delphinia did not like the wire, but it was being used commonly across the West, now, and she herself had helped Amity string the barbed wire around their sheep corral. Fearing her presence on their property might be misinterpreted and wanting to avoid a confrontation with any of the family members, she reined back west in an arch. It saddened her to be avoiding her neighbors, to be feeling she was not welcome by those people who had once been her good friends. Clucking to Slicker, they rode into a steep arroyo and back up the graveled bank that took them into a stand of white-barked sycamores entrenched along the old stream bed. Riding under the leafless branches, she felt the cooling chill of the wind. Winter was coming on. And the thought of winter, when fewer people ventured out, made her more aware of her isolation. Images of the good people in her life flashed through her mind — Amity, Hawk, Jim Hat ton, Jess, and even Buck. All of these people were gone from her life.

"Come on now, Delphinia," she said to herself and then realized she had begun talking to herself more and more lately.

"Forget all this nonsense. You're riding and having a good time with Slicker. Right, Slicker?"

It was as if the crack of gunfire punctuated her sentence — one single shot whanged from a distance north among some bluffs that separated the arroyo from her own land. It was here Delphinia's attention was drawn. The noise of the bullet was followed by a thump, and Slicker fell forward, head first, quivering once. His long mane shone like silver corn tassels. Then down. His front legs pinned underneath his body. De--phinia rolled hard, her hands caught frantically in the tangle of mane. "Slicker! Slicker!" she cried, clinging to his neck and hugging him, her arms wrapped around his warm throat. His large black eyes stared, sightless. A final gasp emitted through his nostrils.

"Slicker!" Delphinia screamed, still holding his head. Stunned, she found the hole in Slicker's left side where the bullet had come through his body, leaving a hole the size of her fist. Bloody and torn, pieces of bone clung to pink lung tissue. A big gun. A buffalo gun. A long gun capable of killing a horse at six hundred yards. Or a person.

Delphinia crawled across the ground and dropped into a depression. Her eyes were glued to the ridge from which the gunsmoke had already drifted away. Nothing stirred. The only sound was the high-pitched, lonely whistle of a hawk. She fingered her gun, knowing it was a useless weapon at this distance if the gunman on the ridge wanted to keep her pinned down. Her eyes settled on Slicker's underbelly fifteen feet away now, and she watched with sickly fascination as the horse's warm, red blood dripped, forming a puddle that attracted a cloud of flies instantly. Then she studied the ridge again. After waiting for any sign of movement for some time, Delphinia decided to investigate the ridge. She crept across the ground to remove Slicker's bridle. That accomplished she stroked the horse's silver mane and tried to close its eyelids. Tears pooled in own her eyes.

"It's my fault, Slicker. You should be home in the corral. I shouldn't have brought you here. Riding away from my own troubles, I killed my best friend."

Giving Slicker one last pat, she rolled the bridle, wrapped the reins around the headstall, and began walking to the bottom of a rocky ledge. She scaled the wall by using the rocks as hand and foot holds. She finally made it to the top of the ridge where she had seen the puff of smoke. She moved with caution, not knowing what to expect. Soon she was satisfied that the ridge was deserted, that the person who had done the shooting was gone. She stood on the ridge top and looked down at Slicker. As with the dead sheep, she was too weak to bury even her favorite animal. The thought of Slicker's body being picked over by preying wild animals filled her with anguish. Then she remembered the day Hawk brought Slicker home to her, a leggy two-year-old full of life. Turning quickly away, she ran.

She scrambled to the highest rock, and, as she stood, trying to catch her breath, she saw an empty bullet casing on the ground. It still smelled strongly of sulphur when she picked it up and sniffed it. When she examined the sandy ground around the rocks more closely, she discovered her assailant's footprints. She followed them, but they told her nothing more than that a person wearing boots had been waiting here in the rocks. Hopping carefully from rock to rock on the north side, she soon located the place where a horse had been tied. A pile of fresh manure was already surrounded by swarms of little black gnats.

Delphinia slunk along the path, winding north and slightly west. The path eventually widened into a trail that broke up into a larger field that bordered her own property. Here, she got a good look at the big horseshoe prints in the soft trail dust. Pressing her fingers along the edge of the prints, she was certain now. There was only one horse around the area with feet that big — Hawk's gelding.

It was early evening when Jim Hat ton again appeared in her yard. He looked as if it had been a long day, and even his horse hung its head in fatigue. Jim took off his hat and wiped the sweat from his brow with the back of his hand. "I'll be having a look around, Delphinia, then I'll be on my way."

Delphinia stood on the porch, wiping her hands on a dish towel. Hawk's gun hung at her waist. She had not changed out of Hawk's pants since her last ride on Slicker and long walk home. She wanted to cry out and tell Jim that someone had killed Slicker, but he was so aloof, she decided to remain quiet. She watched him dismount and then went back inside the house where she distracted herself with mundane tasks that didn't need doing.

In less than twenty minutes, Jim, hat in hand, finally appeared at the door. "I can't find anything unusual out in the yard, Delphinia. It's hard to say who's doing this, or why."

"We both know it's probably Blackjack." She paused and felt a growing frustration with the awkwardness that now existed between them. "You sure you won't have a cup of coffee, Jim?"

"Delphinia, I don't think it's a good idea for me to come into your house again. Missus Brubaker hasn't wasted any time in spreading gossip about you and me to…."

She cut him off. "I'm sorry if it has embarrassed you."

"Me embarrassed! Delphinia, you're the one I'm worried about. What about your reputation? Flapping tongues don't bother me."

"Jim, you probably saved my life. Am I supposed to be angry because you did that for me? As for people talking about me, why should I care? I'm the bounty hunter's daughter to most people. Has anybody worried about me enough to stop by since Amity died? The only people I get around here are snoopers and troublemakers!"

"Well, if you aren't going to be concerned about your reputation, I guess I'll have to make that my responsibility. So, from now on, if anybody rides in, they won't find me inside your house again, unless we have an understanding."

"Understanding?"

"Delphinia, I'm inviting you to Rosalind Sawyer's engagement party next Saturday night. Her father's throwing a small celebration, and he invited me. I want you to go with me."

"Go with you? How will that stop people from talking about us? That ought to stir them up all the more."

"We won't be hiding anything. It's hard for people to gossip about something that everybody already knows. Or, if they're going to talk, let them do it right to our faces." He jammed his hat back on his head.

"You've got nerve, Jim Hat ton."

He smiled at her. "Will you go with me, or not?"

"I will."

He walked off the porch, and his foot was in the stirrup when she blurted: "Jim, somebody killed Slicker today!"

He stopped, his body suspended midway between the ground and his saddle. "What?" he shouted, easing himself back to the ground.

"I was out riding, south along the arroyo, when it happened."

"Were you hurt? Did you see who did it?"

"No, I'm fine. He was hidden up in the big bluffs. I couldn't see who did the shooting, just where it came from. I climbed up to the ridge where I found a bullet casing and some boot prints. And I'd swear the hoof prints I found coming off the ridge belong to Hawk's gelding. There's no other horse around here with feet that size. Besides, when Cholla stopped by a few days ago, he said he was leaving the area because he was being terrorized by Blackjack Parry. He told me he saw Blackjack riding Hawk's horse."

"Cholla was here?"

"Didn't he stop at your office? He said he'd give you a message from me when he went through town."

"Well, he didn't. I haven't seen Cholla in weeks. As far as I know, he's not come through town lately. He said he was leaving?"

Delphinia was puzzled. "That's strange. Maybe something happened to him. He said Blackjack was putting a scare in him, and he wanted to get out of the hills."

"Cholla scared enough to leave his hills?" Jim said, still frowning. "I didn't think anything could scare old Cholla."

Delphinia gripped the porch railing. "Let me know if you find out anything about Hawk's horse."

He nodded. "Listen, Delphinia, I don't like the idea of you being out here by yourself. You sure you won't come to town?"

"I already told you, I'm not leaving here."

"O K, Delphinia. You sure can be hard-headed. Will you at least promise me you'll be extra careful?"

"You have my word on it, Jim."

Chapter Twenty-Three

"I'm sure glad that's over," Delphinia said to Jim Hat ton, sounding like herself for the first time that evening.

"No, I'll admit not a one of those party-goers, except for Jess, looked happy to see you there tonight."

The two had left the engagement party at the Sawyers' well before the festivities were over and were enjoying the leisurely paced ride back to Delphinia's house. In the pauses between their conversation they could still hear the merry-making going on at the house in spite of the distance they had covered on horseback. The closer they got to her home, the more anxious Delphinia became, wondering and fearing what she might find awaiting her with the house unguarded for hours. Yet, no matter what she might find, Delphinia was glad they had gone to the party since Jim now seemed to have been restored to his old normal self around her, the awkwardness having disappeared. Still, she wasn't sure she should test the waters by inviting Jim in for coffee since it had to be close to midnight. As they rode through the night shadows, she debated the idea with herself. After all the cold stares she had received tonight, she didn't think she could handle another rejection.

"We'd better ride in quietly," she told Jim as they neared her homestead. They pulled the horses into the brush behind a big cluster of prickly pear growing along the edge of the arroyo.

"Something is wrong here," Jim said, listening to Delphinia's team whinnying from inside the corral.

"I smell wood smoke," she said, "and I didn't leave a fire burning when we left earlier."

He drew his gun, reining east, signaling for her to separate from him. She dismounted and moved cautiously toward a stand of mesquite before angling through the arroyo and up its banks to the level ground just north of the horse corrals. She saw two horses tied to the hitching post in front of the house. One of the horses in the corral whinnied again and was answered by Jim Hatton's horse, coming in from the east side of the house.

The front door opened with a creak, and Delphinia made out a tall man stepping outside cautiously.

Jim Hat ton rode up suddenly from behind the house, holding his gun pointed straight at the interloper. "Who are you?" Delphinia heard him ask.

"My name is Jesús Parry."

After introductions were clumsily made, Delphinia, Jim, Parry, and a Parry rider found themselves in her kitchen. Delphinia stood by the stove as the coffee spritzed over the rim of the blue enamel coffee pot. She wrapped a potholder around the hot handle and poured the brown liquid into four mismatched cups.

The silence was broken by Jesús Parry. "I hope you do not mind that I took the liberty of entering your home, Miss Estes. But the door was unlocked, and the night is cold."

By way of a response she placed the cup and saucer in front of him. She couldn't help wondering why he had followed her from New Mexico Territory. His companion, one of the cowboys she recognized from the Parry ranch, was now sprawled in the old rocker by the stove, the chair tipped back, an indifferent expression on his face.

Jim Hatton eyed Parry from where he stood at the side of the room. "What brings you this way?"

Jesús smiled slyly at Delphinia. "Miss Estes left my house unexpectedly, and I didn't have the opportunity to say good bye. Not that I blame her. I wanted to let her know that the charges against her for taking a piece of my mother's jewelry have been dropped."

"Charges against me!" Delphinia glared at him, still holding the hot coffee pot in her hand. "I didn't take your mother's jewelry! She lied."

He arched an eyebrow with a sigh. "Understand something, Miss Estes. My mother is the most precious person in my life. Of course, I do not always agree with the things she says or does, but neither is it for me to take a stand against her. Personally, I believe there was a grave misunderstanding,"

"I'll say," Delphinia spit out and turned back to the stove, slamming the pot down so hard that coffee jumped from the spout. The cowboy in the rocker raised his shoulders in surprise, but said nothing. "Whatever happened between your mother and Hawk Estes had nothing to do with me. Your mother is a vindictive, unreasonable woman."

Jesús Parry's eyes narrowed. "I told you, the charges have been dropped."

"Good, they're dropped. But they shouldn't have been lodged in the first place. I'll take responsibility for the things I do, but I don't take kindly to false accusations. I was a guest in your home and...and...to be accused of stealing from. ...well, from anybody...! I'm not a thief, and I don't want this coming back to haunt me. Do you hear me?"

Jesús nodded and reached into his pants pocket and drew out three gold double eagles. "I believe these belong to you. My mother was mistaken about their ownership. We do not keep double eagles around our poor house. And I do not want it to be said that Parrys steal money from their guests." He placed the double eagles in a pile on the center of the table.

Jim Hatton blew his nose on a big red and white handkerchief and walked over to the table. "I guess that settles it. What do you say, Delphinia? You got an apology and your money back, and the man rode a hundred miles to do it."

Jesús Parry aimed a sarcastic grin at the sheriff. "I am glad you are so observant, Sheriff. I have come with bowed head, trying, in the best way I know, to resolve an unpleasant situation between two ladies, both of whom I am very fond."

Delphinia glowered at Jesús, her forehead furrowed. She remembered with distaste his smooth talk and his invitation to spend the afternoon under some shady trees in his horse pasture. "I appreciate your gesture, *Señor* Parry."

Jesús detected a touch of disdain in her form of address — *Señor*. "My *vaquero* and I ride home tonight. I can see there is little hospitality here."

Delphinia crossed her arms stubbornly. "I am a woman alone here. I'm sorry, I have no place for overnight gentlemen guests."

"Fair enough. I am sure there is a hotel in Willcox that can accommodate us for one night." Jesús Parry stated, addressing his comment to the sheriff who nodded in the affirmative. "There is one last thing I want you to know," he said as he got to his feet. "A piece of information that came to me from an unreliable source. Understand that I have no proof of what I am about to tell you, and I cannot give you any details."

Although curious, Delphinia put her hands on her hips in an effort to make clear her hostility toward this man and his family. "What information?"

"It is possible a man has been hired to kill you. A professional gunman who, apart from the temptation of money he has been offered to do the job, has reasons of his own to settle a score with Hawk Estes."

"Who is this gunman?" Jim Hat ton asked, leaning closer into Parry.

"Clay Dunnagan," Jesús answered. "He is easy to recognize.

Has a big scar on the side of his face, and his right ear is missing...shot off, compliments of Hawk Estes."

"Your mother hired him to kill me?" Delphinia accused.

"¡*Caramba!* Do not say such a thing. I am only telling you what I heard whispered. *Cantina* gossip. Men talking who have had too much to drink. It may not be true, but I felt you would be safer warned."

Delphinia turned her back to Parry and stared out the window into the night, turning this piece of new information over in her mind.

Jesús Parry put his hat on and walked to the door. "We must go now, Miss Estes. I am sorry you and I did not meet under friendlier circumstances. Perhaps there will be another opportunity." He sounded sincere.

Turning to face the door, beginning to regret her hostility, she said: "I appreciate your riding all this way for me. I accept *your* apology."

Parry's cowhand stood up, slapped his old hat on his head, and reached for his fleece-lined leather coat, joining his boss at the door. The two men walked out of the house and mounted their horses.

Jim Hat ton grabbed his own coat. "I'll ride to town with them," he whispered. "Make sure they get there and don't come back." He squeezed her arm gendy as if to reassure her, and stepped out of the house without waiting for a response.

Watching from the crack in the door, she saw Jim mount his horse and ride slowly out of the yard between Jesús Parry and the cowboy. She knew Jim might be saving himself from an ambush on the road, and she wondered dully if the rest of her life would be spent worrying about bushwhackers and night riders. She locked the door and then cleared the dirty saucers and coffee cups from the table. She unbuckled Hawk's gun belt and hung it over a chair. She looked wearily at the old laundry tub, standing on its edge behind the stove, and considered whether or not she had the energy to heat water tonight so that she could slip into the tub and soak her worries away. It was then that she heard a slow creak coming from the loose porch board, and it froze her to attention. She rushed to the kerosene lamp and turned down the wick. The flame smothered, she moved to the window, grabbing Hawk's gun on the way, and peeked outside. The only thing she saw were long shadows and eerie gray patches stretching out across the silent yard.

A cold wind was blowing up from the east, carrying with it storm clouds that hovered like slate mantles across the horizon. Tumble weeds rolled across the yard in high, bouncing tangles, the gnarled brown stems and stickers banking against fences, wiggling in the wind, and catching along the sides of the house. The livestock had grown restless, their tails flapping against the cold blasts. Still nothing approaching a human surfaced in her view.

For the next three days Delphinia scurried from house to yard, doing chores, eyeing the dark sky, hurrying back inside the house to warm herself in front of the fireplace. Without the long-handled axe, she was forced to chop wood with the small hatchet, remembering to carry it back into the house each time she was through. She kept Hawk's gun at her side.

On the fourth morning the storm crested in wild high gusts and thunderous bursts of cold rain that finally culminated in a quiet wave of heat, bringing a thick fog and stickiness, settling in humid layers like a white blanket across the land. The garden and barn and corrals were hardly visible from the house. Made uneasy from feeling so cut off from everything, Delphinia looked outside into the milky wall of motionless vapor and shivered. Her goat bleated, the pig grumbled, and the horses whinnied for hay. Reaching for the empty milk pail, Delphinia made her way across the yard, somewhat comforted by the feel of Hawk's gun at her side.

Working her way quickly through her chores, she finally ended with the milking. She talked to the nervous goat who seemed crankier than usual, kicking and even stepping into the milk pail.

"Easy, girl…easy," Delphinia soothed and then reminded herself the goat should be allowed to dry up soon — to recover from the long months of milking, to be made ready for the new kid that would arrive in the spring. It was not long before Amity was killed that she had traded some herbal remedies for a breeding to Brubakers' buck goat. Delphinia tried to remember when that was. It seemed so long ago.

Clamp. . .squeeze. . *.ping!* Clamp. . .squeeze. . *.ping!* The milk squirted in streams against the sides of the pail. "Easy, girl…why are you so nervous today?"

Delphinia finished with the milking and left the barn, walking toward the house in the fog. Mulling over what she would do when she got inside, she tripped suddenly in the murky whiteness and found herself sprawled on the ground, the body of a dead sheep beneath her. The sheep in the middle of the yard was still warm with blood steaming from a long gash across its throat. She flung the milk pail and reached for her gun, her hand skimming along the wool of the dead animal. Confused and frightened, she tried to peer through the heavy curtain of wet fog, shaking, knowing that someone had been in the yard while she had been tending to her chores.

Then the quiet was shattered suddenly by a clatter of hoofbeats coming straight toward her, as if they knew exactly where she was. Yet she could see nothing, strain as she might. Then just as suddenly Hawk's black horse appeared, charging across the yard, brushing so close to her that she had to leap backwards to avoid being trampled. The horse's rider lashed the animal with merciless flails of a whip. But the hunched over rider made no sound. Delphinia could see only the dark shape of a man bundled in heavy clothing, galloping past her and then vanishing in the dense fog cloud.

So surreal were the events and the setting — the fog clouds shifting and swirling in the air around her — that from her sprawled position on the ground Delphinia blinked and rubbed her eyes, not sure if she had imagined the attack. But there it was — the sound of retreating hoofbeats splattering north toward Locust Cañon on the soggy wet trail. Delphinia felt the weight of the gun in her hand but dared not take a shot at something she could not see, fearful that she might kill Hawk's horse. Nor was she sure that she could bring herself to shoot the rider in the back. Holstering her gun, she crawled to her knees. She examined the dead sheep before picking up the empty milk pail, and then she found herself staring into the puddle of white milk bubbles as they were being washed slowly away by the muddy rainwater.

The storm moved on, and the fog lifted some time during the night. Morning came with a wave of yellow sun glowing over the eastern ridges, droplets of dewy moisture sparkling in the welcome light. More determined than ever to get on with her life, Delphinia saddled the chestnut horse and dragged the dead sheep to the arroyo south of the homestead where she had left the first loss from her small flock. At the arroyo she quickly dismounted, loosened the rope, and stepped back. She felt her confidence dissolve as she stared at the sheep and thought of all the waste — two sheep, Slicker — dinners for the wild coyotes.

She rode slowly back to the house, where she unsaddled the chestnut and did her morning chores. It was as if a shroud hung over the homestead. She felt as if her animals, never before so vulnerable, sensed the threat, and in their uneasiness looked to her to be their protector. I can't protect you, Delphinia thought. *You fools! I wasn't able to save Slicker...two of the sheep. And Hawk's horse is gone, ridden now by my tormentor, being used against me.*

Weariness filled her bones, and her head buzzed from lack of restful sleep. She trudged into the house and unbuckled Hawk's holster from around her thinning waist. Only one more buckle hole left in the belt before it would be too big. No longer was she able to eat right, the idea of food making her sick to her stomach, the idea of preparing a meal likened in her mind to the task of climbing a mountain. Blackjack Parry ...Clay Dunnagan...whoever it was out there was doing a good job of terrorizing her, and she had not found a way to defend herself.

In the afternoon she settled under the warm sunlight on the front porch, tightening the tension of the loom ropes, pulling hard, stretching the warp so that it would sing like the strings of a musical instrument. She ran her finger crosswise, testing their tautness. Satisfied the warp was as tight as she could get it, Delphinia sat on he bench in front of the loom and picked up her weft beater. *Thump, thump.*

Laying in the rows of brown yarn, then yellow, then red ...and finally natural gray. The rug took her mind off her trouble. She was building longevity into the fabric, weaving a serviceable piece of material, something tangible that would be lasting. A rug to grace her floor and warm her feet for many years to come. And then what? What if...? Who would remember her labor? *Thump, thump.* What would happen to the homestead if she were dead? Would neighbors go through her house? Pick though her meager possessions? Knock the place down as Mrs. Brubaker had suggested? Disappear with mementos gathered through her family's lifetime of hard work and quiet living? All the lives of the Estes cut short? Who would remember her...Delphinia Estes...the bounty hunter's daughter? *Thump, thump.*

From time to time her eyes, weary of watching the pattern of threads grow blurry, would scan the road leading toward Locust Cañon. But the ground was still wet, and she knew no dust would expose any oncoming rider for at least two days. The fall sun did not dry the ground as quickly as summer sun. *Thump, thump.*

The growing stiffness of her body and the elongated shadows across the porch floor told her that evening was coming on. Over the course of the afternoon her rug had grown to within two inches of the top. It was nearly completed. She had reached the place where she had to quit using sticks to change sheds. She had to begin weaving the remainder of the rug with a long, blunt needle, drawing the yarn in and out, thread by thread, tediously fighting the tension. Only one way to finish her rug. With aching arms and stiffening shoulders, she grunted and quit, one more inch to go. Tomorrow.

She forced herself to her feet, reached for her coat, and floundered her way across the yard to do evening chores.

In the blackness of early night, Delphinia heard the strenuous pounding of hoofbeats and knew by the way the rider dismounted and bolted up the porch steps that it was Jess.

"Jess! What are you doing here?" she said, meeting him at the door. She hugged her shawl around her shoulders. The hem of her blue calico dress bounced around her booted ankles as she shivered with the cold.

"Del! Do you have a hot cup of coffee for a lost cowpoke?" He laughed, brushed past her, and threw himself into a kitchen chair before she could answer. He tossed his hat toward the hat rack and missed.

Closing the door behind her, Delphinia stood by the door, happy for his company. He was smiling at her, laughing in that kid way of his, always trying to be light and funny no matter what.

"*Whooee!* Have we had the rain up yonder. But it looks like it's over with now. How's your stock doing, Del?"

Delphinia walked to the stove, marveling at Jess's ability to show up in her life as though nothing had changed.

She laughed, handing him a coffee cup. She did not want to burden him with the list of all that had gone wrong for her recently — that somebody had shot Slicker or that two sheep had had their throats slit. No need to bother Jess with stories of ruined herbs and missing coyote traps and stolen axes. "I'm all right, Jess. Just doing the usual."

"I was sure glad you came to me and Roz's engagement party last week, Del. Roz was a little pointy nosed at first.... you know...when you showed up, I mean. But she understands you and I are just good friends. There's nothing to worry about."

"Of course, Jess. I thought we had that all worked out."

"Well, saying it and doing it are two different things."

She sat across from him, agreeing, remembering Roz's glaring stares at the engagement party.

"Roz has set the date. Christmas Eve. She figures to decorate the house and have a big celebration all at once. It don't make any difference to me, really, except I always thought of Christmas in a different way, you know, Jesús and the shepherds and all that."

Delphinia let him ramble on, thinking that Roz was calling the shots and Jess was riding along in her pony cart without a say in matters. "That's good, Jess. As long as you both are happy."

He eyed her. "It's going to be a small wedding, just close friends and family. I reckon...well...not too many invitations are being sent out. It won't be a big hoe-down like ...I mean...Del, I'm sorry you won't be invited."

"Jess! You don't have to apologize to me. I don't think it would be appropriate for me to be there...under the circumstances. I've always thought weddings to be private, solemn affairs ...between two people. You really don't have to apologize."

"It ain't that I...we...d-d-don't want you there, Del," he stuttered.

"Jess, it's all right. Don't give it another thought. If the shoe were on the other foot...I mean I wouldn't invite you to my wedding."

His mouth dropped open. "You're getting married?"

"No!" she laughed. "I just meant it as a comparison."

"Oh! I thought there for a second you and Hat ton was getting hitched."

"Jim Hat ton! Why, Jess, Jim and I are just friends." She felt herself blush.

"You and him ain't a secret, Del. Even my ma says she caught him coming out of your house one morning...I mean, like he'd been over here, you know. I figured it was a good idea, after what happened to Hawk and Amity and then Roz and me, you know. Point is, you should have a man in the house, and all."

"Jess! I don't have a man in the house. I got very sick with a bad fever. Jim Hat ton stayed with me when I was out of my head when he couldn't find anybody else to help out. You probably don't know that he asked your mother, and she refused. So he stayed until the fever broke. Nothing more."

He blinked at her, seemingly relieved. "Oh. I guess my ma got the story mixed up."

"I guess she did."

"Delphinia, I just come over to see you one last time. After me and Roz are married, it won't be fitting for me to come here, you know."

"It's not fitting for you to be here now, Jess. Your mother is plenty mad at me already. If she knew you were here now ...well, it certainly wouldn't help matters. You and I both know there's nothing going on between us any more, but nobody else would believe that." Delphinia could see that Jess was having a hard time looking at her. "This is all for the best, Jess."

"I want you and me to always be friends. But I'm caught up in things, Del." He studied the floor at the side of the table now. "There's promises to Roz and her pa. He's making big plans about my running the ranch someday. He's even talking about grandchildren. And my ma and pa are in a big dither over the wedding. Ma's got a new dress. My brother Elmo's already got a job cowboying for Mister Sawyer."

Delphinia leaned across the table toward him. "Big things are going to happen to you from now on, Jess. Don't spoil it for yourself, getting into trouble because of me. I can take care of myself."

He gulped, nodding. "I just want you to know one thing, Del, and then I'm riding out of here. If I thought there was one chance in hell you loved me enough to marry me, I'd tell Roz Sawyer and the whole damn' shootin' match to go to hell. I'd wait for you, Del. I'd wait for you to make up your mind if you wanted me to. It's not too late."

Her throat squeezed tight. Poor Jess. Kind Jess. If he only knew how much his words meant to her now, now, when she felt more alone than ever before in her life. But if she told him that he should wait, it would only be because of her loneliness and the fear she felt in the middle of the night, and not because she loved him in the way he wanted to be loved. She had nothing to offer other than a deep, abiding fondness. Perhaps that was more than Rosalind Sawyer could give him, but at least with Rosalind there were the financial opportunities offered by her family's fortune. All of the Brubakers would benefit from an alliance with the Sawyers. What benefits could be derived from an alliance with the last member of the Estes family? "Believe me, as much as I'd like to, I can't promise you that, Jess. Don't throw things away between you and Rosalind," she quavered, and despite all her efforts tears welled up her eyes. "I'm sorry, Jess."

Unable to listen any more and without a word, Jess rose to his feet, scooped his hat off the floor, and walked out of the house, closing the door softly behind him.

Delphinia pressed hot, stinging tears from the corners of her eyes, wondering if she had not just let the best thing that had ever happened to her ride out of her life once again. That made for two times Jess had attempted to walk away from Rosalind. She listened to the thunder of hoofbeats pounding furiously east in the direction of the Brubaker homestead. She did not move a muscle until the sound evaporated in the lonely night. She did not scream because she stuffed her fingers into her mouth and clamped down her teeth until she tasted blood.

Chapter Twenty-Four

"Delphinia, you all right?" Jim Hat ton shouted as he trotted his lathered horse into the yard, pulling up at the porch rail.

Delphinia looked up at him from the tangled mess she had made at her loom, licking her sweaty upper lip where perspiration had collected. She studied his sagging silhouette in the late afternoon sun and thought he looked tired. "I'm glad to see you, Jim. I had another sheep killed during that storm two days ago. And whoever is riding Hawk's horse galloped through the yard like a ghost...scared me half out of my wits."

A concerned, yet puzzled, expression crossed his face. "Delphinia, don't you know what happened?"

"Happened?" She frowned, placing the long, blunt rug needle across her lap. She saw now that his face actually looked ashen. "What are you talking about, Jim?"

"You don't know then that Jess Brubaker was killed last night," he stated.

The words, one by one, hit her like hammer blows. She attempted to stand, but could not move. Her head drooped, and she muttered: "Jess? Killed?"

Seeing that the news hit Delphinia hard, the sheriff jumped down from his horse and ran up the porch steps. He took her hand as he squatted down beside her. "His horse galloped home about ten-thirty. Jess's father said the family waited till daylight, and, when there still wasn't any sign of him, they started following the tracks that led this way. They found Jess's body on the road about a mile from here."

"Body! My God, what are you saying? What happened?" She gripped at Jim's arms.

"Jess was shot. A terrible wound to his chest. Looks like it was made with one of those old buffalo guns."

"Buffalo gun! That's the kind of gun that was used to kill Slicker! Jim, what's happening?"

"I don't know, but it's sure not letting up. I just came from Brubakers'. They got Jess laid out over there. The funeral will be noon tomorrow, at their place."

Delphinia slumped back into the chair in front of her loom. "I can't believe this. I must go to the Brubakers. Jess.... dead?"

"I wouldn't if I were you. The Brubakers figure he'd been over here visiting you last night." Jim paused, looking uncomfortable. "Was he?"

She nodded dumbly. "Yes. He was here. Just to tell me how happy he was about the wedding, and...."

"And?" His voice was more demanding, as if he thought there was more to it.

The tears finally came, and she covered her face with her hands. "Jess...gone? It can't be. He had everything to live for."

"Well, he doesn't now. You'd be smart to stay clear of all of the Brubakers for a while, Delphinia. That old lady blames you for everything."

Delphinia couldn't believe what she was hearing, and she felt that Jim was putting up that wall between them again, distancing himself from her. "She doesn't think I killed Jess!"

"No. Not with a gun. But she blames you for luring him over here, getting him mixed up in your trouble. She not only lost her son, but her big dreams for the future have been yanked away as well. She's in quite a state, and a lot of people are listening to her and supporting her. So just stay away, Delphinia. Let her cool off. You can pay your respects to Jess another time, not tomorrow."

“What about you, Jim…do you blame me? Do you think I lured him over…?” Before she had finished asking the question, she already knew the answer. She knew the truth even if no one else did, and the knowledge made her sick. She gagged, and, coughing, she stumbled into the house, tipping her chair over in her wake. Crying and pounding her fists on the table, she screamed.

She took the empty coffee cup that Jess had used and that she had not taken the time to clear from the table and hurled it across the room. “Jess, oh, Jess!” Was it only a few hours ago that he’d laughed his way into her kitchen, making fun, cheering her up, professing his love for her one last time? Why hadn’t she made it clear to him the first time he came over that there was no hope for them?

Outside, Jim Hat ton mounted his horse. He listened to Delphinia’s pain, her lashing out of pent-up anger for all the deaths she had seen in recent months. And, in the quiet of the yard, he finally answered Delphinia’s question. “No, no, I don’t think it’s your fault, Delphinia. So just go ahead and cry it out. But whatever you do, don’t go over to Brubakers’.”

As the last of Delphinia’s shrieks echoed through the house, she heard the sound of Jim’s horse’s hoofs trotting west toward town. A different kind of anger washed over her now, and she hated him for not coming inside and holding her, for his selfishness, his self-sufficiency. The tears continued, quietly streaming down her cheeks as she walked, trance-like, into the bedroom. She flung herself on the bed and cried until she was empty of tears. She’d experienced so much heartache and trouble these past months that she wondered if she would ever find peace.

In the evening, she went about her chores without thinking. When, at last, the stock was tended, she bolted the door and started a fire in the fireplace. She listened to the cold wind —

no creaky boards tonight. Throughout the long, dark hours she rocked in the chair by the fireplace like a haunted thing, desperate and lonely, sorry and guilty. Jess. Jess. Poor, young, happy Jess.

At dawn, pale-faced, hollow-eyed, she accomplished her chores and found herself sitting at the kitchen table without any recall of having done them. But the milk in the pail sitting on the kitchen floor showed she had milked the goat. Contented horses pulling hay from the manger meant she must have fed them. Chickens scratched about the yard, and the pig slept in its pen. Hot coffee burned her throat with its heavy, over-boiled bitterness. The caffeine charged her nerves so that she did not want to go back to sleep.

At ten o'clock she hitched the team to the buckboard and then went back inside the house. Opening Amity's closet, she took out the black mourning dress, and put it on. In a matter of minutes she was attired in black from head to toe — long veils covered her face, black, laced shoes on her feet, and, in between, black gloves covered her hands. As she stared at her image in the mirror — a white face ghost-like behind the black veils — she heard the raging inner voices. Jim Hat ton warning her not to go to the funeral. But wouldn't Jess want her there? Wasn't what he wanted most important? The sorrowing Brubakers. The accusing Brubakers. The enraged Brubakers. Didn't she owe it to Jess to face whatever hostilities waited for her? Just two nights ago he had told her he'd be willing to face the wrath of his family and the Sawyers, too, if she wanted him to wait for her. Shouldn't she be there for him now?

The buckboard bounced over the hard-rutted road. Delphinia didn't remember climbing into it. Touching her right side, she realized she had strapped Hawk's gun over her widow's weeds. She stroked the gun and was unable to stifle a sudden and desperate whoop. Her high, shrill laughter caused the team to flick their ears, pulling ahead into a strong trot. Out of control, shaking and wild eyed, she slapped the reins against the big, round croups, urging the horses into a canter, much too fast a speed for the hard-bouncing, springless vehicle, but the jarring slams helped to punish her. Snorting and fighting, the buckboard making so much noise behind them, the horses bolted. Delphinia slapped the reins again, coming up on a black buggy parked alongside the road. A horse stood with its head down. A group of solemn people hovered, stood staring at a dark spot in the road. They pointed, shaking their heads with morbid curiosity. They looked up and jumped aside in terror as Delphinia's buckboard raced by in a cloud of dust and flying stones, her black veils flying. Delphinia understood it was the spot where Jess had been killed. Their expressions prompted her to let out a high shriek, shocking them even more. Gripping the reins, she broke into great, gasping sobs, feeling her chest and shoulders heave in pain as she lashed the horses into an even harder pace.

Far on a low hill behind the Brubaker house a circle of people and buggies and saddle horses were gathered in a cluster. Delphinia drove the team in close, pulling the fighting horses to a shuddering halt just outside the little family cemetery plot that was fenced with barbed wire. Mr. Brubaker's parents and a stillborn child were the only ones buried here. Now a grave had been opened for Jess's coffin that rested, plain and wooden, at the edge of the black hole.

Dropping down from the buckboard, Delphinia made her way slowly toward the crowd, waiting at the fringes, while a minister read the Twenty-Third Psalm. The funeral-goers shook their heads. The men gripped their hats, while women held parasols over their heads against the noonday sun. Frowning faces turned to Delphinia. Silent as smoke, Delphinia wove through the crowd. She held a black handkerchief clamped across her mouth to keep from crying out. She finally reached the coffin and touched its rough edge with trembling fingertips. "Good bye, dear Jess," she whispered.

And then a shriek split the air. For an instant Delphinia thought the cry was her own, but she realized its source when she was pushed against the coffin by the pounding fists of Mrs. Brubaker who cursed her and wailed her frustration at her. She thrust Delphinia to the ground, kicking and hitting until the men dragged the crazed mother away.

"Draw that gun you carry!" Mrs. Brubaker screamed. "Shoot, why don't you? Kill! Kill us all like you killed Jess! You Esteses…killers! You will rot in hell, Delphinia Estes! You killed my son! How dare you come here like a black widow!"

Huddled on the ground beside Jess's coffin, too surprised and guilty to fight back or even to care to, Delphinia sobbed against the earth, hoping Jess would forgive her. Not only for his own death, but for coming here and causing his mother to lose her mind in front of the whole town.

Mr. Brubaker caught at his wife and led her from the scene. No one said anything to Delphinia who lay curled on the ground. She watched as four tight-lipped Sawyer cowboys lowered the coffin and began the terrible filling-in of the grave. *Thump, thump.* Sounds not unlike the thumping of her weft beater at the loom. *Thump, thump.* Solid and forever.

Jim Hat ton, arriving late, was the one who picked her up, holding her gently. "Shhh…Delphinia, it's over. I'll take you home."

As he guided her staggering body from the burial ground, she pushed him away and then crawled up into her buckboard. Without a glance back, she turned the horses and whipped them into a furious race all the way home.

Chapter Twenty-Five

Delphinia turned over in Amity's bed and blinked against the yellow sunlight shafting through the window. As she pulled back the coverlet, she realized she still wore the widow's dress of yesterday. The long veil and gloves had been tossed onto the floor. She rubbed the sleep from her eyes and, shivering, staggered to the kitchen where the cold stove offered no welcome nor had the fireplace been lit the night before. The kitchen door stood wide open, allowing waves of crisp morning air to fill the room.

It was when she went to close the door that she saw it. Her rug was slashed to pieces. Warp and weft sticking out at odd angles in a pile of torn wool, cut from the loom, a summer's work destroyed. Hugging herself, she staggered out the door and down the porch steps, finding only the old chestnut horse standing in the corral. The team was missing. High in the wind-swept mesquites above the barn a cluster of turkey buzzards huddled in quiet watchfulness, eyeing the sheep pen, their black wings drooping.

As she walked across the yard, Delphinia knew now what she would find. The pig was munching quietly on dead chickens whose necks had been wrung, their lifeless bodies flung into the pigsty. Inside the barn she found her goat. Throat slit. Udders slashed. The last four sheep had met similar fates.

Held tightly at her sides, Delphinia's hands curled slowly into fists as she strode across the yard back to the house. There was no hesitation as she walked into Amity's bedroom. She hung up Amity's black dress and carefully put back the veil and shoes in their places. Then she dressed herself in Hawk's pants and shirt, finally buckling on the gun belt.

In the kitchen, she eyed the guns hanging on the wall — the rifle and the old sawed-off. She chose the rifle. In the yard she dragged her saddle from the saddle house and readied the chestnut horse. She was not surprised that the horse was left for her, alive and well. After all, how else could she follow Blackjack? Had he not left her a trail and plenty of reasons to follow him? So it had finally come down to this, he and she together…face to face.

So busy was she with her saddling that she didn't hear the horse come into the yard. She was brought out of her thoughts by a man's voice calling loudly, an edge slicing the air. "You Delphinia Estes?"

Without turning around, she stuck her left foot into the stirrup, mounting with an easy swing up, reining the horse to face the other rider. She took him in with a swift glance. Medium build, stained vest over a red shirt, dark pants, and boots. A hat was pulled low, the brim wide so that his face was lost in its shadow. His right hand hovered above the gun at his side.

"Who wants to know?" she said.

"Don't matter. I have a message for Hawk Estes."

"Hawk's dead," she answered.

"You're the message," he said with a grin, taking his time, showing her he was not worried that she carried a gun. Turning his head to the left, he studied the pigsty and litter of dead chickens. The grisly display held his attention one second too long, so that the dark hole surrounded by white scar tissue that had once been his ear was exposed. Even the reddish hair, hanging around his temple, could not cover the old wound. Delphinia's gaze next caught sight of the scar that ran across Clay Dunnagan's flattened face, which gave him the look of one who had perhaps been hit with a board. He was hollow chested with the cool pale eyes of a killer who survives by outguessing another's next move. The way he studied the scene of dead animals told Delphinia that he was not the one who had been destroying all that she held near and dear, and it gave her the chance to reach for her gun.

Still Dunnagan wasted no time sensing her intentions. His hand flashed to his gun seconds after she had reached for her own. Delphinia pulled, aimed, and squeezed the trigger of Hawk's pistol in one smooth motion that ended with a coughing report. Clay Dunnagan's body slid to the ground with a hard, leathery thud and a hollow ringing of spurs.

The sky was bright blue under the morning sun. In the waste of the rutted mountains, the scrub brush was stunted, growing only two feet high. Delphinia watched for hoof prints as the chestnut's steps crunched over the loose stones on the trail. In time she recognized those of Hawk's horse mingled among those of her led team.

Confident, she stopped for a rest, letting her horse lower his neck while she sipped from the canteen and prepared herself for the events to come. It would end now. Today. She knew. For some time she had felt in her heart that it would have to come to this, but she had put it off, thinking, hoping that maybe it would not have to end this way. Brother against sister. Avenging old family scores about which neither was responsible. *Calm down, Delphinia. Calm down.*

She steeled herself to the task at hand, her senses tingling with alertness, the desire to survive foremost in her mind. Shortening her reins, she leaned forward, making a clucking sound, urging the horse to take up the trail again. They spiraled higher into the mountains, passing sandstone cliffs, tasting the thin, cold air savory with pine sap. She rode past honey oak and brushed under the orange-tipped leaves of sycamore trees.

A brown hawk balanced on silent wind currents above the treetops. Delphinia stopped at another break in the trail, eyed the tracks, and realized it was time to tie the horse in the brush and go in the rest of the way on foot. Perhaps Blackjack was watching her even now. No matter, they would come face to face. She was sure there would be no ambush. Yes, face to face. It would have to be that way.

Sliding the rifle from the saddle boot, she walked deeper into the woods just below the trail, following the forest floor covered with pine needles. Her nose tingled with the smell of damp leaves. At the edge of Cholla's camp she stopped and crouched behind a pile of rocks, observing. Hawk's black horse and her bay team were tethered in the clearing near Cholla's old wooden hut. A thin wisp of smoke rose from the campfire in front of the dilapidated little building. The deerskin flap, hanging in front of the doorway, fluttered. Delphinia tensed, gripped the rifle tighter, and felt the hair on the back of her neck prickle.

Working her way around the clearing, she closed in on the camp from the east side of the hut, listening, straining to peek between the chinks of the thrown-together shack. She found a spot big enough to see inside, but all she could see were a man's legs, stretched across the dirt floor. Seconds ticked by while Delphinia's heart thumped. She licked her lips in an attempt to relieve the dryness of her mouth. Although it would be far easier to shoot through the walls, she could not bring herself to do it. She had to face him. Tiptoeing to the front of the hut, she shoved the barrel of the rifle under the deerskin flap and, taking a deep breath, charged inside. Immediately, she jammed the edge of the gun barrel against his head.

"Uh!" He grunted once but then fell silent. He did not move, except for a slight jerk of his legs. Delphinia hesitated while waiting for her eyes to adjust to the darkness of the room.

Then in a rush she felt something strike the back of her head. It was a blow so hard that she was brought to her knees as red flashes, like lightning bolts, flickered through her head before all became a black nothing.

"Ssstt! You awake yet?" A voice…calling to her. Consciousness was returning. Her head was pounding. Delphinia tried to roll over only to discover that her arms were tied behind her back, the ropes digging into her wrists. Her ankles were bound, too, and, somehow, she was tied by her neck with a noose. The stench of urine and old sweat filled her nostrils as a breeze sailed through the cracks in the walls. Her eyes watered, and sharp pains shot through her head. She tried to shimmy around so she could see who it was that was addressing her. Perhaps Cholla. When she tried to talk, no words came from her dry throat.

"Hey! You hear me yet?"

Now she saw him. Young and blond, a pale face, arms and legs bound like her own. He, too, had a noose around his neck fastened to one of the hut's support posts.

"You," Delphinia whispered, once she managed to adjust herself so that there was some slack in the rope around her neck. "You're Blackjack Parry." She thought back to the attack on the house that had killed Hawk and Amity. She had not gotten a good look at the man who had been holding the horses, the fourth man who had to have been Blackjack, but she recognized him now as if she were looking at herself in a mirror — the eyes, the nose, the arch of the eyebrow.

"That's right, Blackjack Parry. But what in the hell are you doing up here alone? Why didn't you send a posse up here?"

"A posse? I thought this was between you and me."

"You thought *what* was between you and me?" Even in the

darkness she could see the confusion on his face.

"Haven't you been killing my stock?" she asked.

"Killing stock! I've been tied up like a damn' dog for about three weeks. You rode in here once before, bringing food to the old bastard. You surprised him that day. He told me if I made a sound to alert you, he'd kill us both on the spot. If I'd have known what a lunatic he is, I'd have taken my chances then."

"Are you talking about Cholla?" She felt dizzy as the situation slowly began to make sense to her.

"Is that his name? A crazy old prospector with a scar? Talks to himself. Smells like a pig. He sure had me fooled, inviting me to have supper with him one night and then drawing on me. I've been tied up ever since. He took me to another camp for a while…when the sheriff came looking around. We came back here…what?…maybe a week ago."

Delphinia tried to stretch out, groaning against the burn of the ropes on her wrists. "I've made a bad mistake," she said.

He eyed her, trying to rub his bearded jaw against his shoulder. "I haven't got any idea what's going on here."

She turned her head toward him, feeling the knot of the noose when she changed position. "Do you know that you're my half-brother?"

"I know. The old bastard told me your name. But I don't think about that old family crap any more."

"I met your mother and half-brother, Jesús," she said.

"Yeah? How they doin'? Still sitting up there on that *hacienda* counting their money and pretending that they're big shots living in Spain? Actually, Jesús ain't a bad sort. I got along with him all right. But my old lady was either babying me or throwing knives. No in between with her. Never could figure her out. And I hated the old bastard, Parry, my stepfather. And he hated me. I couldn't wait to get out of there."

"What about Hawk?" she asked.

"What about him?"

"I understand he is the one who caught you in New Mexico for stealing a horse...that he sent you to prison."

He shrugged. "Well, what the hell. He didn't know I was with the bunch until he caught us. I was running with a pack. He came after all of us. I was just along for the ride. I haven't got anything against him."

"Did you know it was our homestead you and the Riveras ambushed three weeks ago? That you killed Hawk and my mother?"

"No. Not at first. It was the Riveras who knew what was going on. I thought we were heading for Mexico. I just went along for the ride. I didn't pull a trigger."

"You go along for a lot of rides. Don't you ever make up your own mind?"

He glowered at her. "Look, the only thing I know is I've been held here for three weeks by a crazy old lunatic bastard who says he's going to kill me as soon as you show up. I don't care anything about your problems. I just want to get off this mountain."

The deerskin flap was yanked back, and the silhouette of Cholla stood plugging the doorway with his round-bellied shape. "Lots of god damn' chattering going on in here! You two gettin' nice and cozy? Ketchin' up on old news? Like brother and sister at a family reunion?"

"What do you want with us?" Delphinia asked.

He lashed out at her, kicking the side of her ankle so hard she was certain he broke it. "Shet up, you! Only reason you're still alive is 'cause I've one more thing to kill that's precious to you. Think I don't know about Jim Hat ton?"

"Jim Hat ton!" she cried.

He inched closer, holding a hot coffee pot in his craggy

hand. "Your pa kilt the only thing in this world ever meant anything to me. My son. My only son. And Amity was in on it. Your sweet-prissy ma, sashaying around with her little humming tunes and good works. You think I don't know it was her caused all the trouble? Everything would have been all right if she'd have married my Chauncy, and behaved herself. Did what she was told."

Delphinia did not dare argue with him, tied up on the floor with a scalding coffee pot held over her face. Blackjack kept still, too, watching Cholla like a trapped rodent watches a snake.

Cholla tipped the coffee pot. A steaming splash hit Delphinia's chin. She twisted away with a yelp.

"Ha!" Cholla laughed, throwing back his head so that even in the dim light she caught a flash of his broken teeth. "I waited twenty years, and it's all paid off. The Riveras were kind enough to carry out the first step of the plan. And you, miss, I've been watching you grow up…thinking you should have been my granddaughter, not the spawn of the likes of Hawk Estes. I seen you play through summer days, riding your horse, scampering about the garden…I knew my day would come."

She shuddered, envisioning his spying on her. "You kept Amity scared all these years, didn't you?"

He let out a wild laugh. "She gave me food and nursed my ailments, and she never let on to Hawk. I told her if she did, I'd catch you one fine day and snap your little white neck like a twig. She knew I meant it."

Delphinia recalled the many times Amity had seemed overly protective, not wanting her to go places by herself and fretting whenever she wandered far from home. It was understandable, now, why Amity had refused to leave the homestead to help ailing people, why they had to come to her. Everybody had to come to her…she would not leave Delphinia alone. And why she had sent Delphinia to school in Tucson, rather than have her traveling back and forth to town. It all made sense now.

"Thinking about it, ain't you?" he taunted. "I had that little whore in the palm of my hand. Yes, sweet times. And she didn't want Hawk Estes coming after me, so she kept our little secret. Two Chauncy Kyds on her delicate conscience was more than she could stand."

Delphinia had to bite her tongue to stop from responding. She knew now just how crazy he was — far too crazy to reason with. Too many years of plotting and planning revenge had rotted his thinking. Then, as suddenly as he had appeared, he turned away, clumping heavily out of the hut, the deerskin flap falling back into place except for one corner, allowing a glimpse of the camp to remain in view.

Outside he continued talking: "You two get caught up on old times now, brother and sister. Soon as Hat ton rides in, we'll have us a little party, him and me. After that, it'll be all over for the pair of you. My child for Hawk's two. That sounds 'bout even enough. Especially when you add in all the extras I been gettin'…there was them coyote traps. Nearly got your foot with that one, didn't I, Miss Estes. Eh? And there was the horse and all them sheep and chickens, and, oh, yes, let's not forget your young friend, Jess. He was easiest of all! Dumb little bastard, just stopped his horse to talk with me, friendly. His mistake. Yep, his mistake." His voice died away as he wandered farther from the camp.

Chapter Twenty-Six

"Shit," Blackjack muttered, as he rolled about in the darkness.

Delphinia shifted so she could look at him. "Does he ever take you out of here? You know? For personal reasons?" She did not know how else to put it.

"When he thinks about it, which isn't often. You're liable to be in for a long wait. There ain't no polite way of saying this…so you just go…where you are. It can't be any worse than the idea of doing it in front of him out there in the woods."

"I have to get out of here!" she said as she bucked and thrashed, choking herself in the process, so that she was forced to lie still.

"You need to stop fighting this, miss. But then you haven't spent two years in New Mexico's Territorial Prison. You get used to living like an animal."

"Didn't you hear him? He's planning to kill us. We've got to get loose. Maybe between the two of us, we can figure out some way of escape." She waited for a sign of encouragement from this stranger, her brother. When he merely rolled away in answer to her, she peered through the opening in the doorway, studying the layout of the camp, and then she examined the interior of the shack. "Listen, Blackjack, there're two of us now. I think I can get my feet over by your head, and I want you to use your teeth to untie the rope. Then I'll be able to stand and untie the rope attached to the wall and my neck."

His back remained toward her. "And then what?"

"And then we can work on the rest of the ropes. We'll get ourselves out of here. Now roll over, you stupid…!"

He rolled onto his back and over to his side, doing as he was told. Then he watched as Delphinia jerked the lower portion of her body in his direction. This sister of his was something, he decided, as her boots inched slowly toward his head.

"How'm I doing?" she asked, breathless from her exertion.

"Fine, keep coming…but watch out for my face." The soles of her boots were within inches of his head. "Slow down now. Push yourself up, so I can get my head by the knot…. there."

Delphinia positioned herself so that the rope attached to her neck was slack. She closed her eyes as Blackjack gnawed and bit at the rope that bound her feet. As time passed, she grew impatient, but she knew his task was not an easy one and so remained silent in spite of a strong desire to hurry him on.

He spit and cursed. "My damn' mouth is going numb. Try pulling your feet apart, but easy…not too hard."

Slowly she lifted her right foot away from her left. The rope was definitely loosening. "Keep going…you're getting it."

It seemed another eternity before she heard him say: "Got it!" There seemed to be genuine excitement in his voice.

She yanked her feet apart now, and the rope slid away. "You did it, Blackjack." She pulled her knees up, propping herself on her side before giving her body one big jerk that brought her to a sitting position. Then she was kneeling, then standing. With growing nervousness she tiptoed over to the wall where the rope around her neck was attached to a hook. "Watch the flap, and let me know if you see Cholla coming." Luckily the hook was stationed in the wall at just about neck level with Delphinia. She licked her lips and set to work. Within a matter of minutes she understood why Blackjack had been cussing throughout the process. But considering the choices, she kept at it…biting, pulling, pulling, biting. Finally, when she was at the point where she thought her teeth would fall out, she felt an ease in the piece of rope between her teeth. With one yank the knot was undone.

"You got it?" Blackjack asked.

"Yeah," she whispered. "Now, I'll get your hands free." She scurried over to his side. She knew he was weak, and, as much as she wanted to have him work on her bound wrists, she didn't have the heart to ask him. "Roll on your stomach," she said. Either she was getting better at this, or Cholla hadn't done a very good job tying the rope around his wrists. The work of coaxing the knot loose was halted when she heard Cholla rattling around his campfire. She froze, the rope dropping from her mouth. She saw Blackjack's body stiffen.

"I reckon you two are getting hungry in there? Eh? I ain't one to be inhospitable." He laughed. "Soon as the greens and squirrel are cooked, I'll be offering you young 'uns a bite. But then, maybe not." He chuckled again. "Have to save some for Hat ton, I guess…his last meal and all."

"We've got to hurry up," Delphinia whispered and then, leaning down, bit into the knot of the rope. "You're free," she announced, after spitting out the rope.

Blackjack moved his stiff arms. The rope fell away. He rolled over and rubbed his raw wrists. Then he reached up and loosened the noose from around his neck.

"Quick, my hands," she gasped, turning her back to Blackjack

But Blackjack was otherwise engaged, attempting to free his own ankles. His hands and fingers were so numb from being tied that they were nearly useless. He struggled with the loops around his booted ankles, hissing with frustration when he could not loosen the knot.

"Shhh," Delphinia signaled to him. "Listen! Horse coming."

They both froze.

Cholla's greeting rang out: "Who's there? By golly, if it ain't our sheriff!"

Through the opening in the doorway flap Delphinia watched as the legs of Jim Hatton's horse came into view outside Cholla's campfire. She could hear the leathery squeak of his gear.

"How are you doing, Cholla?" Jim asked. "I heard you left the country. Was heading up to Dos Cabezas."

"I thought about it. But, you know, once this prospectin' bug has got into a man's blood, it's hard to quit. Have a bite with me, Sheriff? Set a spell. What brings you out this way.... still hunting that Blackjack fellow?"

Delphinia shoved her back into Blackjack, who still hadn't managed to free his feet. "My wrists. I need my hands."

She heard Jim dismount. The stirrup leather stretched under his weight with a leathery creak. She strained against her wrist ropes. She dared not scream to warn Jim. Were she to scream, she would probably only confuse Jim and give Cholla the opportunity he needed to shoot.

Blackjack continued to toy with his own leg ropes, seemingly oblivious to her own need to be free of the last of her rope bonds. She couldn't blame him — dirty, sick, held captive by Cholla all these weeks. She was surprised he could think at all. He muttered distractedly, still working his stiff fingers around his knotted ankle ropes.

"You know, Hat ton," Cholla said, "I'm glad you rode in. I've got something I been wantin' to ask you about. It's something I found. It got it over there...by the hut."

Delphinia shrank back, her heart beating so hard she could feel it in her ears. Cholla snatched the side of the deerskin flap, holding it open so that Delphinia could see Jim Hat ton who showed a perfect silhouette in gold between the darkening wilderness and flickering campfire. She saw the angle of his clean jaw, the hat pulled low on his forehead, his smooth hand holding a metal coffee cup near the flames. She could not see his eyes.

Cholla hooked the deerskin open and then backed up to the doorway. His hand reached inside and dug behind the makeshift doorjamb. Several boards pulled loose. "Got it right here, Jim, just hold on." Then slowly his hand emerged from between the boards holding a buffalo gun. "Watch this, girl," Cholla whispered, "watch this and watch good."

When he turned his right side toward the hut and drew the gun toward his body, keeping it in the dark and out of Jim's sight, Delphinia leaped to her feet and, lowering her head, rushed at Cholla with all her strength. She rammed him in the ribs with her shoulder, and the gun went off with a horrific discharge, splitting the night air.

"Look out, Jim!" she screamed, as she and Cholla continued to careen until Cholla tripped over a Dutch oven, sprawling them both to the ground.

"You bitch!" Cholla snarled. "How'd you get loo…."

Delphinia, on top of Cholla and remembering all he had done, pushed her weight at him again, kneeing him in the belly and kicking at his legs and the fallen gun with her heel — trying to kick it clear of his reach. She flew back when Cholla's arm came up, catching her under the chin with his elbow.

He scrambled over her and kicked her in the ribs which knocked the wind out of her. Gasping for his own breath, Cholla pulled out his pistol and took aim just as Jim Hatton's bullet caught him through the neck. Blood spurted from the wound as he tumbled over on top of Delphinia.

Delphinia screamed and called out — "Jim!" — as she tried to squirm away from under the man who had destroyed so much of her life. She jerked spasmodically on the ground, still unable to use her arms as tears of relief and pain poured out from her.

Then, pulling Cholla off from on top of her, Jim was on the ground and at her side. He pulled her toward him and managed both to comfort her and undo the knot that bound her hands. "It's over. You're all right. *Shhhh"*

"It was all Cholla, Jim. Everything. He even hired the Riveras to kill my parents. And Jess…he killed him."

Jim pulled her closer and again assured her that it was over now. He was still soothing her when suddenly his body stiffened, and he jerked out his gun. "Who's in the hut?"

"It's Blackjack Parry," came from inside the shack. "Don't shoot. I don't want any trouble."

"Wait," Delphinia commanded as she pulled at Jim's arm. "It's true. He's not going to make any trouble."

Jim got to his feet and then helped Delphinia up.

"Cholla's held him captive for weeks," she explained as she steadied herself. Her whole body was trembling. "I don't really think he's been involved in most of this."

"Let's go see to him, then." He supported her around the waist with his hand.

She rubbed her wrists as they made their way into Cholla's shack. It took a while for their eyes to make out Blackjack, who now sat on the floor, still fumbling with the ropes tied around his feet.

"A lot of help you were," Delphinia accused Blackjack.

He shrugged, his weakened state more apparent to Delphinia now than before.

"I told you, I'm just along for the ride."

"Let me help you," said Jim as he squatted at Blackjack's feet.

"How did you know to come here?" Delphinia asked as Jim worked the knot.

"I found that hired killer's body, Dunnagan, in your yard this morning. I followed the tracks of your horses up here. There were plenty of them...Hawk's horse's, your team's, and then the chestnut's. You see, I'd ridden out to warn you about Cholla. I got an answer back from a wire I'd sent to Missouri after your trip to Douglas. Old Chauncy Kyd has a thousand-dollar reward on his head from twenty years ago. Rode with a band of raiders after the war. Turns out he was wanted for robbery, murder, and jailbreak. He was one tough customer."

"He was a monster. All those years he tormented my mother ...and then it was my turn. He was bent on destroying everyone, everything that mattered to me." She found it hard to continue. "He enjoyed it...watching me suffer."

Jim and Blackjack sat motionless as the hauntingly pained voice of Delphinia related the facts of the events as she had learned them.

"It's over, Delphinia. You're safe," Jim stated then, his voice unsteady.

She peered at Jim in the semi-darkness. "I never would have suspected that you were suspicious of Cholla the way you came riding in here."

"I figured that was the best way to handle it...acting friendly like I always did with him. I knew you were somewhere around here when I found the chestnut horse tied back there beside the trail. So I wasn't about to come in here shooting."

"I'd say we're all pretty lucky the way it worked out," Blackjack interjected.

Cholla's body was tied, face down, across his burro. The camp was cleared. Between the three of them they'd torn Cholla's filthy hovel to pieces. Delphinia had made a serviceable dinner from the airtights they had uncovered in the camp, knowing Blackjack desperately needed to gain back some of his strength and that he would be well on his way to recovery after having some decent meals in his stomach. As they led the burro out of the camp, Blackjack kept his distance behind the sheriff and his half-sister.

Although she wasn't even sure why at first, Delphinia appealed to Jim to let Blackjack go, provided Blackjack traveled far and attempted to change his life around. "He's all the family I've got left," she said, thinking out loud.

"I guess it wouldn't hurt to talk to him."

When they got to Delphinia's chestnut, Jim told Blackjack to have a seat on a nearby rock. He presented Delphinia's proposal, making it clear that if it hadn't been for Delphinia's suggesting it, he'd be on his way to jail.

"I care enough about Delphinia," he explained, "to want to try and do right by her, considering all that she's been through lately...all that she's suffered. But I don't want to see your face around here again...ever. And so help me, if I ever hear your name connected with something rotten, I might just come after you." He put his foot on the rock on which Blackjack was seated and leaned in close range of Blackjack's face as he asked: "What'll it be?"

"I haven't done much in my life to be proud of, Sheriff," Blackjack said, shaking his head. "But, you know, I'm proud to be the half-brother of someone as fine as Delphinia. Might've been a different person, if I'd grown up with her. But...well, I give you my word you won't see my face around these parts again."

"All right," said Sheriff Hatton, extending his hand, "we'll even shake on it."

Blackjack stood up, shook hands, and then walked over to Delphinia, who was standing near the chestnut horse.

"I want you to take this horse, Blackjack," Delphinia said, handing him the reins.

"I can't take…."

Delphinia didn't let him finish his sentence. "You need a horse, don't you?"

He ran his hand through his hair, letting out a gust of air from deep within his chest. "I'm sorry about your mother…. and about Haw…about our father. I really didn't know what was going to happen. I didn't even know that it was Hawk's home until it was too late."

"Go, before the sheriff changes his mind. I want you to stop at my house on your way and get a new set of clothes out of the bedroom. Hawk's clothes. They're likely to fit you. And there's a crockery jar in the kitchen, a blue one. Take enough money to get yourself started. Then ride out."

He said his thanks to both Delphinia and Sheriff Hat ton as he mounted the chestnut and headed out in the direction of the Estes homestead.

Delphinia approached Jim and pressed her cheek to his chest, leaning into him but with her arms held tightly at her sides, afraid to be so bold as to hold him. When his arms went around her, it was though a flame of hope flickered alive inside of her.

"Let's get out of here, Delphinia," he suggested after some time had passed.

Reining along the dark trail southwest toward town, Delphinia rode Hawk's horse and led the team. She followed Jim, who led the pack burro. "You know I could do with a hot bath and a real meal," she called to Jim.

"How would a steak dinner in town do you? You can afford it, you know. Besides Chauncy Kyd's reward, there was a two-hundred-dollar bounty for that killer, Dunnagan." He turned back to look at her, a teasing smile pasted across his face.

She smiled back at the broad-shouldered silhoutte. “I guess its going to take a while longer before I can stop being the bounty hunter’s daughter, isn’t it?”

He reined his horse and sat waiting for her to come alongside. “You know, if you’re looking for a new title, I’ve got a suggestion you might want to think about.”

She smiled again, bigger this time. “I’ll just bet you do, Sheriff Jim Hat ton. I’ll just bet you do.”

THE END

Made in the USA
Lexington, KY
17 July 2018